The Adulterous Bride

Venice during Carnevale was a different city. From Christmas to Easter, inhabitants donned costumes and masks and partook in many festivities. Filipa wore a dark blue giornea over black, a black, velvet cap, a black cape tied around her neck with a gold chain, and a white Bauta mask which covered her face except her mouth. Fantino was all in black including a black tricorne hat, and he also had a white Bauta mask. Many of the men milling about the streets were in dark or black clothes with masks, while women mostly wore conventional clothing but with masks. In fact with so many in masks it was impossible to tell who was who. You could pass your best friend and not even recognise them.

Piazza San Marco bustled with many entertainers: jugglers, acrobats, clowns, singers as usual but in costume. But it was the preparations for Forze d'Ercole which made the most activity. There was to be the traditional battle between Castellani: the inhabitants of San Marco, Sestiere di Castello and Dorsoduro; against Nicolotti: the inhabitants of San Polo, Cannareggio and Santa Croce.

"Why aren't you battling?" Filipa asked Fantino while rival forces gathered at opposite ends of the piasà.

"I'm not really a battle person," Fantino said.

"I thought every young man would want to prove himself worthy in front of his lover?"

He took her hand. "I thought I was worthy already," he said.

Filipa liked Fantino, which was why he was her escort for Carnevale. "You're worthy as a lover, but there's more to being a man than that."

"I found siór Contarini for you."

"That's true."

"Did that work out well for you?"

"That worked out very well Fantino. I will give you a reward for that later. Now, the battle...."

"Do you want to see me battle?"

"I'm Castellani born and raised, and I want you to defend the honour of my true home."

"Then I will!" he said firmly.

Fantino headed into the throng and Filipa hoped he wouldn't get hurt. The two forces arranged themselves into gigantic pyramids of humanity; layer upon layer, and after much falling and recovery of individuals, they were ready to advance. Everyone in the piazza cheered and shouted for all in Venice supported one side or the other. At first Nicolotti forced back Castellani who then recovered some ground. The battle of the human pyramids ebbed and flowed until, slowly Castellani gained the upper hand, gradually demolishing the Nicolotti pyramid with many falling

2

harmlessly to the ground and struggling to get back up, but unable to climb under the weight of force. Eventually Castellani scattered Nicolotti and it had been a great victory. Filipa was so enthralled by the battle she didn't notice Fantino, until he was right with her.

"Well done mio amore," she said. "You successfully defended the honour of my birthplace."

"Did you see me?" Fantino asked.

"I saw your every move."

"Ha! You didn't see me at all."

Filipa tilted her head. "I didn't mio amore, but I'm sure you did well. Now, let us find a dance. I'm in the mood for dancing!"

Filipa took Fantino's hand and led him beyond the piazza. The bridge opposite was under battle from two gangs: harmless fun as they pushed and shoved each other to gain possession. As a result Filipa led Fantino north to the next bridge at Calle Drio la Cièsa, and there Filipa got the greatest shock. She recognised him by his size and stature despite his face hidden by a mask. Dardi Zorzi celebrating Carnevale was no surprise, but celebrating with a man instead of his wife was a surprise.

Filipa left Fantino and closed on Dardi, who must have sensed her presence, because he turned his head but his mask hid his expression. Instead he took the hand of his companion and headed along the calle. Filipa followed, even

3

more curious that Dardi had seen her and run away. She followed him along the crowded calle, and amongst the throng she lost him. She stopped, quite bemused that not only was Dardi with a man, but they held hands while they got away from her. She wondered why he would do that.

"What is it?" Fantino asked.

"I saw someone I knew," Filipa said.

"Even with a mask?"

"I would recognise him anywhere." It was awkward to be standing in a narrow calle jostled by crowds, and she went that way for another reason anyway. "Let's find a ball," Filipa said.

Filipa led Fantino towards the canal and the many palazzi which lined it. Many headed to Palazzo Gritti just ahead and Filipa followed them. A man servant in a uniform and a mask stopped them.

"Your names?" he asked.

"Signor Fantino de Pesaro and signorina Filipa Barbarigo."

"You can enter."

The reception room was lit by hundreds of candles, and quite full with fifty or sixty dancers or even more. All in their finest clothes and all masked. Servants carried cups of wine on trays, and Fantino grabbed two as a servant passed and gave one to Filipa who sipped at it. Some party-goers had more than sipped at their drinks, and some showed the effects of too much wine. It was boisterous: men laughed and talked too loudly while women giggled stupidly. Men flirted with ladies not their own; both man and woman protected by the anonymity of masks. Filipa was interested by what she saw, she had no desire for anyone but Fantino, but she'd made love with Marino earlier that day, and with many of her lovers during the past week. Wives chained to the one man needed more than that, and a masquerade ball gave the opportunity for flirting at least, and maybe more than flirting if they could find some space and time. Of course some of the masked women were mistresses, with wives abandoned and alone in palazzi.

The band got ready to play and many couples formed into pairs for a bassadanza. Fantino bowed and Filipa curtseyed, and the music played for the slow, stately dance. It was a hand-in-hand procession in time to the music, stopping, bowing and repeating, and stopping, turning as a couple, and returning to the start before turning again. Slow, stately and in time to the music until the end of the song.

Then followed a saltarello. Fantino bowed and Filipa curtseyed, accompanied by music near twice as fast with a more driving energy. It was a more complicated dance of two steps a hop, two steps and a kick right and a kick left, two steps backwards and a hop, and the man pirouetted first and the woman pirouetted. The sequence was repeated until the woman pirouetted first and the man pirouetted, and the sequence was repeated until the man danced a circle around the woman, then the sequence repeated until the woman danced a circle around the man. The sequence repeated until the couple took hands and danced the same steps in a circle before repeating from the beginning. And so it went on; ending in a bow and a curtsey.

Fantino, in addition to his attributes in bed, was a good dancer, and Filipa was pleased to have him as her partner that evening. They danced another saltarello before Filipa guided Fantino away for another drink of wine. She stood on the sidelines to see who was who, or more precisely who was what because there were men and their wives no doubt, and men with their mistresses of course. Maybe other women were nuns of patrician birth enjoying carnevale with their lovers.

"Do you want to have supper at an inn?" Fantino asked.

Filipa was wise to that. "You want to take me to the inn where you rented a room, so we can make love there."

"I suppose making love will follow."

Filipa wished she could kiss her sweet young man, but their masks were in the way. "Let's have supper at the inn, and make love after that."

Fantino took Filipa's hand and led her out of Palazzo Gritti. They would sup together, and make love after. Filipa would share Fantino's room and his bed for the night, probably rise late, probably make love again, and then see what carnevale offered for the new day. Surrounded by so many celebrating carnevale, Filipa decided to make the most of her time in Venice with Fantino.

What They Are Saying About The Adulterous

Bride

What an amazing story! Renaissance Venice told from three different points of view: bright, extroverted Filipa Barbarigo, honest and decent Marin Curri, happily married to the wonderful Blanca, and Dardi Zorzi who has to make the best of an almost untenable situation. Amazing backdrop, amazing story, amazing characters, and the most masterful ending that I have ever come across. **Sarah Holmes – author of Promise of Canaan.**

Other Works by Mark Morey

The Red Sun will Come - June 2012

Souls in Darkness - August 2012

The Governess and the Stalker - July 2014

Maidens in the Night - September 2014

One Hundred Days - September 2015

The Last Great Race – April 2016

The Adulterous Bride

by

Mark Morey

All rights reserved

Mark Morey

http://markmorey.blogspot.com.au

Copyright ©

978-0-9944171-8-3

Published In Australia

October 2016

Life in Late Medieval Times

The following story is set in late Medieval Venice: a prosperous, commercial city at the time. Life for the characters will seem eerily familiar at times, especially when they go to work in shops, or go to work in offices in Palàso Ducale (the Palace of the Doge). The workday seems to have been as long as today: about eight hours. There are many differences though; especially the patterns of waking and sleeping. In late Medieval Times people rose early and went to bed relatively early; probably around eight. They slept naked but wore a cap to prevent loss of body heat through the head.

In the early hours of the morning, people woke at the end of the first sleep. They spent time conversing, socialising or making love. Couples were advised that the best time for making love was between the first and second sleeps. Often families slept in the one room, so children would at least turn their heads to give their parents visual privacy, but actual privacy wouldn't come for many hundreds of years. In the abesia (abbey) of this story, the nuns go to chapel after their first sleep. They would have socialised after the service; before retiring to bed for their second sleep.

When people rose in the morning, they washed their faces and hands, dressed, and were ready for breakfast.

Around the middle of the day they had their main meal or dinner, which is a tradition surviving in Europe to this day. In the evening they had a smaller meal or supper. They washed their hands before and after eating, and after eating they rinsed their mouths and rubbed their teeth with a clean cloth, and used toothpicks. Beyond washing daily, bathing was regular; perhaps weekly. The wealthy bathed in tubs in their homes, and the rest used public bathhouses. In the sixteenth century, bathing was claimed to be harmful in relation to ongoing bubonic plague. Regular bathing, and particularly public bathhouses, fell out of fashion.

Food at the time was often tasty, cooked with spices, herbs and olive oil. Bread was similar to the bread of today, although cakes were more bread-like and usually sweetened with honey. In southern Europe they drank water, wine, and watered-down wine. The wine was coarse and bitter compared to the wine we have today. In northern Europe where grapes couldn't be grown, beer and ale were common drinks.

Love was dangerous and to be avoided, which is why arranged marriages between noblemen and noble women for economic benefit was not only possible, but preferable. Other classes may well have married for love, and probably many did. Once married, couples could have sex in order to conceive and raise children; otherwise sex was a sin. This religious restriction on sex only in marriage only for procreation was reflected in many secular laws of the time. In addition, the Church had many restrictions limiting pleasurable aspects of sex. The existence of penitentials, the penances to be served for breaking Church rules about sex, showed that not all followed these religious teachings.

Bringing new life to the world was hazardous with about 5% of women dying in childbirth, and a further 15% dying from infections associated with giving birth. Infant mortality rates were high with about 30% dying before the age of five. If a person survived to adulthood they had a chance to live to their late 40s, and some even lived to their 60s and 70s.

Even though doctrine of the Church loomed large over many aspects of life; this was not always a bad thing. At the time of this story there were about 30 religious days free of work, so workers then had more holidays than today.

Glossary

During the time of the Roman Empire, a simplified, everyday form of Latin known as Vulgar Latin existed alongside Classical Latin. After the collapse of the Roman Empire, each Italian City-State had its own language derived from Vulgar Latin. Over time the central geographic location of Tuscany, the many written works in Tuscan, and the relative economic strength of Tuscany resulted in the Tuscan language being used as a second language in other parts of Italy. Upon the unification of Italy in the nineteenth century, Tuscan was adopted as the standard Italian language. Previous city-state languages continue to exist alongside standard Italian, and these are now known as dialects.

To maintain authenticity, this novel uses terms from the language of Venèsia, which would have been the case in the Fifteenth Century.

Abasia / Abasie	Abbey (singular / plural)
Adio	Goodbye
Avogadoria / Avogardori	Public prosecutors who defended the legal interests of the city of Venèsia (singular / plural)
Badésa	Abbess
Baxélega	Basilica
Benvegnùa / Benvegnùe	Welcome (female form singular / female form plural)
Baréta	Cap
Bonasera	Good evening
Bondi	Good day (informal)

Bongiorno	Good day (formal)
Calle / Calli	Street (singular / plural)
Caligo	Light sea mist
Calsa / Calsi	Knitted hose. For men calsa were sewn into a single garment similar to today's panty hose, while for women their two calsi were normally calf high and held in place by a garter (singular / plural)
Camicia	A linen slip worn by men and women
Campo / Campi	A parish square (singular / plural)
Canal Grando	The Grand Canal
Capèo / Capèli	Hat (singular / plural)
Cièsa	Church
Él Doxe / Doxi	The Doge (supreme magistrate) of Venice (singular / plural)
Él Consìlio dei Cuarànta	The Council of Forty. A group of 40 elected by the Great Council who oversaw minor administrative and legal issues
Él Consìlio dei Diéxe	The Council of Ten. A group of 10 elected by the Great Council who oversaw diplomatic and intelligence services, managed military affairs, and handled legal matters and enforcement
Él Maggior Consiglio	The Great Council. All male patricians were entitled to sit on the Great Council at age 25. The Great Council appointed members of Él Consìlio dei Cuarànta and Él Consìlio dei Diéxe
Famégia	Family
Fondamenta / Fondamente	Canal with a path to the side (singular / plural)
Gamurra / Gamurri	An under dress which was often partly visible through the giornea

	(singular / plural)
Giornea / Giornei	A dress usually made of a shirt or bodice sewn to a skirt. For men a giornia reached to about mid-thigh while for women it was full length (singular / plural)
Gondola / Gondole	A long, narrow rowboat suitable for the narrow rii (canals) of Venèsia (singular / plural)
Gondoliere / Gondolieri	Rower of a gondola (singular / plural)
Grassie	Thank you
I Siór di Nòti	Lords of the Night. Originally tasked to keep Venèsia safe at night. Later they investigated serious crimes including sodomy
Mio amór / Mia amór	My love (masculine / feminine)
Mulòti	Platform shoes for women fashionable at the time
Mutande	Men's underwear. Women didn't wear underwear at the time
Nadal	Christmas
Palàso / Palàsi	Grand house (singular / plural)
Pàre	Father (priest)
Patrician	Ruling families of The Republic of Venice
Per piasser	Please
Pestilentia	The bubonic plague
Piasà	Square
Piaséta	Small square
Ponte	Bridge
Procuradór	Procurator
Rio / Rii	Narrow canal (singular / plural)
Sbirro / Sbirri	The police force of Él Consìlio dei Diéxe (singular / plural)
Scarpe	Shoes (plural)
Sé	Yes

Séngia	Belt
Siór	Mister
Sióra / Sóri	Missus (singular / plural)
Siórina	Miss
Sòra / Sòri	Sister (nun) (singular / plural)
Stivàl	Skin container for carrying wine and other liquids
Tabàro / Tabàri	Cloak (singular / plural)
Tacolin	Purse
Te vògio ben	I love you
Venèsia	Venice

Chapter One

Filipa gazed from her window at the shimmering canal beneath a sunny sky. It was a magnificent sight with broad Canal Grando surrounded by grand palàsi; stately homes all in bright colours: red, yellow, pink, orange, her home in purple and many more. Down below her mother boarded their gondola from the water door, and Filipa watched Giorgio, their gondoliere, cast off and head along Canal Grando. Their bright red gondola was surrounded by many other colourful gondole, and soon it disappeared out of sight.

Filipa went downstairs and crossed the alcove towards the back door. She opened the door to the narrow lane hemmed in on all sides by looming, brick walls. That lane took her to Fondamenta Duodo o Barbarigo: a narrow canal with a footpath along one side, again lined by tall buildings all but blocking the sun. There wasn't one square inch of Venèsia that wasn't put to good use; either buildings squashed side-by-side crowding calli, fondamente and rii, or compact campi for parish recreation. It was cool in the shade and smelled of salt water, and smelled of cooking from many homes; including her home of Palàso Barbarigo. Filipa walked along the footpath before using a short laneway which led   into Campo Santa Maria del Giglio, which was busy as always. Patrician men and patrician ladies dressed in rich, silk garments, merchants and their wives in fine linen, and the poor, always there were poor, in coarse and worn clothing. At the far end of the campo, fishermen had stalls and were doing a busy trade, while stray dogs foraged for scraps. Cièsa di Santa Maria del Giglio dominated the setting with its columns and its multitude of elaborately carved statues. The campo, the centre of her parish, was truly wonderful on a mild, sunny day. Mid-spring, Monday April six, 1426; Easter had just passed and soon summer would be upon them. Filipa wandered amongst the crowd while glad to be away from her home which was more of a prison.

"Should you be here alone, siórina Barbarigo?" a male voice asked.

Filipa turned around and smiled brightly. "Bondi Dardi," she said.

"Bondi Filipa," he replied.

"When I was young I often came here."

"I know; I used to watch you."

Filipa knew that Dardi Zorzi's eyes had followed her for many long years. That was innocent enough then, but now she was of marrying age and she could use Dardi's attractions to her advantage. Maybe. He was tall, about six foot, and very handsome. About thirty with rugged features, dark eyes and even darker hair. Always well dressed, today in a red giornea over red calsa, and wearing a red, velvet baréta. "You watched me again today," she said.

"We're old friends."

19

"Do you want to be more than friends?"

"You know that's not possible."

"It is possible," Filipa said. She knew how it worked. "If we were to make love and then I was to make a report...."

"How?"

"An anonymous denunciation into the mouth of the lion on Piasà San Marco. We would be tried of course, and you would be given the option of righting that which you did wrong."

"By marrying you?"

Filipa nodded her head slowly. "Sé."

"I can't," Dardi said. "Already negotiations are underway."

Filipa took his hand. "Surely you want to marry someone you like?"

"I have to do my duty. Besides, you don't know anything about me."

"I know I like you."

"I like you too, and because I like you it's best that I marry someone else."

Filipa didn't understand his nonsense. If they liked each other they would have a happy marriage. A happier marriage than her parents. She played with her hair and gazed around the square at the merchants and their wives and even at the poor couples, and felt a twinge of jealousy. They were free to marry whoever they chose. She played with her hair, her long golden hair which had mesmerised Dardi for many, long years.

"You deserve a better man than me," Dardi said. "You should go before you get into trouble."

"I won't get into trouble," Filipa said, smiling brightly. "I went to church to pray for a good husband!"

"I hope you get your prayers answered."

"Who's your family negotiating for?"

"Caterina Cornaro."

"I hope she's good for you."

"I must go," Dardi said. Adio Filipa."

"Adio Dardi."

Filipa watched Dardi head off into the crowd before retracing her route home. She opened the door to their palàso and went to the alcove. The ground floor rooms of their home were spacious with tall ceilings, and the alcove was particularly grand with ornate, sculptured plasterwork across the ceiling and on upper parts of walls. Also grand were the sitting and dining rooms which had large windows facing Canal Grando, and both had sculptured plasterwork although less elaborate than the alcove. The ground floor rooms were painted in muted green with brown trim. Sitting room furniture was typical for a patrician family: two armchairs and a three-seater couch in ornately carved oak, with dark, red, velvet cushions. There were three low-set tables in carved oak, different in style but complimenting the couch and chairs. The dining room had an oak table large enough for 12 matching chairs, with two of those chairs in the alcove along with two armchairs from earlier times, or earlier generations of famégia Barbarigo. The rooms upstairs were less extravagant but very pleasing to the eye, painted in muted blue with darker blue trim. Two bedrooms had large windows overlooking Canal Grando, while the office and the unused bedroom had smaller windows facing the narrow, gloomy Rio de San Maurizio. The servant's rooms on the top floor were very basic. Filipa crept across the alcove towards the polished, timber staircase.

"Where have you been?" her Mama shouted.

"I went to Cièsa di Santa Maria del Giglio to pray," Filipa said.

"You're seventeen years old and not supposed to be outside alone."

Filipa knew her Mama was right, and besides it was best not to antagonise her. "I'm sorry Mama," she said.

"What worries me is that one day you will bring disgrace to this family."

"I would never do such a thing."

"Go to your room Filipa. Help Cristina get ready."

"Ready for what, Mama?"

"Ready to meet her future husband."

Filipa felt dizzy and reached for the wall to prevent herself from falling. "Which husband?" she asked quietly.

Mama sighed. "Silvestro Navagero."

Filipa felt even dizzier. Navagero was a grand family.

"Are you alright?" Mama asked.

"Sé," Filipa said quietly. "I will help Cristina."

Filipa climbed the narrow staircase to the first floor. Her Papa was a patrician and a silk trader, but there was much competition in silk. The family got by well enough, but Filipa wondered how they could afford dowries for two daughters of marrying age. She looked through the door of their shared bedroom at Cristina wearing her camicia, while a fine, blue-coloured silk giornea lay on her bed. Filipa eased away and sat on the floor at the end of the corridor.

* * *

A well-dressed man entered Marin's shop. "Bongiorno siór," Marin said to the gentleman in a red, silk giornea and a red, velvet baréta.

"Bongiorno siór," he replied.

"Can I help you? A haircut and a shave perhaps?"

"Sé, per piasser."

The customer placed his baréta on the stand and sat in the chair. Marin got his scissors and a comb and commenced to trim the customer's black hair. He had a simple, practical cut and Marin trimmed it to his collar and just below his ears. Marin then took a towel and draped it over the giornea of his customer. He took a part-used bar of soap and thoroughly wet this in his bowl of water, before using his fingers to liberally apply soap lather to his customer's face. After wiping his hands dry, Marin grabbed his sharpest razor from the counter and carefully shaved his from the jaw upwards against the grain of beard growth, and from the jaw downwards so as to not nick his throat. Marin finished by using the towel to wipe any traces of soap away, and the customer had a smooth, cleanly shaved face with not a nick or cut.

"Grassie siór," he said. "Well done."

"Grassie siór," Marin replied.

A young man came into the shop and Marin glanced in his direction. Tall with wavy, dark hair and needing a shave. The first customer stood.

"Ten soldi, per piasser siór," Marin asked.

The first customer opened his tacolinn at his séngia and gave Marin a coin. Marin placed it in the bowl on his bench. "Grassie siór," he said.

"Bondi Clario," the first customer said to the second. "Siór shaves very well."

"Bondi Dardi," the second customer replied. "I will have a shave and a haircut, per piasser."

Marin gestured towards the chair and the second customer, Clario, sat, while the first customer, Dardi, sat on one of the three waiting chairs. Marin commenced with the second customer, and soon his hair was cut and he was freshly shaved. After paying his ten soldi, Clario went to

Dardi who stood. Marin eyed them warily. Older and younger and they knew each other well. Maybe there was more than just knowing each other and Marin sensed something was wrong. Marin didn't know what it was, but something was wrong with those two men. Marin made good money from them, but he hoped they didn't come back.

Many customers came to Marin's shop for shaves in particular, and Marin had a good reputation in the parish. Many customers came twice or even three times a week for their shaves, and they chatted about work or home or family, and of course Marin made good money from their business. The light outside faded; the temperature dropped, and the maragona rang to end the working day. Marin took down his sign, closed his door and sharpened his scissors and razor for the next day. He then wiped down the counter before folding the towels and placing them on the shelf beneath. Marin pocketed his takings and pondered whether or not to visit Blanca. He decided he would, and went outside and around the corner to her family's rooms in a building on a narrow lane leading towards Rio de l'Alboro. Marin climbed the stairs and knocked on their door; greeted siór and sióra Agoli and noticed Blanca was just inside. They had a small, two-room apartment which was rather crowded, so Marin asked if he could go outside with Blanca. She was a pretty young lady aged 17, and from Albanian parents like Marin. They were ideal for each other: they were the right age to marry; Marin liked her and he sensed she liked him too. Marin's business was doing well and he could support a wife and children. His apprenticeship had been worth it, even with the pain it brought him.

"How was your day?" Marin asked Blanca while they walked towards the campo.

"I helped Mama make a new dress," she said. Blanca paused. "One day when I marry, I could make my dress for the ceremony."

"Sé you could, and you could make clothes for your children."

"When the time's right I can do that."

She was a clever woman and would make a good wife. Marin thought about that and then realised they reached the campo. He stopped walking and glanced at Blanca: her fair skin, her ruby red lips, her soft features and her delicate build. Blanca was beautiful and Marin wished he could make her his wife. Again he glanced at her, and if he didn't ask it would never happen.

"Blanca," Marin said, and he didn't know what to say. And then he did. "Would you marry me?"

Blanca took his hand and she had a lovely, gentle touch. "I would marry you tomorrow sweet Marin."

Marin felt his heart racing and he wanted to reach out and take Blanca in his arms, but that wasn't possible in public.

All he could do was gaze at her sweet face while she held his hand.

"You must ask your parents to ask my parents," Blanca said.

"Sé," Marin said. "When I get home."

"I hope this can work out for us."

"I hope so too."

"We should go back."

Still holding hands, Marin and Blanca returned to the plain, brick building of her home, and Marin checked all around and saw nobody. He quickly kissed Blanca's cheek and she blushed bright red!

"Adio Blanca," Marin said.

"Adio Marin," she replied, and Marin watched her climb the stairs inside. He returned to the campo where just around the corner were his family's rooms. They had three rooms upstairs: two for sleeping and a living room. Small windows shaded by other buildings made the living room perpetually dark, although expensive candles were reserved for evenings only. Furniture consisted of a timber table with two benches, a timber pantry, and a cupboard also used as a bench for food preparation. At the far end of the room was the fireplace with a pot for cooking. After the salty tang outside, the apartment had a pungent odour of tallow candles, sweaty bodies, and the fish and vegetable stew warming over the fire.

"Did you have a good day?" Mama asked Marin.

"I had a busy day," Marin replied.

"You must have been busy to come home so late."

"I had two customers for shaves and haircuts later in the day, and after that I went to see Blanca."

"Don't get your hopes up with that girl," Papa said over the top of his cup of watered-down wine. "Siór Agoli works at the docks and he could never afford a decent dowry."

"Blanca and I like each other and that's more important than a dowry," Marin said.

"As you know Marin, after you finished your apprenticeship I loaned you money to start your shop, and you need to pay that back in time. You can't do that while supporting a wife who can't pay a dowry for her upkeep."

Marin sat at the bench, grabbed the jug and poured a cup of wine for himself. "Blanca has learned dressmaking and she can use her skills to keep a family in clothing, and could even sell some of what she sews."

"I will talk with siór Agoli and see what he can offer for her."

Papa was a wine merchant and had always lived a life of relative luxury. Marin understood his father, but he also knew that happiness couldn't be found in a sack of coins. Besides, a woman like Blanca had other assets, such as being practical and thrifty. Marin decided to keep that argument for another day, if he needed to. "What's for supper Mama?" he asked.

"Warmed leftover fish stew from dinner," she said and Marin smiled brightly. Warmed leftover for supper as always.

* * *

Dardi lay on his back with Clario cuddled close; his arm across Dardi's chest. Dardi thought back to his encounter with Filipa Barbarigo. She was good natured and feisty, and her parents always struggled against her independent spirit without realising that made her an interesting young woman. She had always been attractive: genuinely pretty with a cute, upturned nose, full, heart-shaped lips, deep blue eyes, and her long blonde hair always braided into a thin plat with the rest hanging free. The past two years had seen Filipa blossom into a beautiful woman. Tall, as tall most men, and she had the sense to wear muīoti of a modest height. Her figure had matured; Dardi could tell beneath her dress, hips and bust in proportion. He hoped Filipa would find herself in a marriage with a good husband.

"What is it?" Clario asked.

"I met a friend at the campo," Dardi said. "She's a spirited young woman, and beautiful too. She invited me to marry her, even though we both know there would be dowry problems. She suggested we make love and she would report

29

it anonymously, and the trial would right the wrong I did to her."

"She really is spirited! Would that work?"

"Sé it would."

"She sounds like an interesting young lady."

"She is."

"She will find herself married to someone not worthy of her. But at least they will be socially acceptable, unlike us who have to sneak around just to have a few moments to make love together."

"This is more than a few moments Clario. We talk, we make love, we talk some more, and we often play chess and other games. A few hours more like it."

"But it's not the same as men and women, even if they are unworthy matches. It's not the same."

Dardi put his arm around Clario and cupped his buttocks. "I know," he said. He turned his head and kissed Clario. "I don't know what I would do without these hours with you."

"Nor I."

"At least we love each other."

"Te vògio ben."

"Te vògio ben."

Chapter Two

Filipa stood with her back against the corner of her room, arms crossed while she glared at her father. There was a strained silence between the two.

"What do you say?" Papa goaded her.

"I won't go!" Filipa shouted at him.

"You will do as I say."

"No I won't!"

"You don't have any choice."

Filipa knew that was true but she didn't want to. The last thing she wanted was to be locked up in an abasia.

"Leave Filipa be," Mama said from the doorway. "Let me talk with her." Silence. "Alone, per piasser."

Papa left and Mama came close to Filipa.

"If we could do this differently you know we would," Mama said. "Many patrician families don't want to spread their wealth amongst many heirs, so they're sending their sons away from Venèsia. We had difficulty enough getting a match for Cristina, and we don't have the money to get someone decent for you."

"I don't want to be a nun," Filipa said.

"I know. You've known Dardi Zorzi for many years, but we don't have the money for a man like him." Mama moved closer. "We don't have the money for a good husband for Cristina," she said quietly.

"What do you mean?" Filipa asked.

"It's not the match we would prefer."

"Cristina will be happier married than being a nun."

"Almost half of patrician ladies become nuns, and we picked a good abasia on the Island of Torcello."

Filipa was startled that the marriage situation was so severe. "Why on Torcello?" she asked.

"I don't know how it works, but maybe on Torcello they have more – freedom than here."

"I hope you're right Mama."

"I hope I'm right too."

"Why me and not Cristina?"

"I don't trust you in an unhappy marriage, Filipa."

Filipa understood.

* * *

Siór Agoli was a short and stocky man, as to be expected for a man who earned his way through physical labour. Dark and swarthy, and it was surprising he had a daughter as fair as Blanca. Siór Agoli and Papa were at the table arguing over ducats; ten to marry Marin but five was all siór Agoli could afford. Maybe nine or maybe six, and then eight but still six, and six was as much as siór Agoli could afford. Siór Agoli departed and Marin's plan was destroyed for the want of two ducats. Marin went to the bedroom shared with his younger brother and his younger sister, and he sat his one of the two beds. A simple timber frame with a mattress stuffed with wool, and overlaid by a sheet and two blankets. There were many young women in Venèsia but marriage with a barber would come at a cost. Because of his trade his choices were limited. Regardless of that, Blanca was as good a woman as he ever would find. At age 21 it was time Marin was married, and after a year working it was time for a home and a family of his own. At age 21 it was time to move on from sharing a bed with his brother.

Vicenzo came home; aged 19 he was in the last year of his apprenticeship to be a jeweller. Cheerful as always when he came into the bedroom, until he saw Marin's face.

"What's wrong?" Vicenzo asked.

"I asked Blanca to marry me but her father can't afford the dowry," Marin said.

"That's too bad. She's a fair woman, one of the prettiest in the parish."

"She has a good heart."

"I've sensed that without knowing her that well."

Laura came into the room. "I'm sorry Marin," she said. "I'm sure you will find someone good." At age 17 Laura was due to be married soon, probably a man from the parish, although she hadn't shown an interest in anyone yet.

"Supper's ready," Mama said, and they went to the table for warmed leftover sardines and rice from dinner. It was a quiet meal that evening. Marin pondered what to do and then he remembered the practical and thrifty side of

Blanca, but it wasn't time to make that argument to his parents. In the next few days he would say that, and talk with Blanca and see what else she could bring to a marriage. Maybe she could help in the shop in some way. After supper, Mama and Laura went to the well in the campo to wash their plates, while Papa and Vicenzo played draughts. Marin went to the campo still busy despite the late hour, and lit from the glow from windows of the homes all around. He saw a pretty young woman in the care of her parents and that brightened his mood. If things didn't work out with Blanca, someone else would come along.

Marin returned home when the church bell struck seven, and Vicenzo had gone to bed; like all apprentices he was worked hard! Hopefully he wasn't abused by his master. Marin bid his parents goodnight and stripped off his clothes before pulling on his nightcap. He slipped into bed beside Vicenzo while Laura got into her bed opposite. Marin lay in the dark and eventually fell asleep.

Marin woke at the end of the first sleep, and Laura was already up with a candle flickering. He rose and dressed while she turned her head the other way, and Vicenzo rose and dressed as well. From the next room he heard his parents awake and murmuring, and then the timbers of their bed creaked, as Marin had heard many times before, especially when the family all slept in the one room. He heard the breathing of his mother heavier and heavier, and then the creaking started regular and rhythmic. Marin thought of other things to give them privacy, and then the answer hit him! It was only two ducats and surely his parents wouldn't mind that much. Even if they did mind, they would get over it once they got to know Blanca better. With regular creaking and gasps in the background, Marin stretched and felt really good.

"You look happy," Laura said.

"Me?" asked Marin as innocently as he could manage.

"Surely you're upset about Blanca. She seems nice and I'm sure she would make a fine wife, if her father had enough money."

"That not necessarily the end of things."

"Do you have a plan?"

"No," Marin lied. "Sé; when time passes we will try again."

"I hope things work out for you."

Silence for a moment, except for his parent's love-making barely muffled by curtains across doorways.

"You still haven't beaten me in draughts," Laura said.

"Let's play," Marin said.

They carried the candle to the living room and set up the game on the table. Things started well for Marin, but Laura had a run of luck and looked like she would win again. Their parents emerged from their room to sit beside Vicenzo to watch the game, where eventually Marin won. And when he won he hoped that soon he would be playing draughts in his own home with his wife. After brief conversations they retired to bed for the second sleep; undressing once more with nightcaps on. Only in the darkness Marin thought about his plan, and his shop would be ideal. Pleased with that thought; Marin rolled onto his side.

* * *

The two gondolieri pulled at their oars while Filipa gazed out of the little cabin, the fieze, across the lagoon towards the Island of Torcello. She knew her history: Torcello was first settled by the Veneti fleeing the barbarians, and the marshes around the island provided salt which they traded. But after a time the canals of Torcello silted up, and the island of Torcello faded in importance relative to the island of Venèsia. But Torcello still contained many palàsi, grand churches and 16 abasie. Filipa was bound for Abasia San Nicolai di Torcello, with her clothes in a trunk as instructed. They closed on the island where the rowers pulled to a busy port with many boats; including several batèla buranele, some laden with goods and some being unloaded, and also peàta, larger transport ships. The gondolieri drifted to a fine, wooden jetty and one jumped out to tie the small craft. Filipa's mama climbed out of the fieze and a gondoliere helped her out. Filipa followed her Mama onto the dock which led to a broad promenade fronting a large but squat building in dark granite, with a tall belltower to the left. Filipa contemplated the grim and austere abasia which had a taller, central church containing a large, central door with a statue of Christ set above, a statue of the Virgin to one side and a statue, no doubt of Saint Nicolai, on the other side. Butting either side of the church were two, lower-set wings with central doorways, and those wings had several windows overlooking the lagoon. A number of tall chimneys poked above the roof line of those two buildings.

Mama went to the grey door of the church and knocked, but there was no response. Filipa noticed a bell chain on the doorway to the wing on the right, and pointed it out. Mama pulled that chain and Filipa heard a bell jangling inside. She shuddered. She wondered if she was going to be locked inside that grim building for the rest of her days, with never a visitor to pull that chain.

The grey door was swung open by a young woman in a long black gown gathered by a cord at her waist, and with her head wrapped in white and then covered by a black hood. "Sióra e siórina Barbarigo?" she asked.

"I'm sióra Barbarigo," Mama said. "This is my daughter Filipa."

"Benvegnùe. I'm sòra Augusta and welcome to San Nicolai di Torcello. Come with me and I will take you to your cell where you can leave your trunk."

Filipa shuddered once more. She didn't think she would be spending the rest of her days in a cell!

They entered a cool, dark corridor which intersected with another corridor half-way along, and headed right along that corridor and passed several grey doors on either side. Then a door towards the end opened suddenly, and a young man bounded out and ran past. A very well dressed young man in a fine, purple, silk giornea over darker purple and red calsa. A young woman came out of the door, giggling, and she was well-dressed in a lovely, yellow giornea. She ran after the young man but stopped when she reached Filipa, Mama and sòra Augusta.

"Benvegnùe," she said. "You must be sióra e siórina Barbarigo."

"Bongiorno," Filipa said. "I'm Filipa Barbarigo with my mother."

"I'm Clara and I'm glad you're here; we need another one like us. Augusta, show Filipa and her mother around and then introduce them to Barbarella."

"Sé Clara," sòra Augusta said.

"I must get after Marco," Clara said. "There's no telling what trouble he will get up to! I will see you soon Filipa."

Clara ran off shouting 'Marco come here' while sòra Augusta led Filipa to an open door, and Filipa followed the sòra into her small room or 'cell'. The two gondolieri put the trunk on the floor at the end of the bed.

Mama turned to face Filipa. "This is your home now and I know they will look after you well. I will visit as often as I can. Adio Filipa."

"Adio Mama," Filipa said, and she watched Mama and the two men head away. Filipa's room wasn't exactly a cell: it had a bed to the left, a simple chair in the corner, a cabinet with a bowl, jug and a towel, and a window which overlooked the lagoon. The only decoration was a simple, wooden cross above the bed. The cell was spacious enough, and almost as big as her room at home.

"Let me show you around," sòra Augusta said.

They walked along the corridor while Filipa was told the all nuns lived in cells along that wing of the cloister. The corridor led into a compact chapel, illuminated by windows high in the walls. The chapel was quite plain inside with white walls and a white ceiling supported by timber beams. There was a dark varnished alter and a lectern, and several rows of dark varnished pews. A doorway from the chapel led into the other, squat wing, and they entered what sòra Augusta called the refectory or the eating area. This was a large, open room with brown walls and a ceiling in white, and quite bright with windows on two sides; some overlooking the lagoon, and other windows overlooking a grassed area. There was one large table with benches on either side, and a smaller table with four chairs. Beyond the refectory was a kitchen, where two nuns and two other women cooked on a hearth many times bigger than Filipa had ever seen before. Cooking implements hung from racks suspended from the ceiling, beneath which were timber benches with pans on shelves below. Many cupboards lined the near wall. Next to the kitchen was the bathhouse with two, large tubs. Beside the bathhouse was the laundry, and then came what was called the necessarium or a large latrine. They left that wing and followed a covered walkway which lined the open, grassed square, and that walkway led to a lower-roofed extension of the chapel. That was the chapter house, which sòra Augusta explained as being the meeting area. That was the grandest so far; all in white inside with a tall ceiling, while windows on both sides allowed light to flood in. Solid timber benches were built into the walls on all four sides. A doorway on the far side of the chapter house led to a second covered walkway which lined another grassed square, and beyond that square was a garden of tall trees which looked quite magnificent. Near the garden was a small, stone building and Filipa asked what that was. Sòra Augusta explained that building was an unused storeroom, which once was used to land and store goods from the lagoon. Next to the chapter house was a smaller building, and sòra Augusta took Filipa to that building; knocked on a grey door and waited. The door opened to reveal a beautiful woman in the most magnificent gown. Through the open door Filipa made out a living room with two comfortable chairs, a desk strewn with papers with its own chair, and a doorway to another room beyond.

"Benvegnùa," the woman said. "You must be siórina Barbarigo."

"Bongiorno," Filipa said. "I'm Filipa Barbarigo."

"I'm badésa Barbarella della Fontana, but you can call me Barbarella. Grassie Augusta," and sòra Augusta left. "Come in," Barbarella said and Filipa entered the light, spacious room painted white, with windows overlooking the grassed area and the tree garden. "Sit, per piasser," and Filipa sat on a chair. Barbarella sat on a chair opposite, and like Clara she wore the most beautiful giornea, but in green silk which almost matched the lush, green grass seen through the windows. "Being newly arrived I understand how bewildering things must seem."

That was an understatement! The abasia was huge and totally run by women, with most dressed in simple black but some in gorgeous outfits. And Clara running after Marco, whoever he was. "You're in charge here?" Filipa asked.

"I am and I'm glad we can give you a home. I hope you will enjoy your life here, and I'm sure we will enjoy having you with us. Barbarigo is a fine, patrician family, and with the good dowry your parents paid, we will look after you as best we can. Did you bring your own clothes?"

"I brought my clothes," Filipa said.

41

"Good. As a patrician you have certain freedoms, and wearing your own clothes is one, and there are others if you feel so inclined."

Filipa suddenly realised what was going on. "Would one of those freedoms be having a man visit?"

Barbarella smiled brightly. "You met Clara."

"I met Clara chasing Marco."

"Before anything like that happens, you and I will have a long talk. And then we can see what happens. In the meantime make yourself at home; I'm sorry that your cell is so austere but we can work on that if you wish. Vespers is at five in the chapel and after that is supper, and you will be eating at my table."

"The smaller table in the refrectory?"

"Sé." Barbarella tilted her head and stared at Filipa. "Sometimes beauty comes at a cost, Filipa," she said.

"Like being sent to an abasia because your family doesn't trust you in marriage?" Filipa said.

"Sé."

Barbarella was about thirty and divinely beautiful: with delicately sculptured features, deep blue eyes, full, dark lips and attractive dimples on her cheeks. Barbarella knew the cost of beauty well enough.

"You can make yourself at home now," Barbarella said, rising to open the door.

Filipa went outside and followed the walkway around to the cell building, and then the corridor inside. Beside Filipa's cell was Clara's cell with the door open and no sign of Marco. Filipa peered inside to a room the copy of her own, but it had a larger bed with a feather mattress, and had a canopy in purple silk above. A tapestry of Venèsia as seen from the lagoon hung on one wall, and there was a shelf with trinkets opposite.

"Do you like it?" Clara asked from behind.

Filipa nodded her head. "It's cosy."

"It doesn't take much to turn a cell into home. Have you met Barbarella?"

Filipa turned around to face Clara, who was merely attractive enough to have any man chase after her. "I have."

"I'm sure you will enjoy your time here."

Abasia San Nicolai di Torcello was not all what Filipa expected, and she was sure she would enjoy her time there.

Chapter Three

Dardi returned to the barber shop near the campo; it had been three days and he needed a shave, and that barber gave the best shaves in the parish. Probably the best shaves in Venèsia. Dardi entered the shop and the barber's eyes met his. Dardi sensed something but couldn't quite put a finger on it.

"A shave siór?" the barber asked.

"Sé, per piasser," Dardi said.

Dardi sat in the chair while the barber got to work. A close shave without a nick or a cut showed great skill, but he was a dour and taciturn young man. Early twenties, a bit shorter than average with medium length brown hear. He was quite formal and didn't say a word the whole time he shaved Dardi. Another customer entered.

"Bondi Mario," the barber said cheerfully.

"Bondi Marin," the customer replied.

"I'll be with you in just a moment."

So the barber's name was Marin, and he was pleasant to some customers at least. Marin finished the shave, wiped the soap away and Dardi paid him for his services. Another customer entered and Dardi turned around to see Clario. Clario sat to wait while the other customer, Mario, was shaved. Dardi sat beside Clario, and Marin the barber briefly turned to face them both. He frowned at them before returning to chat with Mario. Marin finished Mario's shave, Mario paid and left, and Clario took his place. They agreed to a shave and Marin did that efficiently as he always did. Clario settled his money, Dardi stood, and they left the shop.

"That barber's a man of few words," Clario said.

He was with some customers. "Sé he is," Dardi said while wondering why Marin was talkative with Mario. Maybe they were old friends, or perhaps Marin was uncomfortable with the well-dressed. Dardi and Clario walked towards Él Geto in silence. Él Geto was home to much of the Jewish population of Venèsia. Jews were unwelcome in Venèsia and they knew it, so they kept to themselves and didn't make trouble. So if two men happened to come and go from a room in Él Geto; that was either not noticed or wouldn't go any further. In other words Él Geto was safe, or as safe as two men could be.

"How are the arrangements for your marriage?" Clario asked.

"We marry on Thursday at her home, and are blessed on Sunday at her church," Dardi said.

"What will that mean for us?"

"As little as possible, I hope."

"You have to make love with your wife."

"I have to consummate my marriage with Caterina, and I have to make love with Caterina until she's pregnant."

"And then you will see me?"

45

"I will see you regardless."

"When we're apart I will picture you with that woman."

Dardi turned his head. "Don't Clario! This is something I have to do to protect us. If I refuse an arranged marriage or refuse all women, questions will be asked. So I have to marry, and I have to make love with her so I can love you."

"I understand."

"Don't get jealous, Clario."

They reached the building and climbed the stairs to the top floor. Dardi unlocked the door and went inside. Clario followed and closed it behind him. Dardi grabbed Clario and pushed him against the wall and kissed him, and Clario responded with his tongue. They kissed and Dardi broke it off. "When I fuck her I will be fucking you in my mind."

Clario pulled Dardi close and they kissed again, until Clario broke it off. "I know you will."

* * *

Marin lurked in the shadows of the ground floor of the apartment building near Rio de l'Alboro, desperately hoping he wasn't spotted and chased away. It wasn't proper for a young man to be hiding there. Marin sensed someone coming down the stairs and looked around the corner, but he saw an older man and hid once more. Outside was busy in a fading light, while Marin hid from view and pondered those two customers. They brought business to his store but Marin didn't want to be involved with those sorts of men, who for some reason used barber shops to associate with each other. That was a situation he could do without. Marin was so deep in his thoughts that he didn't notice Blanca entering the building until she almost reached the staircase. Marin rushed to her and she put her hand over her mouth with surprise.

"Marin, what are you doing here?" she asked.

"I would like to talk with you," Marin said. "Away from here."

"Where?"

"My shop."

"Alright."

They walked in silence along the calle, across the campo and to Marin's shop in a building painted red, although much faded. Marin unlocked the door and held it open; followed Blanca inside and locked the door behind him.

Marin had rehearsed what to say and the words came out easily. "I want to marry you Blanca," he said.

"I want to marry you too," Blanca said. "But my Papa can't afford the dowry."

"There's another way."

"What other way?"

"Do you really want to marry me?"

She took both his hands and looked into his eyes. "Sé I do."

"Then we can make love and you can tell your Papa."

"And my Papa tells your Papa...."

Marin nodded.

"You'll get into trouble," Blanca said.

"Trouble like that is worth it for you. Besides, this is about two ducats, which isn't so much in a lifetime together."

"Am I worth two ducats?" Blanca asked, smiling.

Marin grabbed her and held her and she felt so good. "You're worth two-hundred ducats."

"Then we must make love."

"Are you sure about this?"

She kissed him. "I'm sure."

"Here and now?"

"Sé," Blanca said very, very softly.

"I don't have a soft bed for you Blanca; just some towels on the floor."

"A bed doesn't matter as long as I'm with you."

Marin let Blanca go and took four of his white towels and lay them on the floor. Blanca looked at them and then she looked at Marin. She removed the black cord at her waist, untied the side of her simple, white giornea and removed that, and unlaced and removed her black gamurra too, and then removed her camicia. Marin had never seen such beauty before, and he quickly removed his clothes.

48

Blanca knelt on the towels and Marin knelt with her. They kissed, the first time they'd ever kissed, and Marin knew they were doing the right thing.

* * *

Sleep at Abasia San Nicolai di Torcello was broken at two with Matins Laud; a service in the chapel between the first and second sleeps. After returning to bed, nuns woke at six with all rising to wash and then to have breakfast, with Barbarella, Clara, Filipa, and the other patrician nun, sòra Anna Molin, at the smaller table, which was really the table for patricians. Breakfast was freshly baked bread and a cup of milk, after which came the second service of the day; Prime at seven. Those who so chose could go to the chapter house to read and discuss the bible with Barbarella, while those who weren't interested in that could occupy themselves in other ways. The next service was Tierce at nine, which was prayer and a hymn in the chapel followed by work for those nuns assigned to work. Work included the kitchen to cook dinner, the laundry, housework and cleaning, or the garden outside. At midday came Sext None in the chapel, followed by dinner, which on Filipa's first day was cuttlefish with rice and a cup of wine. Most returned to work until the bell chimed at five for Vespers in the chapel, followed by supper, which was leftover from dinner, again with wine. Then came the last service of the day at seven: Compline in the chapel lit with candles because it was getting dark. After Compline the nuns went to bed.

On her second full day at the Abasia; the day Filipa turned 18, she took her place at the table for patricians. A servant girl brought bread and a cup of milk, which Filipa sipped. Surprisingly Filipa was looking forward to Prime. The prayer was soothing and relaxing, while the voices of seventeen women singing hymns were uplifting in a way that Filipa had never experienced before. The patrician women attended all services, although they didn't have to work around the abasia.

"How have you found your first day here?" Barbarella asked Filipa.

"I liked my first day very much," Filipa replied, while deciding not to mention turning 18. She felt awkward talking about that.

"I'm glad," Barbarella said.

After breakfast came Prime, with Barbarella leading the nuns in prayer and hymn, and then they went their own ways for an hour. Filipa returned to the chapel for Tierce, and after the service both Anna and Clara put chairs on the grass and sunned their hair. The fashion for women was fair hair, and many women applied lotions and then sat in the sun with broad-brimmed capèli with tops cut away, so the sun would bleach their hair and the brim would protect their faces. Filipa sat in the shade on the low, stone wall of the walkway.

"How do you get your hair so fair?" Anna asked.

"My hair is naturally this colour," Filipa said.

"Lucky you!"

Filipa shrugged her shoulders.

"Is Marco coming today?" Anna asked Clara.

"No," Clara said. "Carlo is visiting today. And you?"

"Francesco tomorrow as usual."

"Of course."

Filipa felt out; really, really out. She wondered about the long talk Barbarella mentioned. The sooner that happened the better. She glanced at Barbarella's room but all was still and quiet. Filipa sat on the stone wall and didn't know what to say. They were women and she was still a girl. She knew men admired her but she was just a girl. She had to get away and was interested by the unusual, tall chimneys anyway. She went to the brick wall separating the abasia from the lagoon, and looked over. There was a furnace under the cloister which must heat their cells. She then went to the little, stone building which had a ramshackle, timber door of peeling paint. Again Filipa looked over the wall, and the storeroom had an opening at the bottom to allow goods to be loaded from the lagoon. Satisfied, she explored the tree garden before returning to the stone wall and sitting in silence. The rest of the day dragged by and the next day too;

where Filipa saw Anna with her man, Francesco. He came to the corridor and she let him into her cell. Filipa fantasised what they would be doing together and wished that was her. The following day over breakfast still nothing was mentioned, and after Prime, Barbarella went to the chapter house as usual. Then after Tierce, Filipa followed Barbarella outside.

"Excuse me Barbarella," Filipa said. "You said we would talk sometime."

"Do you want to talk now?" Barbarella asked.

"Sé, per piasser."

Barbarella invited Filipa in, closed the door, and invited Filipa to sit on an armchair. Barbarella sat opposite.

"Have you liked your time as a nun?" Barbarella asked.

"I like it very much; it's soothing and relaxing," Filipa said.

"The rhythm of prayer and song has that effect. Do you have concerns about the future your family has chosen for you?"

Before she came to the convent Filipa was worried about being locked away behind stone walls, and that was made worse by the patrician nuns living separate lives from the rest. She wondered how to put it, and then it came to her. "I feel cut off from the world."

"All women are cut off from the world in one way or another."

"But married women have a husband and their children."

"And you won't ever have a husband or children."

"The nuns are nice, especially Clara and Anna, but that's not the same."

"What do you think of men?" Barbarella asked.

"I like men of course. I have a friend who I would have like to marry. He's a good man and very handsome."

"Would you like to go through your life without ever touching a man?"

"I wondered about that when my Mama told me I was to be a nun." Filipa looked at the floor. "Sometimes I dream things," she said quietly. Filipa sometimes imagined what Dardi looked like naked, and she fantasised herself with Dardi hugging and kissing her, and feeling his body pressed against her body.

"Do you more than dream?"

Filipa felt herself getting flushed. "Sé I do," she said very, very quietly. Whenever Filipa fantasised about Dardi she felt wet and tingly down there, and when she touched and rubbed she felt the most amazing pleasure which took her to another place. And then she felt empty and needed more. She could pleasure herself whenever she chose, but she needed more than that.

"All women feel the same. That's why Clara and Anna have men visit them."

Filipa understood. "Can I have a man visit me?" she asked.

"You can have as many men as you like. Clara has four men."

Filipa gasped and then looked at Barbarella. "I'm sorry," she said, feeling hot and knowing she was blushing even more.

"You will see Clara's men soon enough."

"We have cells side-by-side."

"Anna has her friend who comes by once or twice a week."

"I've seen him."

"But unlike other women, we can't allow ourselves to fall pregnant. There are ways to avoid that and they're surprisingly effective. The simplest way is to ask men not to ejaculate inside us."

"Men will do that?"

"Some do and some don't; it's not always something they can control. Some men prefer not to control themselves, but there are other options for when that happens. I will show you." Barbarella left for the other room and returned with a cup and gave it to Filipa. In it were many seeds. "These are the seeds of the wild carrot, and if we take some of these seeds in drinks for three or four days after a man ejaculates inside us, that should prevent pregnancy. We grow wild carrot here, and we always have a supply of seeds."

"So men not ejaculating inside us is more to conserve these seeds and reduce the risk of pregnancy?"

"That's right. And if men do ejaculate inside us, then drinks of wild carrot seeds should resolve that problem."

"If that doesn't?"

"The early symptoms of pregnancy are feeling nauseous and not having a monthly cycle. If either of those happens then we will make a hot drink with pennyroyal, and we have pennyroyal growing here as well."

"I understand."

"But the least risky option is to ask men not to ejaculate inside us. Men are used to that and they still enjoy a lot of pleasure before those last moments, and we enjoy pleasure too."

Filipa had fantasised about making love for many years and especially in the past days, and in the space of one conversation she had come closer to her fantasy. "This will make me a woman," Filipa said.

"You're very beautiful Filipa, and your time will come when you're ready."

"When will I be ready?"

"Would your friend take your virginity?"

Filipa thought back to their strange meeting at the campo. "I don't know," she said. "I'm not sure."

"Do you know anyone else?"

Filipa shook her head. "No I don't."

"You could go to Venèsia, find a man and bring him here, and he could take your virginity."

"That doesn't seem right," Filipa said automatically.

"No, it doesn't. Losing our virginity is not the same as a married woman on her wedding night, but it's important to us."

Filipa agreed. "Sé it is."

"This is only your first week here Filipa, so there's no rush. If you want, one of us can take your virginity."

"How?" Filipa asked, confused and dumbfounded.

"I will show you," Barbarella said, and she left the room. She came back with a round glass thing and gave it to Filipa. "With this," Barbarella said.

"Is this what men are like?"

"About this size and pointed at the end like that, but soft and warm and just lovely."

"This is cold and hard."

Barbarella touched Filipa's forehead. "It's what goes on in here that matters."

Filipa knew that was right, like her fantasies about Dardi. What was inside her body didn't matter anywhere near as much as the person she was with. "I understand," Filipa said.

"Think about this Filipa."

"Would you do this for me?"

"I will if you ask me, but not today. First you must think about what you really want, maybe sleep on it and let God tell you in your dreams, and if you still want me then I will help you. If you want someone else I will understand, because this is your decision for your next step in life. If you don't ask me again I will understand."

"You have been good to me today, Barbarella. Can I ask who you were with for your first time?"

"Of course you can, Filipa. Shortly after I started here I met the most wonderful, kind, gentle man."

"I would like Dardi to make love with me, but he was quite strange the other week so I don't know. And you have been so good to me today that I want you to do this for me!"

"Sleep on this Filipa, and if I hear from you that's good, and if I don't hear from you then you have decided to see your friend."

"Grassie. Do you have a man or men at the moment?"

"I have Pietro who comes here a few times a week."

"And glass for other times."

"Do you want one of those?" Barbarella asked.

Filipa wrapped her fingers around it and her heart beat fast. "Sé, grassie."

* * *

The family were startled by hammering at their door while Marin wondered why it took so long for siór Agoli to make his appearance. Papa opened the door and siór Agoli burst into the room dragging Blanca with him.

"Your son stole my daughter!" siór Agoli bellowed.

"Pardon?" Papa asked.

"Your son stole her virginity!"

Papa frowned and slowly he turned his head towards Marin. "Is this true?" he asked.

"Sé it is," Marin said.

Papa sighed. "You did this deliberately."

"We did."

"We have to right what happened," Papa said to siór Agoli. "You reached six ducats for a dowry and we can accept that."

"I originally offered five ducats," siór Agoli said.

"We reached six," Papa said.

"Pay them six, Papa," Blanca said. "Marin owes money for his shop."

"Alright Blanca; six ducats. You'll have your money by Friday."

Papa frowned. "We'll do the contract for betrothal tomorrow at midday with the notary," he said.

Mama went to Blanca and held her hands. "I haven't said anything until now, but I'm glad you'll be part of our family. I'm sure you'll be a good wife and mother, and I'm sure you'll help Marin however you can."

"Grassie sióra Curri. I'll try my best. I'll start on my wedding dress straight away."

"Your mama will help you," siór Agoli said.

"I can see you're a practical family," Mama said. "That will help Marin."

"The ring day will be Thursday next week," siór Agoli said. "I'll speak with the notary tomorrow to arrange his time, and I'll speak to the priest at Cièsa di Santa Maria del Giglio for a blessing on the following Sunday."

"That'll be fine," Papa said.

"We'll leave you now."

They left and Papa closed the door. "You did the wrong thing," he said to Marin.

"Blanca is hard working, practical and thrifty," Marin said. "She's worth much more than the two ducats we couldn't agree upon."

"He's right Daniele," Mama said. "You can see they're happy together, and she will bring much to their marriage."

"I'm pleased for you," Laura said to Marin.

"You have a new sister," Marin said.

"Sé I do, and I'm happy about that. Blanca's lovely."

Marin was quite happy. Soon he would be married and in his own home, and he had to find a room to rent. A good room for the best wife in the parish. He also had to buy a ring for Blanca, and he would do that once the contract was signed. Blanca would sew her dress, while her mother would arrange the wedding feast with her friends and neighbours for Thursday next week. There was so much to do!

"It's getting late and we must eat," Papa said.

As always supper was leftover from dinner, warming in the pot on the hearth. That and watered-down wine. Marin thought that late next week, his wife would be preparing him dinner and supper, and he looked forward to that. He knew he'd done the right thing.

Chapter Four

Dardi Zorzi had recently moved to Palàso Zorzi Bon, fronting Rio de San Severo. Filipa walked to the rear entrance at the end of a narrow lane between two other palàsi, and pulled the chain to ring the bell. A few moments later a servant girl in black opened the door.

"Bongiorno," Filipa said. "Is siór Dardi Zorzi home?"

"Bongiorno." the servant replied. "Who can I tell him is here?"

"Sòra Filipa Barbarigo."

"I'll be just a moment."

Filipa waited and then he heard Dardi running across the timber floor. "Filipa!" he exclaimed. "What are you doing here? And why are you dressed like that? No, I'm being rude; come inside per piasser."

Dardi stood to one side and Filipa entered their grand home, at least four or maybe even six times the size of Palàso Barbarigo.

"Come in here," Dardi said, and he led her to a living room. Filipa sat in an armchair and Dardi sat opposite. "I thought you were sent to an abasia," Dardi said.

"I am at an abasia, but my life there has a lot of freedom. I don't have to wear their clothes, I'm allowed out, and I can have men as lovers."

"Pardon?"

"I can have men as lovers."

Dardi nodded thoughtfully. "There have been rumours of such things at certain abasie, but I never believed them until now."

"You can believe them Dardi."

"You're freer than a married woman."

"I can come and go as I wish, but I won't ever have children."

"That's a shame."

"Women's lives are never as we choose them to be."

"If it were up to me I would change things."

Filipa felt her heart skip a beat; he was such a nice man. "I know you would and that's why I came here. I'm eighteen years old and it's time for me, and I would like you to be my first."

Dardi pulled away. "I can't," he said.

Filipa wondered. "I understand," she said. "You're promised to Caterina Cornaro."

"Sé," he said, but Filipa sensed that wasn't it. It was like at the campo.

"I know the real reason," Filipa said. "You're my friend and I'm you're friend, and that's different to being lovers."

"That's right."

"I'm sorry if I made you feel awkward."

"No you didn't. Well, you did, but you're good at doing that!"

"That's why we're friends."

"Mischievous Filipa Barbarigo who comes up with all sorts of surprises."

"That's why they locked me away, you know."

Dardi chuckled.

"It's true!" Filipa said. "I'm not suited to be a faithful wife. I must go; I really came to Venèsia to pick up my lute."

"I didn't know you played music."

"I'm full of little surprises." Filipa stood. "Grassie Dardi, and you will keep my secret about the abasia?"

"I will."

"We will see each other from time to time."

"Sé, we will. If I could change the rules for women, I would. But I can't, so maybe what you have is as good as it gets."

"I think my new life is as good as it gets."

Dardi stood. "Let me show you out."

Dardi took Filipa to the back door, and Filipa crossed San Marco and reached her old home in about 10 minutes. She unlocked the back door and went upstairs to her old room. She stood at the doorway and it was so familiar, except her bed was stripped of sheets and blankets. She was gone. Filipa put her books in the linen bag she brought and slung it over her shoulder, took her jewellery box, took her lute, and went downstairs. She went outside and locked the door, used the lane to get to Fondamenta Duodo o Barbarigo and crossed Campo Santa Maria del Giglio. At the end a gondoliere waited at the jetty, and Filipa asked him to take her to Abasia San Nicolai di Torcello. She climbed into the fieze while the gondoliere pulled at his oar to guide them into the lagoon for the hour journey to her new home. At Torcello she paid him ten soldi, climbed out of the gondola and he pushed away. Filipa opened the door to the abasia; it wasn't locked during daylight hours, and went to her cell where she placed the lute on her trunk, the bag of books on her chair, and her jewellery box on the window sill. Filipa went outside and along the walkway to Barbarella's apartment, and there she paused. What to say? What she wanted. She knocked on the door and Barbarella opened it.

"Can you make love with me?" Filipa blurted.

"Sé sweet child," Barbarella said. "Come inside."

Filipa went into the living room.

"Do you want a bath to relax?" Barbarella asked.

"Sé, per piasser," Filipa said.

"I will ask the servants to prepare a bath for you."

Barbarella left and Filipa went to the other room; dominated by a large bed with a feather mattress. A green, linen canopy stood above the bed and Filipa imagined herself naked under that canopy. Soon enough. Two servants brought a wooden tub into the bedroom, and more servants carried steel jugs of hot water. They filled the tub while Barbarella watched, and then Barbarella closed the door.

"You can undress for your bath," Barbarella said.

Filipa did and she felt Barbarella's eyes on her, and that made her heart beat faster and faster. Filipa climbed into the bath and Barbarella rolled her sleeve up and washed Filipa with soap and a sponge. Nobody had ever washed her before, and she closed her eyes and relaxed. Yes relaxed, Barbarella was right, a bath was relaxing.

Barbarella fetched a towel and Filipa stood. Barbarella knelt and looked up at Filipa's eyes. There was something strange about her look, her eyes wide open and yet half-closed. "You're a girl and yet you have the body of a woman," Barbarella whispered barely loud enough for Filipa to hear. "I never imagined such beauty existed." Barbarella wiped Filipa slowly and delicately while still gazing into Filipa's eyes, then Filipa climbed from the bath and Barbarella gently wiped Filipa's legs and feet. Filipa watched Barbarella remove her clothes, layer upon layer, until she was naked. Filipa felt awkward: she was tall and slim while Barbarella was a real woman. Barbarella was beautiful and Filipa felt undeserving of such beauty. Only Barbarella arms found their way around Filipa's waist, her hands rested on Filipa's buttocks, and her tongue touched Filipa's lips. Filipa instinctively opened her mouth to allow that tongue inside, and she felt herself riding something which wasn't her.

Hungry tongues touched and explored while Filipa tentatively rested her hands on Barbarella's buttocks which felt firm and yet soft. Breasts pressed against breasts, hands on buttocks, tongues against tongues until Barbarella eased away and climbed onto her bed. Filipa watched, confused, wondering if she should. Her legs knew what to do and she found herself on that bed, kissing once more. Filipa's felt her wetness, she ached down there. She bit the side of Barbarella's neck in frustration, and Barbarella touched between Filipa's legs and that was what she needed.

"Lay down mia amór," Barbarella whispered.

Barbarella licked and sucked, licked and sucked while Filipa's pleasure swelled not of her control, and that startled her. She had no control; just her pleasure growing, swelling and filling her. Filling her and filling her. She felt the glass penis at her, in her, stretching her, and then it stung; it burned and stung!

"Relax mia amór," Barbarella murmured.

Filipa tried to relax but it just hurt! Hurt and hurt and the pain faded. Filipa breathed out deeply and felt the penis moving slowly inside her. Filipa opened her eyes and admired beautiful, wonderful Barbarella.

"Let me make love to you," Filipa murmured, and the penis slowly left her.

Barbarella lay down and Filipa kissed and licked and sucked and grabbed the glass penis covered in blood, and

66

wiped it with her hand before sliding it inside. She rubbed and fucked, rubbed and fucked and Barbarella grabbed Filipa's arm. Rubbed and fucked, rubbed and fucked and Barbarella gasped ever so quietly. Filipa eased the penis free and kissed Barbarella, and Barbarella pulled Filipa to her and kissed her and kissed her. Kissed her and kissed her; beautiful, wonderful woman.

Filipa lay with her head resting on Barbarella's soft body. She felt like all her worries had been taken away and only goodness was left.

"Are you alright?" Barbarella asked.

Filipa rolled over and looked into Barbarella's deep, blue eyes. "I'm good," she said, but that wasn't right. "I feel peaceful. Will I feel like this whenever I make love?"

"You will."

"I want to make love with you."

"I'm the badésa and you're a nun, and I have many other nuns under my care."

"Sé, you do."

"One day we will make love again."

Filipa put her head down and Barbarella played with Filipa's hair. That was nice. Barbarella moved and reached for the table beside her bed. Filipa looked up and Barbarella handed her a book. Filipa opened the book and got the greatest surprise.

"You might find this useful for when the time comes," Barbarella said.

Filipa turned over the pages and some of the positions were complicated. "Is making love with a man really like this?" she asked.

"Not exactly, but this will give you some ideas."

Filipa started from the beginning and turned the pages over until she reached the page 'Julie avec un athelete'. The man was on his back on a pillow and Julie was above him with her back to his face, and with his member inside her. "I like this," she said.

Barbarella looked over her shoulder. "Men like that one," she said. "They can see themselves inside you. That one feels good."

Filipa turned over more pages and then reached 'Mars et Venus', and she felt tingly. The man was on his back and Venus was above him, with his member inside her while she kissed him. "I like this one."

Barbarella looked again. "You like being on top."

"Do men have a problem with that?"

"No, but you can't stop them ejaculating inside you. That doesn't matter though."

Filipa reached the end of the book and Barbarella took it. She turned over some pages until she reached 'Enée et Didon'. She gave that to Filipa. "This one is the most important."

Enée was half-naked and he was clothed, and he was rubbing her sex. "I understand," Filipa said. "Do men use their tongues like we did?"

"Some men do and some don't, and if they don't then they must use their fingers first, and then they can enter you."

"They must use their tongues or their fingers before they enter us."

"That's the way God made men and women to fit together. Keep that book and give it back when you're finished with it."

"Grassie."

Barbarella played with Filipa's hair again. "Until today I hadn't seen perfection," she said quietly. "You're only eighteen and yet you're perfect. Men of patrician birth don't marry until they're about thirty, so there are many good men out there for you to choose from. Choose wisely dear girl."

"I will try."

Filipa looked at the bathtub and felt her eyes go moist. "That bath was most delightful, but it brings memories for me now. Every week in the kitchen; me first and then Cristina."

"Cristina is your sister who's getting married?" Barbarella asked.

"My smart younger sister. Clever Cristina and naughty Filipa."

"I heard you have a lute."

"Oh sé, I can play that and sing. Always tragic love songs!"

"You must be smart to be able to play music and sing."

"I don't know. I brought my books as well; I just love poetry. Long stories bore me but I could read poems all day."

"You're full of surprises Filipa Barbarigo."

"You can borrow my poems if you want."

Barbarella grabbed Filipa and kissed her, and Filipa was surprised by that.

"You are so wonderful Filipa Barbarigo. You better go before I lock you in here and throw away the key!"

"Is that a threat or a promise?"

Barbarella slapped Filipa's bottom. "Go now sòra Filipa or I will do something I will regret."

"Will we make love again one day?"

"Sé we will."

* * *

Late April was a good time for a wedding. The weather was fine but not hot, while everyone seemed more cheerful with the change of season. Campo Santa Maria del Giglio looked particularly splendid that fine, spring afternoon. Tables were in the Campo for the feast to follow the ring ceremony; a feast cooked by many, willing hands. Around the corner, many congregated outside the Agoli family home. Inside,

Blanca looked particularly beautiful in a new, blue dress with a black séngia. Blue for virginity although that wasn't technically true, but her virginity was taken by her betrothed which was close enough. Marin and his parents went inside to meet with Blanca, her parents and the notary, while those on the stairwell were quite noisy, and made many good-natured but explicit suggestions.

The notary asked the three questions: were they of age, did they have parental consent, and were they not related in a way to prevent marriage. The notary then oversaw the vows, where Marin placed the ring on the third finger of Blanca's right hand. Then Marin could kiss Blanca, and they were married to the cheers of the crowd.

After the ceremony it was all busy in the campo. Wine was served from a cask while women fetched food left stewing. A special cake, made of many smaller cakes stacked one on top of the other, layer upon layer, marked the bride and groom's table. Beyond that was a long table for their many guests: family and friends. Marin and Blanca had to kiss over their cake, and after that the rowdy feast was underway. The wine took effect and the good-natured suggestions became even more explicit, but everyone had fun and that was what mattered. They enjoyed the food, the drink and the jokes that afternoon, while the minstrels who frequented the campo paid special attention to the wedding feast which shared their space. Music and songs made the feast even more special as daylight faded.

After a time the crowd got ever more ribald and insisted on escorting Blanca to her new home, as was the tradition. She was hoisted high on many shoulders, laughing wildly while looking absolutely terrified! Marin led the way to the room he rented, just along from his shop. Marin went inside and climbed the stairs to their room, while Vicenzo and Blanca's older brothers, Maffeo and Anzolo, followed Marin to the bed. They dropped Blanca down, and then the single men in the room charged at the bed and groped at her dress, lifting it up and exposing her stockinged legs. Vicenzo won one prize; a garter for good luck, and Marin's friend Piero got the other garter.

"Do you know what to do Marin?"

"Do you know where it goes?"

"Can I watch?"

Marin stood in front of his bed and put his hands in the air. "Grassie tuti everyone for coming, and if you'll leave us be...."

"So you can do what?" Vicenzo asked.

"Do what I'm supposed to do," Marin said.

"We should go," Papa said.

They all left the room, and Marin closed the door before looking towards Blanca all in a mess on their bed.

"Are you alright Blanca?" he asked.

72

"That was a fun wedding," Blanca said. She sat up and straightened her dress. "I like this room," she said looking around. "I will remember my first home for always."

It was a simple room with a table, two benches, a cupboard to prepare food and the bed, of course. In time they would need a better home, but for the while that room was good enough.

Marin knew he would remember two things for always. His first home, and their special night in his shop. But what was to come was more special, given they were now married. Blanca stood and removed the séngia at her waist and Marin removed his séngia too. In parallel they removed their clothes, and then Marin took his wife's hand and helped her back onto their bed. It was time to consummate their marriage.

Chapter Five

Piasà San Marco bustled on a mild, cloudy, mid-spring day.
Beggars and cripples set themselves in any space they could
find, and Filipa wished she could give the worst of the
cripples some coins but she had to make her money last.
There was a puppet show and Filipa stood behind the crowd
for a moment, enjoying the pleasure of the many children
watching the simple treat. Several ballad singers with lutes
performed, and made their livings from coins placed in their
upturned capèli. Closer to Canal Grando were stalls of
vegetable vendors and fishmongers noisily calling for
business, and surrounded by the inevitable stray dogs. On
the far side of the piasà was Baxélega di San Marco, in granite
with multiple arches facing the piasà, ornate statues above
each arch and a high, domed roof behind those statues. In
front of the baxélega were the four, great horses symbolising
the power of La Repubblica di Venèsia. Beyond the baxélega
was Palàso Ducale; already massive and being extended along
the wing facing Piasá San Marco. Palàso Ducale was the
home of Él Doxe, and was the seat of government. Él Doxe
was the supreme magistrate of La Repubblica di Venèsia, but
the palàso was much more than his home. Palàso Ducale was
also the home of Él Maggior Consiglio, the great council, Él
Consìlio dèi Cuarànta, the council of 40, Él Consìlio dèi
Diéxe, the council of ten, Él Colèjo, the administrators of

Venèsia, and Él Consìlio dèi Pregadi who managed foreign relations. Only patricians, the noble class of Venèsia, could hold positions in those bodies; patricians like famégia Barbarigo. Along the south side of the piasà was L'ospìsio Orseolo, a hospice for pilgrims visiting the relics of Saint Marco. The main building along the northern edge of the piasà, Él Procuradi, was the offices of Él Procuradór di San Marco, the administrator of Baxélega di San Marco. Él procuradór was a lifetime appointment made by él doxe, and él procuradór appointed his staff from patricians. A patrician like Filipa truly belonged at Piasà San Marco.

Filipa walked towards Él Procuradi which had shops behind a walkway on the ground floor, and she then headed along Piaséta dèi Leoncini. Just out of the piaséta was Él Lión Biànco, an inn. She went inside and contemplated what to do. The dark-painted inn was crowded, noisy, and smelled pungent after the freshness outside. It smelled of many different types of food, stale wine, and unwashed bodies, while it was gloomy especially being painted in dark brown. Two waiters navigated the crush of tables stacked closely together, each with simple benches either side. Some ate their meals with forks while others, working men, gobbled their food with fingers, and succeeded in getting half their meals onto the tables in the process! Waiters came and went through an open doorway to the right, which led to the kitchen. A woman in black stood behind a simple, timber

75

counter serving drinks, while behind her were wine barrels on a shelf, and cups were stored beneath the counter. Filipa went to that woman and asked for a cup of wine. The woman poured the wine from the tap and Filipa paid two soldi. Again Filipa surveyed the room and there was one smaller table in the far corner with only one handsome young man with fair skin and long, brown hair, and he was well dressed in a red silk giornea with white collars and cuffs, dark red calsa and a black velvet baréta. Perhaps late twenties and not yet of marrying age for a man. Filipa went to that table and bowed slightly.

"Bongiorno siór," she said. "May I sit here?"

"Of course siórina," he said.

Filipa sat. "I'm Filipa Barbarigo," she said.

"I'm Andrea Barbo," he replied.

"I'm sorry to disturb your dinner," Filipa said. He was finishing a plate of shrimp with polenta, and he had a cup of wine.

"No, not at all; you're a welcome distraction siórina Barbarigo."

Filipa smiled sweetly. "Grassie siór Barbo," she said.

"You can call me Andrea."

"You can call me Filipa."

"I haven't seen you here before," Andrea said.

"I haven't seen you here before either," Filipa said.

"It's uncommon for a woman to venture into an inn on her own."

"I know; I haven't done this before."

"What brings you here?"

"I'm looking for a man."

"Which man?"

"A handsome man who can take time away from his labours."

"To do what?"

"To accompany me to my home on the Island of Torcello."

Andrea frowned and then drank some of his wine. "And then?"

"If we get on well together...."

"I understand." Andrea drank a little more of his wine. "I can take time away from my labours."

"Good."

"I must speak with someone first."

Andrea crossed the room to a table packed with six men, all well-dressed and undoubtedly patricians. He bent down and spoke with one who nodded, and then Andrea returned. Filipa finished her wine and stood, and Andrea led her out of the inn to the freshness of the calle leading to the piaséta.

"What work do you do?" Filipa asked Andrea.

"I work for Él Procuradór di San Marco," he said. "I can show you the baxélega and point out some interesting features."

"Grassie Andrea." Giovanni Barbo was Él Procuradór di San Marco, a most prestigious appointment, and Filipa guessed that Andrea worked for his father.

Construction of the baxélega commenced when the remains of Saint Marco, the writer of the Gospel of Marco, were stolen from Alexandra and taken to Venèsia. Parts of the interior of Cièsa d'Oro, the church of gold, were truly breathtaking with many upper surfaces covered in bright mosaics, mostly in gold and blue. Unfortunately the interior was damaged by a recent fire in 1419, and restoration was slowly underway. Andrea was sure that in time the interior of the baxélega would truly represent the wealth and power of Venèsia, but Filipa wondered about the relative worth of wealth and power gained from never-ending wars, and the death and suffering caused by those wars. Her brother Polo had been away for many years fighting the Lombardians. Filipa also wondered about the relative worth of wealth and power, when half the patrician women of Venèsia couldn't afford to marry and were sent to abasie instead. Filipa kept those thoughts to herself. If she were with Dardi she would have said what she thought and he would have been shocked by her outspoken ways, and he would have agreed with her too. But Filipa sensed that Andrea Barbo was more conventional than Dardi Zorzi.

They reached the piasà and Filipa thanked Andrea for the tour, and suggested they find a gondola. They walked to the nearby jetty and Filipa hailed a gondoliere and asked him to take them to Abasia San Nicolai di Torcello. They boarded his bright yellow craft and went into fieze. Once inside Andrea closed the blinds so nobody could see in.

"Can I kiss you?" he asked.

"You can kiss me," Filipa said.

He kissed her; a firm, purposeful kiss and quite different to Barbarella. His strong hands on her face, holding her to him while their tongues touched and explored. His strength, his muscles; Filipa sensed his power. His power in her hands and that made her giddy with excitement. She picked him at the inn and his purpose was to pleasure her. That thought made Filipa feel giddier while the gondola rose and fell over the waves of the lagoon, with water sloshing against the little craft. His hand on her leg firmly squeezing her thigh, and returning to kiss her again. Holding her and kissing her most of the way to Torcello, until Filipa heard the sounds of the port. She pulled away and opened the blinds, and when they docked she paid the gondoliere.

"Andrea, I ask one thing of you," Filipa said while they walked along the promenade. "You must not ejaculate inside me."

"Of course."

"My room is basic and I have plans to improve it as best I can."

Andrea lifted the red ruby pendant from Filipa's neck. It was one of two pendants she owned, and she also wore her four gold rings; two on her left hand and two on her right.

"That's a nice pendant," he said.

"It belonged to my grandmother."

He let it go and Filipa opened the door. She led Andrea through the corridors towards her cell.

"So this is your home?" Andrea asked.

"The choice for women is a marriage without love, or an abasia like this. Few women in this abasia can do as I do."

"Because you're from famégia Barbarigo?"

"Correct."

Filipa opened the door to her cell and led Andrea inside, and decided to have him watch her. Then they would try 'Julie avec un athelete', only for him not to ejaculate inside her.

"Sit on the bed, per piasser," Filipa said and he did. Filipa removed her pendant and placed that in her jewellery box. She removed her capèło and séngia placed them on her lute on her trunk, and then she removed her two inch high mułóti and her calf-high calsi. Filipa loosened and removed her blue giornea and draped it over the back of her chair, and then she untied and removed her white gamurra. She then

80

unlaced and removed her linen camicia and heard Andrea gasp.

"You're beautiful," he said. "Like no woman I've ever seen before." He put his hands on her hips. "Your hips, your breasts, your legs; every part of you."

Filipa felt her hands shaking while she removed his baréta. For the first time she was going to see a man naked. "Stand, per piasser," she asked.

Andrea stood and she removed his séngia and then untied his giornea, and he lifted that off and away. Filipa unlaced his black gamurra and Andrea lifted that off as well. Then his white camicia and Filipa unbuckled the séngia around his waist while admiring the bulge between his legs. Andrea sat on the bed and removed his long, pointed scarpe, his fine, red calsa and his white, linen mutande, and Filipa watched, transfixed, as his cock sprang to full size. It was about the same size as the glass one, but irregular in shape and colour. Andrea stood and Filipa went to him, and he grabbed her buttocks and kissed her while she wrapped her hand around his cock. It was stiff and yet spongy, and hot to the touch. Delightfully hot to the touch. Andrea kneaded her buttocks firmly and that felt good, and he grabbed her breasts and kneaded them too, but more delicately, and then he lightly brushed her nipple before kissing it and flicking it with his tongue. Filipa held his arms and felt his firm muscles, and admired the light covering of dark hair on his body. Andrea guided Filipa to the bed, lay on his back and she knelt above him and bent down to kiss him. He put his fingers on her sex and that sent a shudder through her. But she wanted more so she edged forward and he lifted his head and used his tongue instead. Filipa closed her eyes and slowly, steadily she felt it building and building, until her pleasure burst free and filled her over and over.

Filipa had him just where she wanted him. She looked down and their eyes met. "You must tell me when you're close to ejaculating," she said and he nodded his head. Filipa turned around and put him inside her, and then she stopped to absorb the sensation of being stretched and filled by soft hardness. It was remarkable, and the more she lowered herself the better it felt; the ridges and veins on his cock caressing her, the warmth of him inside her, and the stretching. She took all of him, put her hands on his knees and rode him, and barely believed that was actually happening. She had a man under her power, totally under her power and her control, his hard and yet soft penis filling her and caressing her; his warmth inside expanding and filling her body, until she was warm all over. Filipa looked behind to see him watching, transfixed, and remembered Barbarella's comment about men seeing themselves inside. Filipa smiled at Andrea like a little boy watching his favourite treat. She rode him and felt her pleasure building once more, and she wanted that feeling of cosy, stretched warmness to last forever. He squeezed her buttocks, squeezing her and squeezing her and then he gasped 'I'm close'.

Filipa pulled away and rolled onto her back beside Andrea, and he filled her very, very hard. Then she felt his energy, harder and harder. She felt his strength, his muscles tense. Suddenly she felt his hot cock sliding on her stomach, he groaned, and she felt warm wetness on her skin. Groaning, sliding and then he kissed her, and Filipa held him to her. Their tongues touched and Filipa was content. He was a good man and that had been good. That had been good beyond her wildest dreams.

Andrea rolled aside and Filipa was aware of his liquid on her, and there was so much! She jumped out of bed, grabbed the towel from her washbasin and wiped herself before it made too much mess. Next time she would be better prepared!

"You're the most beautiful woman in Torcello," Andrea said softly.

"Grassie Andrea," Filipa said.

"I really mean it."

"You're very handsome Andrea."

"Grassie Filipa."

"I really mean it." Filipa wondered what came next. Did he go? She would invite him back but she wanted to try other men too. But for Andrea to go after just an hour together was too soon. And then Filipa knew. "Do you want me to play some music?"

"Aren't you tired?"

"No; I feel fine. I can play for us." Filipa put her capèlo and séngia on the floor and took her lute, and she opened her jewellery box and took her quill. "This will take time to tune," she said. Filipa sat on the bed and tuned her lute by ear, and as always every string was out. Eventually she got it right just as the bell chimed four, and she still had time.

"Breeze, blowing that blonde curling hair, stirring it, and being softly stirred in turn, scattering that sweet gold about; then gathering it, in a lovely knot of curls again.

"You linger around bright eyes whose loving sting pierces me so, 'till I feel it and weep, and I wander searching for my treasure, like a creature that often shies and kicks.

"Now I seem to find her, now I realise she's far away, now I'm comforted, now despair, now longing for her, now truly seeing her.

"Happy air, remain here with your living rays: and you, clear running stream, why can't I exchange my path for yours?"

"That was a sad song," Andrea said.

"Most songs for the lute are sad love songs. I can sing another."

"Sé, per piasser."

84

"It was on that day when the sun's ray was darkened in pity for its Maker that I was captured, and did not defend myself, because your lovely eyes had bound me, Lady.

"It did not seem to me to be a time to guard myself against Love's blows: so I went on confident, unsuspecting; from that, my troubles started, amongst the public sorrows.

"Love discovered me all weaponless, and opened the way to the heart through the eyes, which are made the passageways and doors of tears:

"So that it seems to me it does him little honour to wound me with his arrow, in that state, he not showing his bow at all to you who are armed."

"That was lovely Filipa, Andrea said. "I don't know what I did to deserve this."

Filipa put her lute and quill down and kissed his lips. "You let me have my way with you," she said.

"You said you wanted to improve your room."

"A larger bed with feather mattress would be more practical, and a canopy over the bed would be nice. Blue is my favourite colour, so I would like a canopy in blue silk. I would like curtains, and a shelf for my books and other things. I have a few books, and next time you come I can read you some poetry."

Andrea leaned out of bed and rummaged through his clothes for his séngia, and he opened his tacolinn. He gave Filipa a twenty lire coin which she put in her jewellery box.

"Grassie Andrea; I will save this for a bed and mattress. Can you come again next week?"

"I can come tomorrow."

Filipa laughed. "You're too greedy! No, next week."

"Monday at the same time?"

"Come to this room after dinner on Monday."

"What are you doing tomorrow?"

"I'm not sure," Filipa said although she was sure. She would return to that inn.

Time was running out and Filipa needed to get ready.

"I should go now," Andrea said. He dressed and Filipa dressed too, and then he kissed her. Filipa watched him leave and then Clara came from her room.

"Was he nice?" she asked.

"Andrea was very nice," Filipa said. "He will be back."

"I heard you singing; you have a lovely voice. But such sad songs!"

"Isn't love meant to be sad or even tragic?"

"I suppose it is."

The bell chimed five.

"We should go to Vespers," Clara said.

"We must." Filipa laughed. "How many sins do I have to pray to God for forgiveness? Fornicating. No, adultery because I'm a bride of Christ! Encouraging a man to spill his seed!"

Clara laughed. "I will race you there."

Laughing loudly, they ran along the corridor much to the surprise of Barbarella. Filipa and Clara joined the group of nuns in black, and more reverently they filed into the chapel.

* * *

Filipa stood just inside the doorway of Él Lión Biànco and looked over the room. The tables were mostly large and crowded although there were two smaller tables in the far corners of the room; one where she met Andrea and another. Both were taken and, surprise, one was taken by Andrea and another man. Another patrician and that was an opportunity. Filipa went to the counter and bought a cup of wine from the woman, almost certainly the innkeeper's wife, and women were capable of more worthy pastimes than loveless marriages or being sent to abasie. Many women worked in their husbands businesses; shops and inns, or did other work as they could find it.

Filipa went to Andrea dressed in her favourite colour blue, with the other man just as handsome and dressed in patterned green silk: light green with darker green shapes. A dark green baréta and green calsa looked rather fetching, and like Andrea this man had fair skin, long, brown hair, and was, perhaps, in his late twenties.

"Bondi Andrea," Filipa said.

"Bondi Filipa," Andrea replied. "Filipa, this is Marco."

"Bongiorno Marco. You don't mind me calling you Marco?"

"No, not at all. Bongiorno Filipa."

"I don't know if Andrea has told you anything, but if he has then it's all lies!" and Filipa laughed.

"He said he met the most beautiful woman in Venèsia, and he wasn't lying about that."

"I'm not beautiful."

"This is crowded for three," Andrea said. "I will go and you two can talk."

Andrea left and Filipa took his place, and she placed her cup on the table. She thought about what to say because that day, Tuesday, was quite different to Monday. "This is my second time in this inn and you know what happened last time. I don't want to go into that; rather I want to know what you want out of life."

"I want to do the best I can at everything I do," Marco said. "I do my work as well as I can, I try to be as good a friend as possible, when the time comes I will be as good a husband as I can manage, and I will be as good a father as I am able to be."

"That's worthy and realistic Marco. When the time comes I'm sure you will make a good husband and father. When you're a husband and a father, remember that the women in your life, your wife and your daughters, are as important as life itself. If you let the women in your life into your heart, deep into your heart as your equals, they will bring you more joy than you ever thought possible."

"Grassie for that Filipa, and when the time comes I will remember what you said. You have been treated badly?"

"No, not badly; my mother, my sister and I have been treated like any other wife and daughters in Venèsia. But we could have been treated better and all would have gained from that."

"Andrea told me you're in an abasia."

"I'm like many women of my station. I don't know if there's a solution for the cost of dowry and the shortage of patrician men for marriage, but perhaps there's an alternative to unhappy marriages or sending women to abasie. When the time comes for your daughters, maybe you can find a third way. Marriage away from Venèsia perhaps."

"With patrician families from other cities?"

"That could be worth looking at."

"I will remember that Filipa and grassie again. I think I like you."

"I'm just a young woman making the best of my situation." Filipa sipped her wine and watched Marco sip his. He was young, he was handsome and he was decent. He was good enough. "Do you want to come with me to Torcello?"

"Sé, grassie."

"Let's go."

They went outside into a mild, cloudy day, but deathly still. Filipa loved spring; winter's cold had passed and summer's heat had not yet arrived. Spring and autumn were her two favourite times of year.

"What work do you do, Marco?" Filipa asked.

"I work for Él Procuradór di San Marco," Marco said.

Filipa was quite startled by that. "Are you Marco Barbo?"

"I am."

"Older or younger?"

"Younger by two years. You don't mind?"

"That you're brothers?" Filipa couldn't think of anything wrong with that. "No, not really. It's quite sweet that Andrea thought enough of me to arrange this. What did he say?"

"To go with whatever you want."

That was peculiar. She was 18 and they were about 10 years older, and then it hit Filipa. For 10 years or more they'd been fucking prostitutes who just didn't care. Fortunately she had Barbarella who taught her. "The one thing I ask is that you don't ejaculate inside me."

"I understand."

"Are the any more brothers?" Filipa asked. She didn't want any more than two.

"No."

They reached the jetty and Filipa asked the gondoliere to take them to Abasia San Nicolai di Torcello. They climbed into the fieze of his blue craft and the gondoliere pushed away from the wharf. Filipa closed the blinds and kissed Marco and he kissed her back, but without the muscular, manliness of Andrea. Filipa supposed all men were different and Marco was gentler, and she used her tongue more than he used his. Their kissing was nice though and his gentle holding of her shoulders was nice too, and then his cupping of her buttocks. Men loved women's buttocks! They kissed and hugged passionately but gently all the way to Torcello. Upon arriving, Filipa paid the gondoliere, and walked with Marco along the promenade and into the cloister. There Filipa saw Anna take her man into her cell and close the door behind her, and much debauchery was going to happen at Abasia San Nicolai di Torcello that afternoon! Filipa was fascinated by men's cocks and she wanted to do something different that day anyway. 'Mars et Venus' would suit Marco, although she wasn't sure how she could finish him. She led Marco along the corridors and into her cell, and closed the door. Like with Andrea she made Marco sit on the bed while she undressed, and then she undressed him except for his calsa and mutande which he had to remove himself. Like yesterday he kissed Filipa and grabbed her buttocks too, only Filipa eased away and knelt before him. She licked his hard, erect cock and then took it in her mouth, and for a few minutes she imitated fucking it but with her lips. Marco's heavy breathing and his hands on her head showed he liked that. She let him go and lay on the bed with her legs spread.

Marco lay between her legs and soon she was on her journey to that wonderful, wonderful place. Slowly, steadily and then it drenched her with pleasure. Filipa held Marco away until she got her breath back, and then she nudged his shoulder. He understood and rolled over. Filipa climbed above him with her knees either side of his buttocks.

"You must tell me when you're close to ejaculating," she said.

Filipa put him inside her and she stopped to absorb that remarkable feeling of being stretched by hard softness. She lowered herself and was stretched and stretched by his warm, hard softness; caressing her inside while she took all of him. Filipa bent down and kissed him before she rode him, and Marco kissed her with more purpose, much more purpose, while he held her shoulders and matched her with his hips. Their kiss was magnificent, truly magnificent, and Filipa wished they could stay like that forever: him inside her, caressing and filling her, and kissing with tongues inside each other. With that kiss Filipa went beyond merely fucking to making love. He held her face while their tongues touched on a steady rhythm of love. Forever and ever joined together, and Filipa never wanted to leave him.

Eventually Marco broke their kiss. "Any moment," he gasped, and Filipa lifted herself off his cock, wrapped her hand around it and stroked it hard. Marco rolled his head to one side and Filipa felt his cock burst into life in her hand! Again and again he sprayed over her hand and over him. Again and again, less and less until he was finished. Filipa sat back with the biggest, biggest smile. She never imagined ever doing that to a man. Marco sat up and kissed her and she still had his hard cock in her hand. She let it go and kissed him, before grabbing the towel from her bed and wiping his stomach and her hand.

"That was fantastic!" Filipa exclaimed, and it really was. She barely believed she'd actually done that.

"No woman has ever done that before."

"What?"

"Make me come like that."

"Was it good?"

"That was the best ever."

"You sweet man."

"I like you Filipa."

"I like you Marco. Do you feel good?

"I feel great."

"Do you like poetry?"

"I've never bothered with poetry."

"Let me read you some."

The bell chimed three and Filipa still had time. She pulled out the most appropriate book, a collection of love poems, and turned to the poems of Guido Cavalanti. She sat on her bed cross-legged and read his six, untitled poems. They made her heart ache, as always, and when she was finished she put the book down.

"That was marvellous," Marco said.

"You're just saying that," Filipa said.

He put his hand on her thigh and Filipa shuddered with his gentle touch. "I have never experienced an afternoon as pleasant as this one."

Filipa looked into his eyes and didn't know what to say.

"Who's biggest?" Marco asked.

"What do you mean?" Filipa asked, confused.

"Andrea or me?"

Filipa laughed. "You're both about the same size."

"Who lasts longer?"

"Does that matter?"

"I suppose not."

"When you come back next week, I will borrow an hourglass and I can time you both!"

Marco chuckled.

"Are you free next Tuesday?" Filipa asked.

"Sé sweet girl," Marco said.

"Come to this room after dinner on Tuesday, and don't ask about size or time!"

"I won't. Are you going to Venèsia tomorrow?"

Filipa felt peaceful and contended and three days in a row was too much. "No, not tomorrow."

"Someone I know speaks highly of Albano Capello, and I can introduce you."

"Grassie for that Marco, and I will speak with you when I'm ready."

Time was running out for Vespers. "Let's dress," Filipa said.

They dressed and Filipa felt embarrassed about her humble room, and especially the hard bed. "I have plans to improve this room when I can," she said. "A new mattress to start."

Marco reached into his tacolinn and gave Filipa a twenty lire coin.

"Grassie Marco," Filipa said, and she kissed his cheek before putting the coin in her jewellery box. "I will walk you to the door."

* * *

After Tierce, Anna and Clara took chairs from their rooms and placed them on the grass next to the cloister. Protected by their broad-brimmed capèli with no centres, they sat in the sun to bleach their hair. Filipa took her lute and quill and sat in the shade on the low, stone wall of the walkway. Sitting in

95

such peaceful surroundings, nobody would suspect Anna or Clara of anything less than pure virtue, especially with Anna embroidering. Anna was maybe mid-twenties, average height, average build, a bit plain with a sharp nose and firm jaw, and quite dark. Her black hair defied the sun! Clara was older than Filipa and younger than Anna, and was also average height and average build, quite fair and pretty, and she had lovely, long, brown hair. Filipa tuned her lute and then noticed a man on the walkway adjacent to the chapel. The man, in his thirties and modestly dressed, walked to Barbarella's room.

"Pietro," Anna said. "Monday, Wednesday and Friday."

Filipa was interested by that. "What about our menses?" she asked.

"Go to the fish market and buy some sponges. Cut them to size and put them inside."

Filipa nodded. "Grassie," she said "Where do I get arsenic and quicklime for hair removal?"

"Ask in the kitchen."

"Grassie Anna."

"We women have to do so much with our hair! Cleaning and styling long hair, bleaching our hair in the sun, removing all our body hair."

"That's true."

"What are you embroidering?"

"A cover for my bed."

"Anna embroidered a tapestry for my cell," Clara said.

Filipa remembered that tapestry and it was a fine
work indeed.

"Would you like a tapestry for your cell?" Anna asked.

"Sé, per piasser," Filipa said.

"What would you like?"

"Campo Santa Maria del Giglio."

Anna nodded her head. "The centre of your parish.
You and I can go there and I will make some sketches."

"Grassie tuti Anna."

"De niente."

Filipa took her quill and strummed her lute. "Blessed
be the day, and the month, and the year, and the season, and
the time, and the hour, and the moment, and the beautiful
country, and the place where I was joined to the two beautiful
eyes that have bound me:

"And blessed be the first sweet suffering that I felt in
being conjoined with Love, and the bow, and the shafts with
which I was pierced, and the wounds that run to the depths
of my heart.

"Blessed be all those verses I scattered calling out the
name of my lady, and the sighs, and the tears, and the
passion:

"And blessed be all the sheets where I acquire fame, and my thoughts, that are only of her, that no one else has part of."

Filipa looked up and their mouths were hanging open. She sang another song and then put her lute down.

"That was very nice," Anna said.

"Grassie Anna," Filipa replied.

"How are you enjoying your time here?"

"I've enjoyed these past weeks very much."

"You have been busy," Clara said.

"Today I will rest."

"You told me the first one will be back. What about yesterday?"

"Andrea and Marco both will be back, but I'm not finished yet," and Filipa wondered why. And then it hit her; the power she had over men. Women were subservient to men, except for Filipa Barbarigo. She already had both sons of Él Procuradór di San Marco, the most prestigious appointment in Venèsia, and there were more men; more patricians to come.

"I know what you want," Clara said.

"I'm content with Francesco," Anna said. "He's a nice man and he looks after me. He's a cittadini and he's a carpenter."

Cittadini were citizens of Venèsia but not patricians. "I'm glad for you," Filipa said.

"And your two?" Clara asked Filipa.

"Andrea and Marco Barbo," Filipa said. "Both work for Él Procuradór di San Marco." Filipa wondered how to explain her attraction discreetly. "They let me have my way," she said.

"Brothers; that's interesting."

"They're quite different to each other."

"I have Marco who you saw, and I think he does as little as possible. Also I have Luca, Carlo and Mario. Marco's a young patrician and he's a lot of fun, Luca's married and I give him what his wife doesn't want to, and I enjoy that myself. Carlo and Mario let me have my way. Luca's a cittadini and maybe my age, and so is Carlo."

Filipa picked up her lute.

"Lirum bililirum, li-lirum, lirum, lirum. Ah, sound the muted instrument.

"You hear me well, Pedrina, and not just out of duty.

"Lirum bililirum, li-lirum, lirum li. Ah, sound the muted instrument. Ah, sound the muted instrument.

"I have loved you for six years, and been a good servant to you,

"But I've been waiting for you so long, that I shall end by bursting with love.

"Ah, don't give me more grief; you know well that I speak the truth."

In the background Pietro left Barbarella's room and followed the walkway to the corridor and disappeared from view. A few minutes later Barbarella came around and sat on the stone wall.

"We have been talking about our lovers," Clara said. "Filipa has two brothers and they will be back, and she has plans for more."

Filipa felt herself go red.

"When I was new here," Barbarella said. "The badésa of the time, Sofia Canal, couldn't read or write, so she used a scribe from town for her legal documents. A family was arranging a dowry for their daughter and Sofia's scribe had taken ill, so she sent me to find another. I asked around and found Pietro Blanco, and I accompanied young Pietro back to the abasia. He was easy to talk with; he had a nice, relaxed manner and he was quite handsome. When we reached the cloister, I showed him my cell for when his business with Sofia was complete. And now I'm badésa and I still have Pietro, whose been married and widowed and has always found time for me."

"That's been nice for you," Filipa said.

"It has been."

"What happened to Sofia Canal?"

"She had a relationship with Antonio Balbi, and when Antonio's wife died in childbirth they married."

Filipa's heart skipped a beat. "So there's hope?" she asked.

"Don't have unrealistic expectations Filipa, but there's always hope."

Chapter Six

Filipa entered Él Lión Biànco and looked around the room. She recognised Marco just as he came to her.

"Bondi Filipa," he said.

"Bondi Marco," she replied. Marco arranged for Filipa to meet with Albano Capello, who was in his thirties and married. Filipa had initially been curious about having an older, married man and what she could gain from his experience. And then she thought about how Cristina would be hurt if her husband had a relationship with another woman, and how Albano's wife was in the same situation. But then Filipa thought that if Albano wanted another woman then he would find one. Prostitutes, a mistress; Albano would find someone. She wasn't giving him the benefit of the doubt, but would speak with him before making up her mind.

Marco took Filipa to one of the big tables where a well-dressed man was sitting alone towards one end. He stood and kissed Filipa's cheeks. Average height, quite handsome, especially with short, straight, brown hair and a neatly trimmed brown beard; dressed in a green sleeveless giornea over a white, silk gamurra, and purple calsa.

"Bongiorno Siórina," he said.

"I'm sòra," Filipa replied. "But you can call me Filipa."

"You can call me Albano."

"Bongiorno Albano."

"Would you like a cup of wine?"

"Grassie Albano."

"Sit per piasser."

Filipa sat while Albano got her drink. He was handsome indeed, and very well presented.

"What work does Albano do?" Filipa asked Marco still standing.

"He works in the family business," Marco said.

Filipa was glad he wasn't from Él Procuradór di San Marco.

"I will go now," Marco said.

"Adio Marco," Filipa said.

"Adio Filipa."

Marco left just as Albano returned with her wine. He sat opposite and Filipa tried to concentrate while there were several noisy young men at the other end of the table; just a few feet away.

"I'm glad you can meet with me," Albano said. "Marco said you were very beautiful, and he was right with that."

"I'm not beautiful," Filipa said before sipping her drink. "Beauty is superficial anyway. Marco told me you're married."

"I am."

"Tell me about your wife."

"Gia is twenty-three years old, we've been married for five years, and we have two children, two boys. We won't be having more children. We get on well enough, but like many marriages there's a distance between us."

"What makes you think you will be closer to me?"

"Meetings for a few hours every now and then are quite different to living together day and night, and frustrations and incompatibilities are unlikely to surface."

"What's the distance between you and your wife?"

"I like intellectual pursuits like chess and backgammon, and Gia doesn't. I like balls and dancing and Gia doesn't. Gia sees sex as a wifely duty and is quite passive, and while we've talked about this many times we haven't gotten anywhere."

"Could you try harder? Surely a woman wouldn't turn her back on the pleasures that are available to her."

"I've tried everything, but Gia takes Church teachings quite seriously."

Filipa understood. The Church taught that sex wasn't for enjoyment, there was only one suitable position, man on top, only certain days of the week and certain times of the day, not when a woman was pregnant, menstruating or breastfeeding, no oral sex, not at many times of the year and many other prohibitions. Filipa sipped her wine and felt sorry for Albano. It wasn't his fault and it wasn't the fault of his wife either. "I don't want to come between you and your family," Filipa said. "A few hours with me shouldn't do that, and if things go well maybe once a week." Filipa thought of something she should know. "Have you seen other women?"

"I've seen prostitutes."

"What was that like?"

"They're comfortable with sex, but it's empty and superficial."

"Your two choices are passive or superficial?"

He nodded.

"You can come with me to Torcello," Filipa said. "As long as you agree not to ejaculate inside me."

"I can do that," Albano agreed.

"Do prostitutes ask for that?"

"No."

Filipa guessed they must take remedies to prevent pregnancy. She finished her wine and stood. "Come with me Albano," she said.

They left the inn and crossed Piasà San Marco. "You work in the family business?" Filipa asked.

"We buy and sell silk," Albano replied. "I can get silk for your clothes."

Filipa smiled brightly. "I have a history with silk."

"Everything from the East passes through Venèsia, including silk."

They reached Canal Grando and Filipa boarded a gondola. She asked the gondoliere to take them to Abasia San Nicolai di Torcello. They climbed into the fieze and Filipa closed the blinds. Albano held her hand and looked into her eyes, and she sensed his admiration. That was nice, and better than being groped. An older man *was* different in a nice way.

"I meant it when I said you were beautiful," Albano said quietly.

"Grassie Albano," Filipa said. She'd been aware of men's eyes following her for many years. She sometimes wondered if there was any worth in being thought beautiful. He kissed her cheek and Filipa turned her head. He lightly kissed her lips and that was nice too. He seemed a nice man and not in a hurry like a younger man. Albano held her hand and kissed her from time to time, all the way to the abasia. There Filipa paid for their fare and led Albano to her cell.

"I have plans to improve my cell," Filipa said. "I bought a new bed, and next I will buy curtains and a canopy."

Albano reached into his tacolinn and gave Filipa a twenty lire coin.

"Grassie Albano," Filipa said, before putting the money into her jewellery box. She turned around and contemplated Albano who wanted something more intimate. The most intimate of all was man on top: body to body and eyes to eyes, but the Church prescribed that as being the only

Albano was with a young man with a dishevelled mop of black, curly hair beneath his baréta. Filipa went to them and they both stood. Marco briefly kissed Filipa's cheeks while the young man, Fantino da Pesaro, held her hands while he kissed her cheeks with more enthusiasm. He was tall, slim and a little gawky, with a big bright smile. Beautifully dressed in a red giornea with puffings of red and white silk at the shoulders, and over he wrapped a broad, black silk scarf, a black velvet baréta with a peacock feather, black calsa, and the longest scarpe that Filipa had ever seen, matching in red.

"Bondi Filipa," Marco said.

"Bondi Marco," Filipa replied. "So you're young Fantino."

"I'm older than you," he said while smiling.

"Not by much."

"Do you want a drink?" Marco asked.

"Sé, per piasser," Filipa replied.

He left for the woman at the counter while Filipa sat opposite young Fantino.

"Tell me Fantino, "Filipa said. "What do you do for a living?"

"As little as possible," he said while still smiling.

"And what can you bring to me?"

"Youthful enthusiasm."

Filipa chuckled. "You're modest," she said.

"I'm known for my modesty."

Marco returned with a cup of wine and Filipa thanked him. He then bid them adio and left. Filipa sipped her wine, and thought she may be able to do things with young Fantino, even if he wasn't old enough to have much experience. Or no experience at all. "Have you made love yet?" Filipa asked.

"Sé; with the maid."

Filipa gasped with shock.

"Oh it was consensual," he said. "She came into the room without realising I had just risen, and one thing became another."

"How old was she?"

"About forty and very attractive for her age."

"Did she show you what to do to her?"

"Sé."

"If we make love, and I'm not sure if we will; but if we make love you must do what I tell you."

"I promise I will."

"The first rule is you must not ejaculate inside me."

"I can try to not do that."

Filipa thought trying was better than nothing at all. She wasn't going to get intellectual stimulation from Fantino, but she didn't need to. She had Andrea, Marco and Albano, and Fantino might make an interesting counterpoint. "I will try you out."

"Like you try a horse before buying it?"

Filipa tried not to smile.

"Who's doing the riding?" Fantino asked.

"I might ride you," Filipa said.

"Be my guest."

Filipa finished her wine and stood. "Let's go Fantino."

He stood and he really was quite tall; about six feet. It was nice to be with a man taller than she. They crossed the piasà and Filipa asked a gondoliere to take them to Abasia San Nicolai di Torcello. They climbed into the fieze and Filipa closed the blinds.

"Do you want me to kiss you?" Fantino asked.

"Sé," Filipa said.

He held her head and kissed her lips, and Filipa touched his lips with her tongue and their tongues met. They kissed with Fantino mirroring her, and Filipa felt quite excited. She was young and inexperienced, yet she had to teach a young man about pleasure. That was interesting. They kissed until Filipa eased away, and he held her hand instead.

"Women have nice hands," he said.

"Men and women are different," Filipa said. "Women like a soft touch and men like a firm touch. When we make love, just go with what I say."

"I understand."

"Are you excited?" Filipa asked.

111

"Sé. And you?"

"A little."

They reached the abasia where Filipa paid ten soldi, and she led Fantino inside.

"I have plans to improve my cell, when I get sufficient funds," Filipa said. "I bought a new bed, and next I will buy curtains and a canopy."

Fantino reached into his tacolinn and gave Filipa a twenty lire coin.

"Grassie Fantino," Filipa said.

"This is very quiet," Fantino said while they walked along the corridor.

"Most of the nuns are working."

Filipa led him into her cell and closed the door.

"This is nice," he said.

"Grassie Fantino," Filipa said. "You can kiss me again"

He held her and kissed her, and it was nice being kissed by a man taller than she. He was learning at kissing too. Eventually Filipa eased away and removed her capèlo, her séngia, and the rest of her clothes. Fantino watched with studious intensity, and when she was naked he hugged and kissed her again, and she liked his smooth, soft hands on her buttocks. They kissed for a while before Filipa moved away once more.

"Let's get you ready."

112

Filipa helped him undress, and while she did that she thought of something he could do. She was sure he would. When he was naked she climbed onto the bed on her hands and knees, and Fantino looked at her with his mouth hanging open.

"What is it?" Filipa asked.

"There's something about you like that;" Fantino said. "But I don't know what it is."

"Kneel behind me."

He did.

"Rub my sex lightly," Filipa said.

He put his hand between her legs and stroked her just right.

"Touch my arsehole with your thumb," Filipa said.

He did and Filipa shuddered with the sensation. Once or twice men had brushed her there and that had felt great, and now it felt magnificent.

"You have a gorgeous arse," Fantino said. "Let me kiss you."

He put his mouth there and licked her arse with his tongue, and Filipa couldn't believe how good that felt. And when he rubbed her sex! She hurtled towards her pleasure, and when it filled her he kept going. Fingers and tongue and again it burst free but brittle and hard, painful even, but a nice pain. And still he kept going, and she felt it again, like waves washing into shore, and again, painful but nice. Wave upon

113

wave of pleasure, never ending, just complete and total pleasure. On and on but she felt sore. She pushed his fingers from her sex and he stopped kissing her too.

"Fuck me Fantino," Filipa gasped and he entered her from behind, and holding her hips he fucked her. Deliciously slowly, and then he rubbed her sex. Filipa was hurtling towards her pleasure once more, only it was a fuller pleasure that cascaded over and over. Only when her pleasure faded did she realise his cock was between the cheeks of her buttocks, and his warm, wet fluid was sprayed on her back. Filipa collapsed on the bed in near exhaustion, and he wiped her with the towel. That was sweet.

"Did I pass my test ride?" Fantino asked.

"That was almost perfect," Filipa said.

"Almost?"

"I would have liked you to come inside me, but I don't want to fall pregnant. It's a pity that sex causes pregnancy."

He laughed. "If sex didn't cause pregnancy; we wouldn't be here."

Filipa giggled. "That's true," she said.

Filipa rolled onto her side and Fantino brushed a strand of hair from her face. "Can we meet again?" he asked.

"I don't know," Filipa said mischievously.

Fantino grabbed at her stomach and tickled her, and Filipa writhed to get away while laughing uncontrollably.

"Can we meet again?" he asked.

"No!" she shouted, and he tickled her more. "Stop it Fantino!"

He tickled her again, and Filipa struggled to get away from his menacing fingers.

"I'll get you!' she shouted, and reached for his stomach and tickled him, and he let her go to protect himself. She tickled him amidst flailing arms, with Fantino laughing wildly. He rolled closer to the edge of the bed and fell to the floor, and Filipa was alarmed. She got off the bed and helped him to stand.

"Are you alright?" she asked.

He grabbed her and tickled her, and Filipa backed to the door. Still he tickled her and she tried to tickle him back, and eventually succeeded. He drew away with Filipa after him.

"Truce!" Fantino shouted.

"You started it!" Filipa shouted in reply.

She tickled him once more, and he picked her up bodily. She wrapped her arms and legs around him while he cradled her buttocks, and she kissed him.

"You can come back sweet man," Filipa said. "Thursday afternoon next week."

"Do you want me to kiss your arse again?" he asked.

She squeezed him tight with her legs.

"Something else?" Fantino asked.

"I will think of something," Filipa said.

"I'm getting tired." Fantino turned around, bent over, and laid Filipa on her bed. She moved away from the edge and he lay on top of her, and he kissed her. She could have made love with him again if that were possible, and his erection probing at her made that quite possible.

"Make love with me per piasser," Filipa murmured.

He entered her and made love with her, kissing her until the last moment when he pulled out and rubbed his cock to spray his juice on her stomach. Then he collapsed on her, and she hugged him.

"You're exhausted," Filipa said quietly.

"You're a bad influence," Fantino said.

"Thursday next week."

"You have something planned?"

"I will think of something, young man."

"I'm older than you."

"Not by much."

"How long can I stay?"

"Not so long, but we will see each other again."

Still he lay on her and she ruffled his unkempt, curly hair. Sweetly soft hair.

"Do you want me to go?" Fantino asked.

"I don't want you to go, but you should," Filipa said.

Fantino climbed out of bed and dressed while Filipa watched him for a moment. Then she dressed. She took his

116

hand and led him to the promenade, and gave him a kiss on his cheek. "Come to my cell next Thursday afternoon; this door's always unlocked."

"Adio Filipa."

"Adio Fantino."

She watched him head down to the jetty, and a nearby gondola closed to pick him up. Filipa turned around and headed inside.

"You two had a lot of fun," Clara said.

"His name's Fantino and he was fun," Filipa replied. "I will see him again."

"Do you want to go outside to where it's nice?"

They went to the grassed square and sat side-by-side on the low, stone wall.

"Now you have four, like me," Clara said.

"I'm satisfied with four," Filipa said. She almost said 'for now' but decided not.

"Men are frightened of the insatiably lustful nature of women's sexual desires."

That was a well-known fact and Filipa nodded in agreement.

"Women get more pleasure from sex than men," Clara said. "Our breasts, our nipples, between our legs, inside...."

"Our arseholes," Filipa said.

"There too. Have you had a man suck your feet?'

117

"No. I will get Fantino to do that next time. Have you had a man lick your arsehole?"

"Is that what Fantino did?"

"It was amazing."

"I must try that with Marco. All men have is their penis, which you can stroke, suck or fuck."

"I like men's penises."

"I do too, but women have much more. I believe that God wouldn't have given us these pleasures if they weren't meant to be used."

Filipa thought that was an interesting point. "It's like delicious food that you're not supposed to eat."

"Or a relaxing bath that you're not meant to have."

"You and I are insatiably lustful," Clara said.

Filipa laughed. "We're the women that men are frightened of!"

"We're the true nature of the feminine."

"My men enjoy making love with me."

"Mine too."

"Does enjoying pleasure with four men cause harm?" Filipa asked rhetorically.

"Not at all."

"Then I will continue."

"Me too."

Filipa thought that much good came from sharing pleasure with her men. Andrea always enjoyed making love

118

with her, and playing cards later. Marco was kind and gentle and he enjoyed making love with her too, and he enjoyed listening to songs or poems after. Albano enjoyed the intimate love-making he was denied at home or with prostitutes, while Fantino clearly enjoyed everything they'd just shared. For sure Filipa would continue with her four men, or more.

Chapter Seven

Every day seemed like a miracle to Marin, and his transition from single to married was so easy that it seemed like he'd always been married to Blanca. Every working day when the bell chimed 12, he went home to find his dinner stewing over the hearth, and Blanca greeted him with a big smile and then a hug and kiss. On Wednesdays and Fridays he brought used towels home from the shop, and Blanca washed and folded them ready for their next use. She kept their room spotless, cleaner than when they moved in. Marin gave her enough money to buy cloth, and she'd already made and sold three giornei and gamurri for children. Marin still shared a bed, but a large bed with the most beautiful and good-natured woman in the parish. He was the luckiest man in the parish, and his good fortune was worth much more than two ducats.

On Saturday Marin arrived home after his half-day of work, and took six soldi from his tacolinn so he could leave his tacolinn in their room. On a fine, warm day they headed to the bathhouse, where Marin paid the woman attendant and they were allowed in. Inside was warm with the heat of hot water, and was busy and bustling as always, with men, women and children of all ages undressing, bathing, drying and socialising. Marin and Blanca undressed and slipped into the large tub amongst many other bathers. Marin reached for a bar and soaped Blanca, and while he did so he thought that no matter what he did, he couldn't get away from bars of soap! Blanca took the bar and soaped Marin, and feeling cleaner he put his arm around his beautiful wife who rested her head on his shoulder. Blanca was the most beautiful woman there, and almost certainly the most pleasantly natured. After a time they left the water, took towels and dried, and put their wet towels with the other wet towels before dressing. Then they went home for dinner stewing slowly over a low fire in the hearth. Marin thought a game of draughts would make for a pleasant afternoon. Later that evening or between the first and second sleeps, they would make love. They always made love on a Saturday clean after bathing, and made love on many other days too!

Just as they finished a game of draughts, there was knocking on the door. Marin opened the door to greet his friends Carlo and Piero. Marin invited them in and they talked for a while, before going outside to grab Vicenzo to play gameball at the campo. Blanca watched, and it was a fine game with the two Curri brothers beating Carlo and Piero.

On Sunday Marin and Blanca went to mass at Cièsa di Santa Maria del Giglio, with the patrician families in the front pews, and the patrons of the church, the Barbarigo family, in pride of place. Mass started with the introit sung while the three priests entered the church, followed by the kyrie sung three times; then came the gloria hymn in Latin, and the prayer for collect.

121

The priest went to his lectern and said the epistle would be from Romans chapter one, versus 24 to 27. "So God abandoned them to do whatever shameful things their hearts desired. As a result, they did vile and degrading things with each other's bodies. They traded the truth about God for a lie. So they worshiped and served the things God created instead of the Creator himself, who is worthy of eternal praise! Amen. That is why God abandoned them to their shameful desires. Even the women turned against the natural way to have sex and instead indulged in sex with each other. And the men, instead of having normal sexual relations with women, burned with lust for each other. Men did shameful things with other men, and as a result of this sin, they suffered within themselves the penalty they deserved."

After that came the second hymn and the sung allelujah. The priest returned to the lectern where he read the next, designated gospel. The priest then strode to the pulpit for the sermon, while glaring at the congregation on his way. Marin sat while not looking forward to being lectured once more.

"Yet again we see the procession of terribly scarred bodies taken away while pestilentia continues to ravage our parish," the priest said. "For almost a century pestilentia has cursed this grand city, but the real curse comes from God. It's His wrath which brings the devastation of pestilentia, because some amongst us choose not to follow His way. The story of Sodom tells us what happens when we adopt unnatural practices. In the city of Sodom, Lot was unable to find ten good men. Instead, the men of Sodom wished to fornicate with other men, and as a result God destroyed the entire city with fire and with brimstone. And today in Venèsia, God's wrath over men fornicating with men progressively destroys our great city. It's beholden on every man here not to engage in unnatural sex with men, and it's beholden on every one of you to report to the authorities any man who engages in unnatural sex with men. Only by ending sodomy can we rid our city of pestilentia, and that relies upon the actions of each and every one of you. Let us pray."

After that dramatic sermon came the offertory collected from the congregation, after which the priest made his silent prayer. Then came the pater nosta by the priest and congregation, the angus dei by the priest and congregation, and dismissal through 'ite, missa est'.

The congregation filed into the campo with Marin thinking about pestilentia and sodomy. For as long as he could remember they'd been ravaged by pestilentia, and everyone had learned to live with thought that their lives could be taken in a moment. The outbreaks continued on and off, sometimes worse and sometimes not so bad. While never as bad as stories of the first, great outbreak of pestilentia in times past, there seemed to be a never ending

123

stream of victims. Marin expected to go to work, come home to greet his wife, and greet his children in time, but that could be over in a moment. Marin had paid little notice to previous sermons linking pestilentia to sodomy, but that was before he was married. That Sunday when he looked at Blanca at his side, he realised he had much more to lose.

"What is it?" Blanca asked.

"I was thinking about that sermon," Marin said. "I don't want to lose you."

"I don't want to lose you either."

"We must keep our eyes and ears open for sodomy."

"I'm not so sure about that. There are many sins which bring God's wrath and sodomy is only one sin. I think we should live good and fruitful lives and rely on His mercy."

"Why do you say that?"

"Sodom was destroyed in a moment with fire and brimstone, but I see no fire and brimstone here. What I know are the terrible stories of pestilentia of times ago, and what I see are those who get sick with those awful sores that burst open, and they always die a few days later. But that isn't fire and it isn't brimstone. If this illness is God's wrath, then surely we must live decently and respectfully to protect ourselves from that wrath."

"No it's sodomy," Marin said.

"If it isn't sodomy but just sin in general, we risk a terrible mistake."

"I believe it's sodomy," Marin said, while remembering his master from a time not so long before. The master who took Marin to a bed and did terrible, unnatural things to him. Marin had no choice because he was little more than a boy, but to Marin all sodomites were evil, wicked men who corrupted the innocent and brought death and destruction to Venèsia. We would kill every one of them, if he could.

"We should agree to differ on this." Blanca said. "There's no doubt that sodomy is a sin, and if we come across sodomy we should report it. And it's just as important to avoid other sins, and to live decent lives."

Marin looked at Blanca with shock, because that was brilliant. "Sé we will do that, starting now."

"That will make conceiving our child difficult."

"Why?"

"Wednesdays, Fridays and Sundays are days of sin, as are Saturdays before communion."

Marin thought about that. "We have all the other days of the week, including tomorrow."

"I will hold you to that."

Marin was more than ready for that challenge.

* * *

Caterina stood with her hands on her hips glaring at Dardi. She was an attractive woman, but not with her face twisted in anger.

"I don't know why you got married!" she shouted at him.

"I married because I had to, like you," Dardi said.

"At least I try to make this work, unlike you!"

"I try; you don't know how hard I try."

"When we make love you're a hundred miles away. Making love is beautiful but I feel like you hate me!"

Dardi winced because that was too close to the truth. "I'm sorry and I will try to be better when we make love."

"And this house! You're from a wealthy family and we have a home suitable for paupers."

"I don't believe in acquiring useless things."

"A little luxury won't go astray."

Dardi sighed. "Go and buy whatever you like."

"Now you fob me off."

Dardi jumped to his feet. "No matter what I do it's not good enough! I don't buy things and that's not good enough; I let you buy things and that's not good enough either! I just can't win!"

"Marriage isn't meant to be a battle."

"You're making it a battle, Caterina." Dardi stood with his heart racing. She stood in front of him with her face still twisted in anger. "I'm going out until you calm down."

"You're always going out."

"Shut-up Caterina!"

Dardi stormed out of the room to the back door, and banged the door behind him. He stomped through the crowded streets straight to Clario's lodgings. Up the stairs and hammered on his door. Clario opened the door wide-eyed, and Dardi pushed his way into the room and closed the door behind him.

Dardi grabbed Clario and kissed him hard; so hard he tasted blood. He kissed while he tore at Clario's séngia, and released it and tossed it aside. Still kissing hard he pushed Clario onto his bed, and then reached under his giornea and tore his calsa down and his mutande away too. Dardi quickly loosened his own séngia before shedding his calsa and his mutande, and then he lay on Clario and kissed him hard again.

"I want to fuck you," Dardi growled.

"I want you to fuck me," Clario murmured.

Dardi rolled Clario over, no oil so he spat on his cock, and rammed it home. He fucked him hard, hard all the way, and then he lay on Clario shaking and sweating. He realised what he'd done. "I'm sorry mio amór." Dardi got off. "I'm sorry mio amór," he said.

"What happened?" Clario asked.

"Canterina's been at me again."

"I'm sorry for you, mio amór."

"It's not fair to take my troubles out on you like that."

Clario sat up and hugged Dardi, and Dardi burried his wet cheek against Clario's shoulder. "You had to marry her and that's been terrible for you."

Dardi looked into Clarios clear, brown eyes. "You're so good."

"You're good too, but you've been put in a bad place."

"I never knew marriage would be so hard."

"When she falls pregnant that will be better, and when she has a child that will be better still. When she has her child she will leave you alone."

Dardi felt the tears welling and he hugged Clario again. He was so good, so kind and just as importantly, so sensible. "I can't make her pregnant today and that will be another argument, but I will try tomorrow and for the rest of the week."

"Take a break from me, and when she's pregnant that will be better for all of us."

"I will."

"I liked that," Clario said quietly.

"Liked what?" Dardi asked, confused.

"You fucking me like that. So powerful."

Dardi hugged him again. "We will do that again one day."

"I hope so. But first make her pregnant and give her a child."

Dardi felt tears once more, and he was glad he could cry with Clario. When you loved someone you could do anything. Love forgave all; the good and the bad. They held each other for so long until Clario told Dardi he was a married man and he should be home.

Dardi went down the stairs and returned home the way he came, but strangely felt someone was following him. He hoped someone wasn't following him. Dardi edged into Calle Pinelli to the side and scanned all around, but saw nobody suspicious. He continued home and that strange feeling returned. He got all the way to the lane that led to the back door of his home, and stopped just around the corner. He peered around the edge of the building expecting to see someone, but nobody was there. His mind was playing tricks. He walked to the back door and let himself into his home. Like past arguments, a few hours' separation would allow Caterina to calm down. That wasn't her fault, and if he could change things for her, he would. Dardi felt really, really sorry for Caterina. Maybe Clario was right. Maybe a child would fill the emptiness in her life. Almost certainly a child would bring joy to her life. All Dardi had to do was make love with her regularly, almost every day if possible. Dardi entered the sitting room and Caterina was on the couch, embroidering. He felt really, really sad about her enduring their unhappy marriage. He sat beside her and kissed her cheek.

"I'm sorry mia amór," he said. "I will be better starting now."

"I know you're trying mio amór," she said. "Marriage is harder for you than for most men for some reason.

He held her soft, slim hand. She really was pretty. "I know it's harder for me, but I will try."

She kissed his cheek. "Try for me," she said softly.

* * *

Anna, Clara and Filipa sat at the small table in the refectory with quills, pots of ink and sheets of paper; a recent invention and much cheaper than parchment. Filipa read the letter from her parents and contemplated what to write in reply.

'To revered Michele and Brisca her parents, humble Filipa your daughter. I am pleased that life treats you well, and that business is prosperous. In answer to your question, life at the abasia treats me well, and I am content with the life of a nun, especially prayers and hymns because you know how much I like music. I am treated well and I have certain freedoms which I cherish. I thank you both for choosing Abasia San Nicolai di Torcello for me. It is possible for you to visit me here, and we have the most magnificent meeting room where I can entertain you. If you do plan to come, send me a letter and I can bake special treats for your visit. Even though the badésa treats me as well as her own daughter, I do miss seeing you both and I would like you to come here. I can show you around and I am sure you will be surprised by what you will see. The tree garden is particularly beautiful. I wish you good tidings for now and for always.'

Filipa put her letter aside and read the letter from Cristina, and wondered how to reply.

'To beloved Cristina her sister, humble Filipa your sister. I was pleased to hear your good news, and I now pray that you will have a good pregnancy, a safe birth and a healthy child. You will be in my prayers every night. In answer to your question, life at the abasia is pleasing to me. The badésa treats me like her daughter, the nuns are close friends, and I have certain freedoms. I understand that you cannot come here in your condition, and I am sure your beloved husband has your best interests at heart when he says you cannot travel nor receive visitors. Time will pass, and when you have your child then you will be freer to travel, and to receive visitors. One of my freedoms is to travel, and it is possible for me to visit you. Of course I must visit you in time, because you will have your son or daughter, and I will have my nephew or niece. If in time you can come to the abasia, send me a letter and I can bake special treats for your visit, and when you come I can show you my new life. I wish you a safe pregnancy and a good birth, and I wish you good tidings for always.'

Filipa folded her letters and wrote their addresses, and then she opened her letter to Cristina and felt quite sad.

"Is there bad news?" Anna asked.

Filipa sighed. "No, quite the opposite. My sister was married a short time after I came here, and now she's pregnant. But her husband won't let her travel to see me, nor will he allow me to visit her."

Anna's expression changed quite dramatically, with the edges of her mouth turned down. "That's quite sad for your sister."

"Many marriages are like this."

"Sadly they are."

"I'm hopeful my parents will visit me, and I even promised to bake for them!"

"Ha!" Anna laughed. "We're a good influence on you!"

"I've seen you both baking cakes and sweets for your families, and I can't not do that. But I don't like baking!"

"When your parents come I can help you bake."

Filipa was so relieved. "Grassie tuti Anna. I'm looking forward to my parents coming here because I want to show them all around. This is the most magnificent home, especially with my good and dear friends."

"Grassie Filipa. I see you as my sister more than just sòra."

Filipa felt a stab of joy in her heart. "Before I came here I had one sister, and now I have three."

"It's quite sad about your sister, although in time she will have a child and that will be good for her, and good for you too."

Filipa thought about that. "I hope she gets happiness from her child," she said, while wondering if having a child would make up for all the things Cristina had lost. Through their letters they would keep in touch, and if Cristina's husband continued to forbid travel and visitors, then Filipa would go there anyway! Cristina wouldn't expect anything less! But enough of that, and Filipa took the next letter she received. She had many cousins of course, and she'd received seven letters. She would invite all of her cousins, and they would come as the three families of Barbarigo. That would mean more baking for Anna and her. From what Filipa saw of Anna and Clara, her parents and her cousins would visit her from time to time. That would keep her as a part of Venèsia beyond the men she knew, and she needed that in her life.

Chapter Eight

Marin's Friday started like any other day, with breakfast for
Blanca and he; bread bought from the baker with watered-
down wine. But it was Friday June 23 and Saint John's Day; a
day of rest for Marin. For sure he worked for himself and his
shop was closed so he wouldn't make any money, but all
barber shops were closed and customers would come on
Saturday morning or on Monday instead. There was always
business for barbers: haircuts, shaves, tooth extractions,
minor operations and bleeding those who were sick, and
customers would come when Marin was next open.
Although Saint John's Day was one of the most important
saints' days and the beginning of summer; like any Sunday or
any other saint's day, not so many in the parish went to
church. Marin and Blanca were dressed in their finest for
church that morning. Others stayed indoors or congregated
in the campo ready for festivities to follow in the afternoon,
while Marin and Blanca went to Cièsa di Santa Maria del
Giglio to pray to the Lord to give them a child.

After the service, the campo was busy on a warm but
cloudy day. Blanca suggested they buy food from one of the
many vendors, and she chose the man grilling skewers of
meat, with cups of wine bought from a vendor doing a busy
trade. They wandered amongst the crowd until Vicenzo
caught up with them. After exchanging greetings and

commenting on the fine weather, Blanca's brothers, Maffeo and Anzolo, then arrived at the campo. They too exchanged greetings before Maffeo offered to pay the vendor who'd set up a bocce court, with the Curri brothers against the Agoli brothers. They played bocce amongst much eating and drinking, particularly drinking by many at the campo, with the Agoli brothers beating the Curri brothers. After that Marin asked all to return to his room where they played cards for a time.

It was getting late when their guests departed, and Marin suggested returning to the campo to buy supper. It was still busy towards the end of a holiday Friday and still warm too, so they bought fish and more wine and ate outdoors. As the evening's light faded, Canal Grando in the near distance looked a treat. They walked to the waterway and admired the view before returning to their room.

"This has been a great day," Blanca said.

"This has been a great day," Marin agreed.

Time spent with family always made for a great day.

* * *

Filipa waited in her cell, and as soon as she heard the bell ring she strode to the door. There she was greeted by her Papa who held her shoulders and kissed her cheeks like he always did, and she was greeted by her Mama who hugged her like she always did.

"Bondi Papa e Mama," Filipa said.

"Bondi Filipa," they said together.

"Come inside and I will show you my cell."

Filipa led her parents along the corridor to her cell, and inside. Her Papa went to the window and looked outside. "You have a nice view," he said.

Filipa nodded in agreement.

"I like your room, or is it a cell?" Mama said.

"It's really a cell," Filipa said. "But I think of it as my room."

"You have a nice big bed, a soft mattress, nice blue curtains, and your lute of course."

"Music is a big part of a nun's life and my lute is part of that. I sometimes play and sing during services in the chapel."

"I was always proud of your music," Papa said. "When I think back you were as smart as anyone with the things you liked: music, dancing, reading, writing, and your lessons in Tuscan. And you showed little interest in things you didn't like: board games, baking and embroidery. But a woman can get by if she doesn't bake cakes or embroider."

"I can bake," Filipa said. "I baked a cake for your visit, with the help of another nun."

Papa came close to her and Filipa eased away sensing he wanted to hug her. "Your greatest gift is to be friends with everyone who crosses your path. You could have been a good and affectionate wife to the right husband."

"How's Cristina?" Filipa asked to change the subject.

"She's glowing, like all women in her condition," Mama said.

"I will see her sooner or later," Filipa said quietly. "Come with me and I will show you around."

Filipa showed them the chapel first, and then the refrectory, the kitchen, the bathroom, the laundry, and through the tree garden which she thought was especially special. They came around the grassed square with her father admiring the beauty of her home, and it was beautiful. There was little greenery in Venèsia, and much greenery at Abasia San Nicolai di Torcello. Filipa took her parents to the chapter house, and there she introduced them to Clara and Anna waiting. They spoke for a moment, before Clara and Anna left.

"You have nice friends," Mama said.

"We're more like sisters," Filipa said.

"Like Dardi was your brother?"

Filipa giggled at that.

"You made a nice cake," Papa said.

"Anna helped me," Filipa said. "Sit, per piasser."

They sat on the bench with the cake on a table, and it was still warm from the hearth.

"I'm proud of you my daughter," Papa said. "You've made this your home and you've put on a wonderful party for us." He stood and Filipa went to him, and he hugged her.

He hugged her and hugged her, and then he let her go to look into her eyes. "You were only eighteen; the day after you came here."

"Women grow up faster."

"But still it's a big change to set out on your own in a place like this, and to become a part of it. We will see you often."

"I would like to see you often. My cousins have promised to come, and I'm looking forward to seeing them all. Perhaps I'm better here," Filipa said while grasping for the right words. "I mean.... I mean marriage is sometimes not as good, and I have my friends and my family and that's good for me."

"I know what you mean," Mama said.

Papa sat down and ate more of the cake, and he'd been getting bigger for a while so he couldn't afford to eat so much! But it was delicious with the help of Anna, and Filipa was pleased that her party was such a treat.

Sunday passed uneventfully, but on Monday Filipa was sure something was happening. Anna and Clara disappeared after Tierce while Barbarella took Filipa to her room to talk about her first few months. Filipa assured Barbarella that she still enjoyed her life at the abasia, she enjoyed the prayers and the hymns, and she enjoyed the freedoms she had. After a time, Barbarella took Filipa to the chapter house where it should have been obvious. Anna and Clara baked a cake for Filipa's name day!

"How did you know?" Filipa exclaimed.

"Your parents told me," Barbarella said. "This isn't within our vow of poverty, but a name day is a name day."

The cake looked delicious, and Filipa went to Anna and hugged her. "Grassie tuti Anna," she said before hugging Clara. "Grassie tuti Clara."

"Grassie tuti Filipa, for being part of our family," Clara said.

Filipa sat on the bench and ate some of the cake, and it was quite lovely.

"Do we always celebrate name days?" Filipa asked.

"For us we do," Clara said.

"When are your name days?"

"I'm on July twenty-six, Anna is on August eleven, and Barbarella is on December four."

"I will help you bake," Filipa said.

"Grassie Filipa, especially as we know how much you like baking!"

"With practice I will get better." Their little celebration, just the four patricians, reminded Filipa how happy she was in her new life. Barbarella, Anna and Clara were her family as much as they were friends, she could come and go as she liked, her real family had visited and more of her family would be coming, and she had four nice men in her life. Filipa couldn't imagine being happier.

* * *

It was a summer wedding for Laura and Angelo, after a romance which began when they talked together one Sunday morning after church. Angelo Tanto, youngest son of Bianco and Maria, had been around the parish for as long as Marin could remember, but hadn't shown an interest in Laura until that day, but to be fair, Angelo hadn't had much to do with any other woman before then. Marin had met Angelo twice since then, and wasn't sure what to make of him. Angelo was besotted by Laura and Laura was quite taken by that, but such intensity of feelings developed in such a short time didn't seem realistic. Angelo held Laura's hand, gazed into her eyes, whispered in her ear and she either laughed or turned red. Angelo was an architect currently working on rebuilding Palàso Zen for one of the Contarini family, and that met with Papa's approval. Papa was more than happy to have his daughter married to a successful, young man. An expensive dowry for a successful man was not a problem for Papa.

The ring ceremony was held at the Curri home of course, and Laura wore a new, blue dress, bought not made at home, as befitted the daughter of a merchant. Marin kept to the background, and after the vows were exchanged and the ring placed on Laura's finger, they decamped to the Campo where the feast was to be held. Angelo was 21 like Marin, medium height, medium build, had fine, brown hair and a slightly hooked nose, looking similar to his older brother Marco, and to his father. Angelo's mother had deeply lined skin and black hair with grey at her temples, which made her look older than her years and quite different to her daughter Angela; the youngest in their family and not yet married.

In the campo the wedding feast got underway, with Marin still contemplating his new brother-in-law.

"You're quiet Marin," Blanca said, and Marin knew what she meant.

"Do you think this is quite sudden?" Marin asked.

"No, not at all. Sometimes these things happen fast. I mean we didn't take so long, maybe five or six months after you first talked with me."

"I suppose so," Marin said, while still not convinced.

Blanca smiled big and bright. "You're being a protective, older brother," she said.

Marin didn't comment, but he hoped Blanca was right.

After food and drink; jokes and music, it was time for the newly married couple to go to their room, not so far from the campo. Marin joined in to pick up Laura and carry her to that room, which was quite a long way up a narrow staircase. When she ended up on her bed Marin stood back for the younger men to get their prizes, and Laura took that well in her good-natured way. She was a good person and Marin hoped she would be happy with her new life. Marin went down to Blanca in the campo, and took her hand and led her home.

"It seems longer than just a few months since our wedding," he said.

"It does," Blanca agreed.

By the time they reached their room it was time to sleep, with Marin thinking they should make love between the first and second sleeps, like they usually did when they could. He briefly thought about Laura's new life and glanced at Blanca, and they would make love between sleeps.

Chapter Nine

The nuns came out of chapel into the corridor after Prime, with a strong wind blowing rain outside. It was a day of contrasts: Nadal; celebrating the birth of Christ the saviour, and terrible, terrible weather. Most nuns headed to the chapter house and Filipa thought her cell was too miserable on such a wet day, especially a day of celebration, so she went with them.

"Filipa," Maria said. "I'm glad you can join us."

"This is a special day for us all," Filipa said.

"We're singing hymns today."

Filipa was pleased. She liked music and she particularly liked hymns.

"Filipa," Isabella said. "Could you accompany us with your lute?"

"Of course I can, but as you know a lute is a quiet instrument."

"If we have just one or singer at a time...?"

"That will work. I will fetch my lute."

Filipa went into the awful weather and grabbed her lute from her cell. Protecting it from any rain blowing under the shelter, she returned to the chapter house and sat on the bench. "I must tune it first," she said. Her teacher used to say that more time was spent tuning a lute than playing it! Filipa got the five courses in tune and looked at the group.

"Who wants to sing?" she asked.

"I will," Margarita said. "Laude Novella is a most suitable song for today."

Laude were simple, folk songs celebrating the birth of Christ. "Margarita; you sing the first verse and I will pick up your tune," Filipa said. "And then we can start again."

"How do you pick up my tune?"

"Just by ear. Start and I will follow you."

Margarita started with the first verse "New praise is sung to the great woman crowned!" and Filipa got that.

"Now we can start again," Filipa said.

They started over. Margarita sang the lauda with Filipa accompanying the repetitive tune. They reached the end and Filipa looked up from her lute and got the greatest surprise. Every single woman intently focused on the two of them. Filipa felt embarrassed. "Do you want to sing another?" Filipa asked, and Margarita sang the first verse of 'All We Can Even Praise Is Holy'. They started over with Filipa accompanying, and then they went onto 'Sweet Love Father' followed by 'Hail Holy Woman'.

"Does anyone else want to sing?" Margarita asked.

"I will," Diana said, and she stayed in the realm of laude with 'And Those Who Do Not Lose Too Much Time Love You' followed by 'Blessing Also Praised'. By that stage Barbarella joined the audience. Rain beat against the windows but inside was safe, and perhaps full of love.

144

Battista sang 'New Star Amongst The People' in a clear voice, and at the end she bowed to the nuns and to Barbarella, and then turned and bowed to Filipa. Filipa nodded in response. Filipa knew the words to one lauda, 'My Lady Saint Mary', and she sung that to her own accompaniment.

"Filipa, congratulations on such a fine celebration for Nadal," Barbarella said.

"This was Isabella's idea," Filipa said and then she thought about it. "We will do this again one day. If I could spend all day praying and singing; I would." She strummed her lute. "To me, music is God's gift to man. Music separates us from beasts in the fields. Music is unique compared to God's many creations. Music can make us feel happy, music can make us feel sad, and sometimes music puts us in awe of His greatness and power."

The bell struck nine and already it was time for Tierce. Filipa put her lute down and followed the other nuns out of the chapter house.

"We will use your musical abilities again," Barbarella said.

"That will be my honour," Filipa said. "I was a poor student until I had the opportunity to learn music. Then I changed. I took notice of my teacher, I practiced every day, and now I'm a competent player."

They went outside into the cold, wet, windy day and Filipa got the greatest surprise. There was Andrea; absolutely drenched.

"What are you doing here?" she snapped.

"Today's my day," he said.

"Today's Nadal; the celebration of the birth of our Lord. How dare you can come here?"

"I'm sorry."

Filipa sighed. "I would send you home but you're soaked. Go past the other side of the chapel to the kitchen where the hearth will warm you. It's over the far side there," Filipa said, pointing. "After the service I will find you dry clothes, and then you must go."

"I'm sorry Filipa," Andrea said, looking down to the ground. "Can I see you again one day?"

Filipa shook her head in bewilderment. "You're a friend and I like you, so of course I will see you again. Next Monday when it's not Nadal. Now go to the kitchen to warm up!"

He went away.

"I'm sorry about that," Filipa said to Barbarella.

"I think he loves you," Barbarella said.

"He loves my sex," Filipa said. "I was going to sing more songs in the chapter house after the service, but Andrea has mucked that up!"

146

"We will sing songs tomorrow," Barbarella said. "I have songs I would like to sing. But now we must go."

They went into the chapel on a cold, wet and windy Nadal.

* * *

Dardi worried about Caterina; the past week she'd been terribly sick, especially in the mornings. He went down to the informal dining room which had a small, rectangular table and six, simple, wooden chairs. The table was draped with a white linen cloth embroidered at the ends, and there were two pottery cups, a pottery jug of milk, bowls of apples and pears and a plate of bread sliced by the maid. He sat and poured some milk which was most refreshing. He took a slice of bread just as Caterina came into the room.

"Bón Nadal" Dardi said.

"Bón Nadal," Caterina replied.

"How are you this morning?"

"I'm feeling queasy, but that's good news for us?"

"How so?" Dardi asked; confused by that.

"I'm pregnant."

Dardi was startled. "That's wonderful!" he exclaimed. "I'm so happy."

"What do you want?"

"A healthy, happy child."

She smiled at that. "You knew the right thing to say."

"A healthy, happy daughter like her beautiful mother."

147

"That's in the hands of God. When we go to church we can pray for a good pregnancy, a good birth and a healthy child."

Dardi took her hand. "We should go to Cièsa di Santa Maria del Giglio."

"Your parish; that's appropriate."

He looked at her. "If I were a woman I would be scared."

"That's in the hands of God."

"But still...."

"I know mio amór, and I'm a little scared myself. But I'm also looking forward to being a mother."

"I'm looking forward to being a father."

She looked at him blankly and Dardi felt cut.

"It's terribly wet out there," Caterina said.

"You wear your best tabàro so you won't catch a cold."

"I'm pregnant Dardi; not an invalid. Life goes on, and even making love."

"Does it? I thought that was a sin."

"Which married couples take notice of sin in marriage? When we have large enough family, we will still make love and not have any more children, like all couples."

"Is sex safe for you?"

"You don't want to; do you?"

"I didn't say that." The past months had been hard pretending to be affectionate when, if he didn't fantasise he was with Clario, he wouldn't be able to get hard and to come. Sometimes sex worked just through Caterina, but for every time it did, he had to close his eyes and be somewhere else.

She shook her head and drank some milk, and Dardi felt terrible.

"It's Nadal mia amór," he said. "We will go to church and later, when we come home, we can make love together."

She took his hand. "Te vògio ben."

Dardi wanted see Clario just to talk things through, and he would do that when he was able. Caterina was so happy and perhaps even glowing with happiness, and it wasn't right to hurt her. For her sake he would do what he could, even if it was hard for him. And buy her a present too. She deserved a special present for all she had to put up with. A special present for the most important woman in his life.

* * *

The jeweller placed the pendant on Dardi's palm. It was gold in the shape of a cross with four equal length sides, and had bright blue gems near each point, and a bright green gem in the centre. Four pearls were arranged equally around the centre, while twenty or more small diamonds were set around the ends of each arm of the cross, and around the centre. It was big, heavy, chunky and beautiful. Dardi reached into his tacolinn and paid four lire di grossi as agreed. For such a pendant that was good value.

Dardi left the jewellery shop in Él Geto and went around the corner to their room. He unlocked the door and let himself in, and sometime later he heard footsteps outside. Clario entered the room and Dardi stood and kissed him, and they hugged and kissed.

"I've something to show you," Dardi said. He picked up the pendant and Clario took it from him.

"She will love this," Clario said. "Remember what we agreed."

"I will take her out more; especially dancing."

"The only affection she gets from you is in bed, and you need to broaden your marriage beyond that."

That was a good idea by Clario and Dardi liked dancing. He wondered why he hadn't thought of that before. Well, better late than not at all.

"One thing you and I will never do is go out together, and dancing is quite out of the question. We can show affection in bed though."

Dardi hugged and kissed him. "Sé we can."

Chapter Ten

Fantino insisted the gondola sail the full length of Canal Grando. He had something he wanted to show Filipa, although she wasn't much interested on a cold, winter's day. Indeed, since they left Torcello, she was preoccupied with thoughts about their journey. Andrea guessed she was returning to the inn, and he introduced her to his brother Marco. Marco then asked if he could introduce Filipa to Albano Capello, and Albano then asked if he could introduce Filipa to Fantino da Pesaro. Then after quite a few months, Fantino asked if he could introduce Filipa to Marino Contarini. She wondered why he did that after so long. Marco introduced Filipa to Albano a week or two later, and Albano introduced Filipa to Fantino a week or two after that; then eight months later Fantino wanted to introduce her to Marino Contarini. She wondered if Marino heard about her, and used the youthful Fantino to get an introduction.

"Here it is on the left," Fantino said.

Filipa looked across and was surprised, but not in a nice way. "That building site?" she asked.

"Sé. Palàso Zen was part of the dowry for Marino, but he has bigger plans than an old palàso. He's tearing it down and going to build the grandest home in Venèsia."

"Oh that's good," Filipa said, totally unimpressed. Although she was patrician she came from a humble home, and that home had proven sufficient a family of five and their servants.

"Contarini is one of the twelve founding families of Venèsia," Fantino said. "The family has produced three doxi and a bishop of Castello. Like all patricians, Marino is entitled to sit on Él Maggior Consiglio, but he found little joy in that role. So he had himself emancipated from his father before the age of twenty, and set himself up in commerce. Before long his interests ranged throughout the Mediterranean, across to Spain and down to Alexandra in Egypt."

"That's interesting," Filipa said; her interest spiked by this successful man. "How old is siór Marino Contarini?"

Fantino frowned. "Forty or forty-one."

Much older than Filipa's lovers to date, which might make things difficult.

"He's one of the richest and most powerful men in Venèsia," Fantino said.

"This is why you wanted to show me the building site of his grand palàso?" Filipa asked.

"Sé. He's worth many hundreds of thousands of ducats. Maybe he's worth more than a million ducats."

Filipa gasped. She never, ever, imagined making love with a man so rich and successful. That was going to be a totally different experience and Filipa wasn't sure how to handle it. Filipa could give younger, inexperienced men her one rule, and they could abide by that or leave. But that wouldn't work with Marino Contarini. At least she prepared something which would work. Clara confided what she shared with Luca, and Filipa would use that, if siór Contarini allowed her. But apart from that she wasn't a prostitute, and love-making was for her pleasure. The young men liked that, but Filipa wondered if siór Marino Contarini would accept a woman less than half his age making things how *she* wanted them to be. His wealth and power meant little unless she could conquer him, and if she didn't conquer him then she was nothing more than an unpaid prostitute. It had to be her way or there wasn't any point.

They closed on the jetty and the gondoliere berthed his craft just past Ponte de Rialto. Fantino paid him, and, side-by-side, they crossed Ponte de Rialto and walked towards Calle del Sturion and Palàso Locando, where siór Contarini obviously met people away from his wife. Filipa was not his first and would not be his last. Fantino rang the bell while Filipa's heart beat fast and her hands felt sweaty. A servant girl, Filipa assumed her to be a servant girl because her blue uniform was very grand, opened the door and said she expected them both. The servant girl led them into a luxurious living room painted in a glorious hue of red close to purple. Magnificent furniture: a couch and two matching armchairs with gold-coloured velvet faced an exquisitely sculptured low table, which had a top so polished that it reflected like a mirror. At the end of the room was an ornate mirror with a frame of gold leaf, with two statues of dark women in short, gold leaf dresses either side, and each woman held five candles blazing. Tall vases with decorative flowers, paintings, more candelabras; it was a sumptuous room.

Sióz Marino Contarini wore his clothes well. Some younger men went too far, but he was right for his age in blue over blue calsa, a simple, blue velvet baréta and simple, black scarpe. He was older and looked it, but not too much. Actually quite handsome with lovely lines around his eyes when be smiled brightly. He kissed Fantino's cheeks before holding Filipa's arms and kissing her cheeks. "Grassie for coming," he said.

"Grassie for inviting me," Filipa replied.

"Has anyone told you that you're beautiful?"

Filipa smiled sweetly.

"You will find siórina Barbarigo to be good company," Fantino said.

"Grassie Fantino," Marino Contarini said.

Fantino left.

"Would you like something to drink, siórina?" Marino asked.

"A cup of wine siór, per piasser," Filipa said.

"You can call me Marino."

"You can call me Filipa."

154

"Sit, per piasser."

Filipa sat on the soft couch; the most comfortable chair she'd ever sat upon. Marino left the room momentarily, and shortly after the servant girl came with two cups of wine on a tray. She placed the cups on the polished table and silently left. Marino sipped at his cup and Filipa did the same, and the wine was rich and full-flavoured and not at all like the bitter-tasting wine normally served.

"Fantino told me you like poetry," Marino said.

"I like poetry very much," Filipa said. "I also sing to sonnets written by Francesco Petrarca and others."

"I bought this for you," Marino said, and he reached behind his armchair and pulled out a large book bound in leather.

Filipa put the book on her knees, opened it, and it was nothing but poetry. She flicked over a few pages and was quite stunned. "Grassie tuti Marino," she said. "I love this." He looked pleased with that, and Filipa got up and kissed him on his cheek. "Grassie tuti," she said again. "This is the most wonderful book you could have bought for me. It's like this room which is the most wonderfully decorated room I have ever seen." Filipa was there for one purpose, conquering that man for her pleasure, and she was impatient to see how that would play out. "I'm sure the rest of your home is just as tasteful."

Filipa put the book on the low table and followed Marino from room to room, and eventually they reached a bedroom warmed by a fire blazing in the hearth. It was an attractive room in shades of green: pale green walls with highlights in darker green, and a brown and green rug. A large, beige-coloured bed with a beige, silk canopy, brass candleholders, candles not lit, and a window overlooking Ponte de Rialto. Filipa untied the cords and let the heavy, dark green velvet drapes swing closed, but she put she put her foot between so there was a gap letting in some light when she turned away. She went to Marino and put her arms over his shoulders because she was as tall as he. "Now Marino, we can make love. I want you to sit on the bed and watch me." He didn't move. "Marino, sit on the bed per piasser, and I will show you."

He sat on the bed and watched Filipa take her capèlo and séngia put them on the end of the bed. She untied and removed her red, silk giornea without any hurry, and then untied and removed her black, silk gamurra; still taking her time. She untied and removed her camicia, and when she sat on the bed to remove her mulóti and calsi, she saw Marino's eyes fixed upon her.

"Come to me," Filipa said, and he did. She removed his baréta and tossed it aside, unfastened his séngia and let that fall, and then unlaced his blue, silk giornea. He removed that and Filipa untied his white, silk gamurra and he removed

156

that, and Filipa helped Marino remove the remainder of his clothing until he was naked. He didn't have the youthful firmness of her other lovers, but he wasn't so bad.

Marino grabbed Filipa and kissed her hungrily, holding her arms so tight it hurt! She grabbed him more to push him away, and that worked! She responded to his probing tongue, and it was almost as if he couldn't get enough of her. When he grabbed her buttocks that was good, and his tongue was most insistent. He stopped kissing and suckled on her breast instead, and she touched his thinning, grey-streaked hair. He was rich and powerful and could buy and sell her a thousand times over, but he was old and human too.

"I want you to get on the bed," Filipa murmured, and he suckled her nipple. "If you go to the bed we will do something special."

Marino went to the bed where he was ready for her, and well-proportioned too. Filipa opened the stivàl attached to her séngia and smeared olive oil on her anus, before climbing to where Marino knelt. He was insistent with his aggressive kisses, but Filipa had enough of that and pulled away. "Lay down because I have a special treat for you," Filipa whispered in his ear, and Marino lay on his back. Filipa bent over and took his hard cock in her mouth, and used her lips as she'd mastered with her other men. She sucked him for a while and then put her sex above him, and he grabbed

157

her buttocks and licked her. Filipa gasped with his hunger, even hungrier than his kisses, she felt light-headed and a little woozy. His attentions took affect and slowly, slowly her pleasure built; tingling at first and then more insistent. Bigger and bigger, throbbing and throbbing, and then that wonderful cascade of pure delight. Filipa then straddled Marino's hips facing away, put him inside her and rode him with his warm, hardness stretching her and caressing her. He squeezed her buttocks, really squeezed them hard, and Filipa enjoyed his hard attentions. It was as if he wanted to climb inside her. She looked over her shoulder at him watching as men always did, and she turned away and smiled. Filipa let him go, turned around, and put his cock inside her again. She put her hands on his chest and rode him while watching him watching her. Rode him and rode him, but she couldn't let him come.

"I want you to fuck my arse," she said firmly.

He swallowed.

"Fuck my arse, per piasser," Filipa asked.

Filipa climbed off and got onto her knees, and looked over her shoulder at Marino looking at her, transfixed. He knelt behind her, grabbed her hips, and she felt him at her. He felt like when she practiced with the glass penis; stinging and burning. He pushed and he seemed too big for her; much too big for her. Filipa put her head down and breathed deeply while he pushed into her. Filipa breathed slowly and deeply while he thrust slowly. He squeezed her hips and thrust into her, and the pain eased to a delightful fullness. She felt full and stretched of him; much more stretched and full than when he was in her vagina. Faster and faster and Filipa kept her head down while he fucked her. Fucked and fucked her, harder and harder, more and more desperate, and then he squeezed her hard when he came. Less and less and then she was empty. Filipa lay on her side and watched him watching her.

"This is the best part of making love," Filipa said. "These wonderful moments of peace and calm when nothing else in the world matters."

"Sé; you're right," Marino said.

"Give me your hand."

He did, and Filipa looked deep into his dark eyes. "I've never done that before."

"Did it hurt?"

"Not so much. After a time not at all."

According to Clara the oil along with her juices on his cock would make it possible, and Filipa practiced to make sure. Clara was right and it was quite easy, naughty, and safe from pregnancy.

"I like you Marino Contarini," Filipa said.

"I like you Filipa Barbarigo," Marino said.

"One day, I would like to make love like that again."

"That can be arranged."

Filipa stretched. "Fantino told me you're a rich man with interests all the way to Spain and Egypt."

"That's right."

"How much time does a rich man have?"

"Fantino told me that you're the most beautiful, young woman in Venèsia, and I should give myself enough time to enjoy your company. Perhaps we can do something together. Do you like playing chess?"

"I don't have the patience for it. I do play cards though."

Marino looked shocked; after all ladies didn't play cards. "No wonder young men enjoy your company," he said.

"Do you play cards?" Filipa asked.

"Sé I do. I will get the servant to get some. And some wine as well." He pulled a cord. "We should get dressed."

"We should play like this," Filipa said.

"No clothes?"

"We made love together naked, and now we can drink wine and play cards together naked."

He smiled brightly. "I like that."

Knocking on the door and Marino opened it just a fraction. He asked for a deck of cards and two cups of wine which came a short while later. Filipa sat cross-legged, and

Marino sat opposite her and then he looked her over.

"There's an attraction in not wearing clothes," he said.

"We can play tréntaun," Filipa said. "You deal."

"What if I win?"

"I will come back next week as your prize."

"What if you win?"

"I will come back next week to claim my prize."

Chapter Eleven

Venèsia during Carnevale was a different city. From Nadal to Easter, inhabitants donned costumes and masks and partook in many festivities. Filipa wore a dark blue giornea over black, a black, velvet baréta, a black cape tied around her neck with a gold chain, and a white Bauta mask which covered her face except her mouth. Fantino was all in black including a black tricorne capèlo, and he also had a white Bauta mask. Many of the men milling about the streets were in dark or black clothes with masks, while women mostly wore conventional clothing but with masks. In fact with so many in masks it was impossible to tell who was who. You could pass your best friend and not even recognise them.

Piasà San Marco bustled with many entertainers: jugglers, acrobats, clowns, singers as usual but in costume. But it was the preparations for Forze d'Ercole which made the most activity. There was to be the traditional battle between Castellani: the inhabitants of San Marco, Sestiere di Castello and Dorsoduro; against Nicolotti: the inhabitants of San Polo, Cannareggio and Santa Croce.

"Why aren't you battling?" Filipa asked Fantino while rival forces gathered at opposite ends of the piasà.

"I'm not really a battle person," Fantino said.

"I thought every young man would want to prove himself worthy in front of his lover?"

162

He took her hand. "I thought I was worthy already," he said.

Filipa liked Fantino, which was why he was her escort for Carnevale. "You're worthy as a lover, but there's more to being a man than that."

"I found siór Contarini for you."

"That's true."

"Did that work out well for you?"

"That worked out very well Fantino. I will give you a reward for that later. Now, the battle...."

"Do you want to see me battle?"

"I'm Castellani born and raised, and I want you to defend the honour of my true home."

"Then I will!" he said firmly.

Fantino headed into the throng and Filipa hoped he wouldn't get hurt. The two forces arranged themselves into gigantic pyramids of humanity; layer upon layer, and after much falling and recovery of individuals, they were ready to advance. Everyone in the piasà cheered and shouted for all in Venèsia supported one side or the other. At first Nicolotti forced back Castellani who then recovered some ground. The battle of the human pyramids ebbed and flowed until, slowly Castellani gained the upper hand, gradually demolishing the Nicolotti pyramid with many falling harmlessly to the ground and struggling to get back up, but unable to climb under the weight of force. Eventually

Castellani scattered Nicolotti and it had been a great victory. Filipa was so enthralled by the battle she didn't notice Fantino, until he was right with her.

"Well done mio amór," she said. "You successfully defended the honour of my birthplace."

"Did you see me?" Fantino asked.

"I saw your every move."

"Ha! You didn't see me at all."

Filipa tilted her head. "I didn't mio amór, but I'm sure you did well. Now, let us find a dance. I'm in the mood for dancing!"

Filipa took Fantino's hand and led him beyond the piasà. The ponte opposite was under battle from two gangs: harmless fun as they pushed and shoved each other to gain possession. As a result Filipa led Fantino north to the next ponte at Calle Drio la Cièsa, and there Filipa got the greatest shock. She recognised him by his size and stature despite his face hidden by a mask. Dardi Zorzi celebrating Carnevale was no surprise, but celebrating with a man instead of his wife was a surprise.

Filipa left Fantino and closed on Dardi, who must have sensed her presence, because he turned his head but his mask hid his expression. Instead he took the hand of his companion and headed along the calle. Filipa followed, even more curious that Dardi had seen her and run away. She followed him along the crowded calle, and amongst the

164

throng she lost him. She stopped, quite bemused that not only was Dardi with a man, but they held hands while they got away from her. She wondered why he would do that.

"What is it?" Fantino asked.

"I saw someone I knew," Filipa said.

"Even with a mask?"

"I would recognise him anywhere." It was awkward to be standing in a narrow calle jostled by crowds, and she went that way for another reason anyway. "Let's find a ball," Filipa said.

Filipa led Fantino towards the canal and the many palàsi which lined it. Many headed to Palàso Gritti just ahead and Filipa followed them. A man servant in a uniform and a mask stopped them.

"Your names?" he asked.

"Siór Fantino de Pesaro and siórina Filipa Barbarigo."

"You can enter."

The reception room was lit by hundreds of candles, and quite full with fifty or sixty dancers or even more. All in their finest clothes and all masked. Servants carried cups of wine on trays, and Fantino grabbed two as a servant passed and gave one to Filipa who sipped at it. Some party-goers had more than sipped at their drinks, and some showed the effects of too much wine. It was boisterous: men laughed and talked too loudly while women giggled stupidly. Men flirted with ladies not their own; both man and woman protected by the anonymity of masks. Filipa was interested by what she saw, she had no desire for anyone but Fantino, but she'd made love with Marino earlier that day, and with many of her lovers during the past week. Wives chained to the one man needed more than that, and a masquerade ball gave the opportunity for flirting at least, and maybe more than flirting if they could find some space and time. Of course some of the masked women were mistresses, with wives abandoned and alone in palàsi.

The band got ready to play and many couples formed into pairs for a bassadanza. Fantino bowed and Filipa curtseyed, and the music played for the slow, stately dance. It was a hand-in-hand procession in time to the music, stopping, bowing and repeating, and stopping, turning as a couple, and returning to the start before turning again. Slow, stately and in time to the music until the end of the song.

Then followed a saltarello. Fantino bowed and Filipa curtseyed, accompanied by music near twice as fast with a more driving energy. It was a more complicated dance of two steps a hop, two steps and a kick right and a kick left, two steps backwards and a hop, and the man pirouetted first and the woman pirouetted. The sequence was repeated until the woman pirouetted first and the man pirouetted, and the sequence was repeated until the man danced a circle around the woman, then the sequence repeated until the woman danced a circle around the man. The sequence repeated until the couple took hands and danced the same steps in a circle before repeating from the beginning. And so it went on; ending in a bow and a curtsey.

Fantino, in addition to his attributes in bed, was a good dancer, and Filipa was pleased to have him as her partner that evening. They danced another saltarello before Filipa guided Fantino away for another drink of wine. She stood on the sidelines to see who was who, or more precisely who was what because there were men and their wives no doubt, and men with their mistresses of course. Maybe other women were nuns of patrician birth enjoying carnevale with their lovers.

"Do you want to have supper at an inn?" Fantino asked.

Filipa was wise to that. "You want to take me to the inn where you rented a room, so we can make love there."

"I suppose making love will follow."

Filipa wished she could kiss her sweet young man, but their masks were in the way. "Let's have supper at the inn, and make love after that."

Fantino took Filipa's hand and led her out of Palàso Gritti. They would supp together, and make love after. Filipa would share Fantino's room and his bed for the night, probably rise late, probably make love again, and then see what carnevale offered for the new day. Surrounded by so many celebrating carnevale, Filipa decided to make the most of her time in Venèsia with Fantino.

* * *

Dardi showed his invitation to the servant who nodded in acknowledgement. Dardi held Caterina's arm and led her into Palàso Morosini, joining many other guests for a great, Carnevale ball. The large room had walls of frescoes and a high ceiling for spaciousness, and was lit by a hundreds of candles in large, wooden frames suspended from the ceiling, and by many candelabras attached to walls. All furniture was removed to make room for the hundred or so guests, who mingled with notable hubbub. A band was at one end of the room for the dancing that was to follow, while waiters drifted around while holding trays of wine cups. A waiter came to Dardi who took two cups and gave one to Caterina.

Dardi sipped his wine while surveying the room, and got the greatest surprise. Although her face was mostly hidden by her mask, Filipa Barbarigo was unmistakable. He took Caterina's hand and crossed the room to her.

"Bonasera Dardi," Filipa said, smiling brightly.

"Bonasera Filipa," Dardi said. "Filipa Barbarigo, this is my wife Caterina,"

Filipa took Caterina's hands. "Bonasera Caterina; I'm so glad I can meet the wife of my oldest friend. Dardi and Caterina Zorzi; this is my friend Fantino da Pesaro."

They greeted each other.

168

"Dardi is your oldest friend?" Caterina asked.

"How long has it been, Dardi?" Filipa asked.

"You were a baby in a cot," he said.

"You were younger then."

"Sé I was. How's life at the abasia?"

"Life there is good. I like the cycle of prayer and hymn, I like many of the nuns, and I'm able to get away from there as well!"

"How did you get an invitation for this ball?"

"We didn't! We just walked in like we belonged!"

Dardi chuckled and some things never changed. "We have good news," Dardi said. "Caterina is with child."

"Oh that's wonderful!" Filipa exclaimed, taking Caterina's hands again. "I will pray every night for a good pregnancy, a good birth and a healthy child for you."

Silence and clearly Caterina was startled by that. "Grassie Filipa," she eventually said quietly. "You're a nun?"

"I am."

"I'm glad you're happy with your life."

"I'm very happy with my life. I love music, and there's so much music in our abasia. We sometimes discuss the bible together but I don't like that so much. The old book is all about wars and pestilence and fathers killing sons and brothers killing each other. That makes little sense to me. The new book is quite different; it's about kindness, forgiveness and love; except our church is unkind, has little forgiveness and doesn't know anything about love."

"Filipa!" Dardi exclaimed.

"It's true! Look at the rules they put around married couples. Not during daylight hours. Not Sunday, Wednesday or Friday, or Saturday before communion. Not during the entire period of Lent! Not Advent, Easter, feast days or fast days. If you followed those rules you wouldn't be with a child!"

"Filipa!"

"You're right," Caterina said. "We didn't follow those rules."

"We call it making love for a purpose," Filipa said and she put her hand on Caterina's heart. "What matters is what feels right here."

Caterina held Filipa's arm to her and Dardi was surprised. "We won't be following other rules either," she said.

"When you do that, your child will sense the love you feel for each other." Filipa took away her hand and touched Caterina's pendant. "That is beautiful," she gasped.

"It's a gift from Dardi."

"That can be your good luck charm for childbirth."

"It will be." Caterina touched Filipa's pendant and it was quite beautiful. A gold cross similar in shape and size to Caterina's, with a red gem in the centre and bright blue gems, like her deep blue eyes, at each point of the cross. "That's a beautiful pendant."

"It's a gift from a friend."

"Fantino?"

"No, Marco." Filipa faced Fantino. "I know you're not in a position to buy me jewellery, but you're the best dancer in Venèsia and you have many, other talents."

"I know; mia amór." Fantino said.

"But first we must dance!" She faced Caterina. "I wish I could see your face." Caterina took her mask off and Filipa grabbed her shoulders. "You're absolutely beautiful," she said. "Dardi, you're a lucky man." Filipa took her mask off and Caterina gasped lightly.

"The band is getting ready, so now we must go." She kissed Caterina's cheeks. "Adio Caterina, and you will be in my prayers. Adio Dardi."

"Adio Filipa e Fantino," they both said, and Dardi watched them merge into the crowd while Filipa put her mask back on.

"She's amazing!" Caterina said. "You should have married her!"

"I couldn't."

"Dowry?"

"That and other things. Te vògio ben Caterina."

"So you say. The band is getting ready, so now it's time to dance."

Dardi took Caterina's hand and led her to the centre of the room. "I'm a lucky man to have you," he said, but he could tell she didn't believe him. They danced a bassadanza and then a saltarello, before Caterina said she wasn't feeling well. Dardi knew what the problem was; she'd been rattled by Filipa Barbarigo. By comparison any woman lacked personality, and by comparison any woman looked plain. That hadn't been Filipa's intention; on the contrary. Dardi led Caterina from the ball, and he sensed many couples noticing them leaving early. In the centre, Filipa exuberantly danced another saltarello with her friend Fantino.

* * *

Blanca's pregnancy showed after four months, and she was fit and healthy and in good spirits. On Martedi Grosso, the day when the biggest celebrations were held, Marin took Blanca out for Carnevale. Throughout the city, rich patricians and merchants were dressed in their finest. Many men and some of the women even had capes; many rich women wore their best jewellery, and they all wore masks. At Campo Santa Maria del Giglio there was a stall selling masks, and Marin bought two. Blanca looked grand in her blue dress from their wedding and a white mask, while Marin wore his best outfit and his mask. At Piasà San Marco there was a band playing and couples dancing in an open air ball. A family of black imps frolicked between those disguised only by white masks; a man stood dressed in a white cape, over which was stretched a fishing net, while on his head was a model sailing boat. Along the Piaséta a strange figure with witch's capèlo and different coloured ribbons hanging below black wigs, squirmed and moved round a pillar in the strangest, perhaps most obscene way. Many stalls sold pork-based dishes, because Martedì Grosso was the last day before the fasting of Lent. Puppet shows were set up for the delight of the many children there, and Marin imagined their son or daughter enjoying Carnevale in years to come. They stood behind a crowd of children and watched a show before heading to the food stalls where Marin bought dishes of grilled pork. Then they moved towards the ball where the well-dressed, all hidden by masks, danced magnificently. Marin wished he could dance like that.

The highlight of the afternoon was the float parade which was truly spectacular. Much effort had gone into building and decorating the many floats, and while they passed Marin felt good to be alive. Venèsia was the greatest city in the world and he was lucky to live there, and even luckier to share the highlights of the greatest celebration in the world with his lovely wife. It was getting dark when they walked home along bustling streets, passing a group of young men staging a mock battle for possession of a ponte. That harmless fun added to the atmosphere of the day. It was well dark by the time they reached home, and nearly time for bed sadly just for sleep. Marin wished they could but they couldn't, and that was their lot for perhaps a year. Marin wanted to make love with his beautiful, wonderful wife, but that was a sin and he couldn't.

* * *

The servant led Filipa into the sitting room where she waited by the fireplace. A few moments later Cristina entered the room and Filipa hugged her, and Cristina tentatively hugged Filipa in response. Filipa hugged her younger sister for a while and then let her go.

"How are you?" Filipa asked.

"I'm good," Cristina said, and she looked good.

"How's Sara?"

"She's sleeping in her room."

"I'm jealous of you!"

"You're an aunt now."

"You must keep me away from your daughter because I will be a bad influence!"

"How's life at the abasia? You look good."

"We're allowed to wear our own clothes, and we're allowed out."

"Sit, per piasser," Cristina asked.

Filipa sat on a floral-covered armchair and Cristina sat on a chair next to her. "We must be quick before Silvestro comes home for dinner," Cristina said.

"Surely he wants to see his sister-in-law?" Filipa asked.

"He likes to keep to himself."

174

Filipa was still surprised by that. "I understand," she said. "Now, do you have plans for more children?"

Cristina shook her head. "We have Antonio and Marco from Silvestro's first wife, and now Sara. There won't be any more."

"Of course; three's a good number for a family."

"That's right. I have my daughter and I'm happy with that."

"And I have my niece."

"Sé you do, and you will be a bad influence on her, even though you're a nun. Have you taken your vows?"

"I wish I didn't have to because that's like locking me away, but I had to take them after a year."

"Has it been a year already?" Cristina asked; looking quite shocked.

"You got married just after I went to the abasia, and now you have a daughter."

"Of course. Do you have friends at the abasia?"

"There are other patrician nuns and I have friends outside."

"If you can come and go and have friends; you're better off than me."

"Friends aren't the same as a husband and family."

"I'm not so sure about that. Have you been to Carnevale?"

"A few times. And you?"

175

"Silvestro doesn't like such things. You went with your friends?" Cristina asked.

"I went with a friend. We went dancing together."

Cristina put her hand over her mouth. "A man?"

"I know men but they're just friends."

"Men can never be just friends to a woman."

"I suppose not."

"You're lucky Filipa."

Filipa didn't want to say anything more about her friends. "Can I see Sara?" she asked to get away from that subject.

"Sé, but don't wake her."

They went upstairs to a large bedroom with a tiny, tiny cot, and in that cot was a tiny, tiny baby wrapped in swaddling and sleeping soundly. Sara was perfect and Filipa wanted to pick her up and hold her. But she couldn't. Filipa watched Sara sleeping until Cristina moved away, and they went down to the alcove.

"She's just like you," Filipa said.

"She might have fair hair later," Cristina said. "Then she will look like you."

"She might. I wish I could have a daughter or a son."

"You would make a good mother."

"Do you think so?"

"A child would calm you down! It's been nice seeing you my dear sister, but you should go now."

"I will, and I will see you again soon." They both stood and Filipa kissed Cristina's cheeks. "Adio Cristina."

"Adio Filipa."

Filipa was on the path by the rio and really quite stunned. The reality was worse than Filipa imagined from Cristina's letters. Cristina was not so much ruled by Silvestro as frightened of him, because she all but threw Filipa out of her house lest they cross paths. Poor Cristina. Married women were not allowed to socialise alone, and if her husband didn't dance or partake in carnevale and other recreations, there would be little in Cristina's life apart from Sara. Poor, poor Cristina. Filipa retraced her steps to the jetty and asked a gondoliere to take her to Abasia San Nicolai di Torcello, and all the way Filipa was lost in thoughts about a beautiful baby and a lonely mother. She felt sad for her younger sister, only 17. Cristina deserved better; she deserved an affectionate husband, but for the rest of her life she would just be a mother to a growing child; like many wives. But not all wives, because some arranged marriages were warm and affectionate. Perhaps it was luck, like a card game. Draw the right hand and you win, but draw the wrong hand and you lose.

Filipa reached the abasia, and still felt down when she entered the corridor, so she went outside instead. She walked around the corner and knocked on Barbarella's door. The door swung open and Barbarella looked quite shocked.

"What's wrong?" she asked. "No, come inside per piasser."

Filipa entered the room and closed the heavy door behind her. "I went to see my sister Cristina today," she said.

"Is there a problem?"

"Not a problem, but she has a miserable life."

"Sit on the bed and tell me."

Filipa sat on the big, soft bed and didn't know where to start. "Cristina has her daughter Sara, but the rest is — quite sad. She's the clever one, smarter than me, and now she's just a prisoner in a palàso."

"What did she say?"

"Nothing specific but I can tell she's unhappy. Even unhappier than our mother."

"That's the way of life."

"But she has her child."

"And you won't ever have a child?"

Filipa put her head down and nodded slowly.

"You can come and go as you wish, and take men as your lovers, and if they don't treat you well you can tell them not to come back," Barbarella said.

"I have one half of it and Cristina has one half of it, but only men have the whole," Filipa said.

"That sums up life for women."

"Men lock us up in palàsi or lock us up in abasie, or put us in other places as prostitutes."

178

"They're scared of women," Barbarella said.

Filipa frowned; that didn't make sense.

"We have more power than any man," Barbarella said. "We bring life to the world, we can take many men to be our lovers, and they preen and pout and have one shot only."

Filipa giggled at the one shot comment.

"That's true," Barbarella said. "If they didn't control women and lock women up, they would be almost irrelevant."

"Not quite irrelevant," Filipa said.

"Not in total, but any one man is irrelevant."

Filipa understood and Barbarella lay down on her bed. "Come," she said.

Filipa lay down and hugged Barbarella and that felt good. They lay in a silent embrace.

"Some men are good," Barbarella said. "My Pietro...."

"I don't have anyone like that," Filipa said.

"My Pietro is attracted to you."

"It's the way of men to want what they can't have."

"He's been faithful to me for a long time now, and I feel sorry for him."

Filipa looked into Barbarella's eyes. "Do you want me to make love with him?" she asked in surprise.

"Do you want us to make love with him?"

Filipa contemplated those words. "Are you sure?"

"That would be fun and it would brighten your mood."

"Men like the beauty of women," Filipa said. She remembered their time together. "Women like the beauty of women."

"For a man, the only thing more beautiful than one woman is two women."

"When's your Pietro coming to visit?"

"He's taking me to Carnevale this afternoon for Martedi Grosso, so any time."

Knocking on the door, light and discreet.

"Now?" Barbarella asked.

Filipa felt dry and she swallowed. "Sé," she said in a husky voice.

"One thing; he's big."

Barbarella slid out of bed and went to her door while Filipa wondered how Pietro could be big when he was slim. Slim and dark: olive skin, black hair, dark eyes and a perpetual two-day's growth of beard. Barbarella led Pietro into the room and his face changed with the most amazing expression that Filipa had ever seen. Mouth open, eyes wide; complete and total shock.

"Bongiorno Pietro," Filipa said.

"Bongiorno sòra," he replied.

"You can call me Filipa."

He nodded.

"You can sit on the chair, per piasser," Barbarella said.

He sat on the chair and Filipa climbed off the bed. Barbarella came to Filipa and took her in her arms and kissed her, and tongues touched and Filipa felt hands on her buttocks, squeezing and kneading. Filipa grabbed Barbarella gorgeous and soft, and sensed Pietro watching them. They kissed and kissed, until Barbarella eased away and removed her séngia before untying her giornea. Filipa watched with her heart racing ready to burst, and glanced at Pietro transfixed. Filipa removed her séngia and untied her dark red silk giornea at the sides, and sensing Pietro's eyes on her, she peeled the tight gown over her hips. Under she wore a black gamurra with white trim, and she untied that from the front and allowed that to fall away as well. Under that was a simple, linen camicia and Filipa unlaced that and allowed it to drop to the floor. Naked but for her black calsi and her mulòti, Filipa hugged Barbarella and they kissed with more urgency, Filipa's passions running faster and faster. They kissed and kissed until Barbarella moved away and climbed onto the bed.

Filipa removed her mulòti and calsi before joining Barbarella, and they knelt and kissed once more, but Pietro was a man and Filipa knew he would be impatient. Filipa rolled onto her back and Barbarella put herself above, and Filipa shuddered when Barbarella touched her with her tongue. Filipa sensed Pietro watching her and that made her heart beat even faster. She was going to come fast, she felt it, and she cascaded over the edge and fell away with the pleasure. She looked up at Barbarella's gorgeous buttocks, her hairless folds of skin, and women were beautiful everywhere. She licked just so, and licked and licked and felt Barbarella too.

"Come here and make love with Filipa," Barbarella said.

Pietro climbed onto the bed and Filipa got the greatest shock. His huge member; dark red and angry-looking. A massive cock: as long as a forearm and almost as thick; she wrapped her fingers around it and they didn't even touch. Barbarella moved away and Pietro took her place, and Filipa shuddered with delight when Pietro filled her. She closed her eyes and turned her head to absorb the pleasure. He made love to her slowly and steadily, and Filipa felt stretched and caressed like never before; each stroke like going to paradise. Slow and steady and Filipa wished he would never stop. He fucked her faster and that felt just as good. Faster and faster and she felt his energy; she opened her eyes to see the concentration on his face. Still fast and Filipa felt those familiar stirrings. Still fast and Filipa was close, and she was swept into pleasure so intense that she didn't notice he'd come until she realised his cock was on her stomach and his juice was running from her skin.

Filipa head the slap of skin against skin and realised Barbarella had spanked Pietro's arse. "How was that?" Barbarella asked.

"Good," he said.

"Good?"

"Great."

"Great?"

"I won't forget that for as long as I live," Pietro said quietly.

"I won't forget that either," Filipa said.

"I knew that would brighten your mood," Barbarella said.

Pietro lay beside Filipa and Barbarella lay on the other side. He bent over and kissed Barbarella, and Filipa thought that was sweet.

"I didn't realise that two women together were like us together," Pietro said quietly.

Filipa wondered what he meant and then she understood. He was right, of course. Filipa stretched and she felt comfortable and relaxed. She had Fantino coming that afternoon to take her to Carnevale for Martedì Grosso, with more love-making that evening. Fantino would never know about Pietro the same day and Barbarella was right. Men were the weaker sex.

Chapter Twelve

It was good to see the sun and feel the warmth of spring.
Well into spring on Saturday the fifth of May, 1427. The
eldest sons of eleven patrician families were invited to a hunt
by the eldest son of the most noble of the patricians: Marino
Contarini, to be conducted on Contarini lands on the
mainland. They gathered on the Friday while expert hunters
searched the hunting grounds for the wild boar which would
be their quarry. The Contarini family put on an evening feast
for the hunters and their wives, and hunting was one activity
where wives were able to socialise, or even participate in
secondary hunts for more docile prey like wolves or foxes.
Caterina was restricted by her pregnancy, which was a shame
for her.

After a simple breakfast of bread with wine, the
twelve male hunters were each given a horn and a spear, and
they all had their daggers, and then they readied their horses.
In the meantime noisy hounds were positioned along the path
the selected boar would most likely take, while other hounds,
barking ferociously, were kept aside to set off with the
hunters. The hounds were essential for a good hunt. They
would sniff out the prey and guide the hunters, and then with
their barking, they would flush the boar into the open where
the kill would be made, ideally by Marino. Boars were big,
wild animals with tusks, and very dangerous. They would

charge a horse, and for a hunter to be unsaddled close to a wild boar was a perilous place to be. The hunters gathered around their horses talking casually and even joking, as a mask for the nerves that each and every man felt. Once the hunt was underway those nerves were replaced by something else: concentration for self-preservation. But while the hunters waited amidst noisy, barking hounds, they all pretended that morning was no more serious than a morning walk to work. In the background ten women readied their parallel hunt for a wolf, also with horses, hounds, horns and spears, while Caterina and Margarita, the wife of Marino, were to keep each other company for the next few hours.

Marino blew his horn as a signal to be off, and they all mounted their horses while the twenty or more dogs were released. In no time the hunters were riding through forest trails; riding over uneven ground while dodging branches impinging on their space. It was wild and dangerous, with Andrea Barbo failing to clear a fallen tree and hitting the ground. They rode into a clearing of soggy, mushy grass while the hounds lost the scent. There was much milling about before they were away again, riding carefully over a brook before heading towards forest in the near distance. Again they rode along forest trails while dodging hazards and being careful not to get into other riders' ways. The chase went on accompanied by the incessant barking of hounds, until Dardi spotted the boar just ahead. They chased the boar on and on until the boar burst into another marshy clearing, and with dogs all around it seemed not to know which way to go. Momentarily it charged the riders, but then turned and headed towards the forest they just emerged from. Marino closed on the boar, as the leader it was his responsibility to kill the beast. All was going well until the boar suddenly charged Marino's horse; the horse reared, and Marino was in all sorts of strife just staying in his saddle. Andrea Barbo rode in and speared the boar that went berserk, and Dardi closed and also speared the boar which brought it down. With the boar disabled, Marino dismounted and finished it with his dagger. The other hunters dismounted and helped dissect the dead animal to feed it to the hounds, as was the tradition. The riders took a break and chatted casually while the dogs ate. The dog handlers rounded up the hounds, the riders mounted their horses, and all headed back through forest to the villa, which had stables and a large kennel to one side. There was a large, open area with a table set up for the evening meal, where Caterina and Margarita were embroidering.

Shortly after that the women hunters returned from their quest, and there was much conversation between husbands and wives over what they'd just experienced. Dardi poured a glass of wine and sat with Caterina at the table.

"How was your hunt?" she asked.

"It went well," Dardi said. "We cornered the boar and both Andrea and I speared it, and Marino finished it off. Nobody was hurt so it was a good day."

"We had a quiet day of course."

"That was a shame."

"You can't hunt when you're many months pregnant, although I would have liked to. It's been a long time since I've ridden."

Dardi was interested by women riding and hunting. He was oldest of three boys, and the closest he had to sister was Filipa Barbarigo. "Obviously women are taught to ride...."

"Most patrician women are taught to ride, but more importantly we're taught to read and to write."

"Do you read Tuscan?"

"No I don't and that's a shame. The best literature's in Tuscan, and many patrician women speak the language but I don't."

Dardi knew Filipa spoke and read Tuscan and had several books of Tuscan poetry. "Do you want to learn?" he asked.

Caterina turned her head in surprise. "Well, you're never too old to learn and it would be nice. Reading's a fine pastime, and I would like to learn Tuscan."

"I will ask Siór Barbarigo who they used for a tutor."

"Grassie Dardi." Caterina said.

"In Tuscan it's Grazie."

"That's not so different."

"Much of the language is similar, but there are differences to learn. Did you learn music?"

"I learned to play the harp."

"Filipa learned the lute."

"Oh the lute is so lovely!" Caterina exclaimed. "It's particularly good for accompanying singing, as you have seen at campi and Piaséta San Marco."

Dardi had seen many singers with lutes over the years. Caterina had been taught to embroider, something Dardi knew that Filipa didn't like, often professing she didn't have the patience for it! Caterina played chess quite well, she read Venèsian, she played backgammon and other board games, she played music and she could ride. In many ways she was a quiet achiever. In the background the hunters showed off and bragged about the hunt, and eventually all occupied the large table while servants brought out the evening meal which, fittingly, was roasted pork. It had been a great day, it was nice to get away from the cramped confines of Venèsia and socialise, before returning home the next morning. Perhaps the best part was to return to Caterina waiting patiently for her husband. Dardi knew he was a lucky man to have such a wonderful woman for his wife. It was a pity he couldn't give her all she wanted from him, but for some reason that wasn't him. He tried very hard to give her all he

188

could, but he only go so far. That was a shame, but as much as Dardi wanted to, that wasn't in him.

Chapter Thirteen

The fine spring weather continued for Dardi's walk to the barber shop late on Tuesday afternoon. The barber, Marin, did his usual close shave without a nick or cut, and as previously agreed, Clario came from his work as a painter. There was much opportunity for good painters in Venèsia, especially painting frescoes. Clario was currently working on a large and complex fresco. He waited on the chair near the door, and they exchanged chairs for Clario to get his shave. Clario paid and they headed out the door together.

"This is a particularly nice spring day," Dardi said.

"You seem cheerful," Clario said.

"Indeed I am. Caterina's pregnancy's going well, and she was pleased I made love with her while we could. That's too difficult now, but she's focussed on what's to come for her."

"I wouldn't want to be a woman."

"Me neither, and I don't know how they do it. We treat women badly in almost all ways, and yet they go through so much just for survival and the next generation. We should get on our hands and knees and worship all women."

"I agree absolutely. Not only that, but women are pleasing to the eye."

"Sé they are."

They reached Él Geto, and climbed the stairs to the room above the butcher shop. Dardi unlocked that room and went inside, and Clario closed the door behind him. As soon as that door closed Dardi grabbed him and kissed him, quite differently to how he kissed Caterina. A proper kiss, hard and masculine, the way kisses were meant to be. They kissed for a while but Dardi wanted to give more, much more. He pulled away and, looking at Clario, removed his capèo and séngia and the rest of his clothes. He had plans, and went to Clario and removed his capèo and séngia, and then unlaced his giornea, and Clario helped Dardi remove his clothes.

Dardi grabbed Clario and kissed him again, muscular body pressed against muscular body, fingers running through coarse, dark hair, hands on firm buttocks. Dardi eased Clario towards the bed and nudged him lightly, and Clario sat. Dardi knelt before him and looked up into Clario's eyes. He deserved what was coming for his kindness, his patience, and for just being him. He deserved what was coming a hundred times over for just being him. Dardi wrapped his hand around Clario's hard cock for a moment and fantasised what was to come. He then took it in his mouth: salty. Salty and just right. Lips first then tongue, then sucking; imagining how good that felt. Taken away from the moment and transfixed by giving pleasure to the man he loved. Losing track of place and time until Clario erupted, throbbing in his mouth with a salty, salty taste. Dardi swallowed and then let Clario go to look up at the peace on his face. Eyes closed and far away, until those eyes flickered open. Clario smiled in acknowledgement, and Dardi felt a stab of pleasure in his heart. That had been more than good.

Suddenly the door burst open and Dardi looked up at a stranger in dark clothes. He scrabbled to his feet in a panic; his heart racing. Who was that man and what did he want?

"Dardi Zorzi and Clario Dudo; what do we have here?"

"Who are you?" Dardi blurted.

"I'm someone very bad. You," he said, gesturing at Clario. "Get your clothes on and get out of here. Now!"

Dardi went to push at the stranger who backed away. "I wouldn't do that if I were you. Sodomy's a heinous sin, as you know. And a married man with a pregnant wife.... That would be difficult for her."

"Difficult in what way?" Dardi asked.

"Difficult when you get executed for sodomy."

In the background Clario quickly dressed. "Don't go," Dardi said.

"He has to go because this is between you and me. If you do the right thing, Dardi Zorzi, nothing ever happened in this room and nothing will ever happen again. Your wife will be protected and you will be free to see your lover. But if you do the wrong thing...."

192

"You should go," Dardi said to Clario.

Clario left, and shut the door behind him.

"I will dress now," Dardi said, and gathered his clothes into order. "What's your name?"

"Roberto Geni," the stranger, Roberto, replied. Maybe forties with grey-streaked hair; cheap linen clothing, dark blue and dark green; haggard, big nose, thin lips, quite ugly.

"What do you want from me?"

"In your job at Palàso Ducale you handle correspondence from the war against Lombardia. I want you to substitute correspondence from me."

"Giving a false view of the campaign?"

"Sé."

Dardi rubbed his chin and that was quite wrong. Treason. But sodomy was wrong and he had Caterina, pregnant Caterina, to consider. All it took was an anonymous accusation and two witnesses, and he would be arrested, interrogated, tortured, tried, convicted and executed. Caterina was from a wealthy family and would get by financially, but she would never get the stain of it from her. And their child, when Caterina gave birth, would never get away from the stain either. Son or daughter wouldn't matter; just the offspring of a sodomite. Dardi didn't want to be executed. Dardi didn't want to be tortured and he didn't want to be executed. Particularly he didn't want to be tortured. "I will do it," he said.

"Good."

"Nobody will ever hear of this?"

"They will not hear of today, or of any day past, or of any day in the future. I know how persistent these relationships can be." Geni took a folded parchment from inside his giornea and gave it to Dardi. "This goes in place of the next report from Francesco da Carmagnola."

Dardi nodded.

"I will come to this room every Monday afternoon, and if I have more urgent correspondence I will meet you at the barber shop you like to frequent. Adio Dardi Zorzi," and he left the room. Dardi heard footsteps on the staircase, less and less and then silence, as was the way in Él Geto.

Dardi sat on the bed and held the folded parchment; sealed by Francesco da Carmagnola. The seal was an excellent forgery. Dardi slipped the parchment inside his giornea, left the room, and locked the door behind him.

Chapter Fourteen

Filipa knelt astride Donato while amused by his soporific peace and calm. She felt calm and peaceful, but not sleepy like a man. Donato's eyes eased open.

"How are you?" Filipa said.

"I'm great," Donato said. "How are you?"

"I'm good."

"Come here."

Filipa lay down and he cradled her in his arms. She felt protected and loved, although she knew that wasn't love. They lay together until Filipa squirmed and moved away. She sat cross-legged.

"What do you think of my humble room?" Filipa asked.

"I like the tapestry on the wall," Donato said.

"Another nun made that for me. It's the campo at my parish."

"It's very good."

"I was thinking of something else for this room, to make it more personal. What do you think?"

Donato frowned while he looked around. "Your portrait."

"That's pretentious."

"As a patrician you deserve to have your portrait painted. How many portraits of patrician wives and daughters have you seen?"

Filipa didn't have to think hard about that. "A lot," she said. "I should find a painter."

"I know of a painter here on Torcello. Pietro Vercius."

"I will see signor Vercius on Monday." Filipa wondered how much a portrait would cost and how she could pay, but first she would speak with signor Vercius. "Now Donato; do you want to visit me again sometime?

He smiled brightly and nodded his head.

"Next week on Saturday?" Filipa offered.

"Sé Filipa. Can I come here?"

"We can't go to your home; your family might get upset."

"My family would get very upset."

"Here after dinner next Saturday.

Donato stretched and sat up. "I must leave; my family will be wondering what's happened."

"I will walk you to the door."

They dressed and Filipa walked with Donato to the door, and kissed him on his cheek for farewell. Young, handsome and well-dressed; like all her men except Marino, who was older, handsome and well-dressed. Filipa watched him for a moment before returning to the corridor.

196

"Will he be back?" Clara asked.

"Donato Donato will be back," Filipa said.

"How many does that make?"

"Six."

"How do you remember who and when?"

"I remember well enough

"You should write a list."

Filipa giggled. "I can manage."

"Do you confess your sins?" Clara asked.

Filipa confessed once a year as was required. "My God; I am sorry for my sins with all my heart. It has been a year since my last confession, and since then I committed the following mortal sins. I committed adultery with six different men, many times."

"What penance do you get?"

"Like you it's substantial, and like you it's worth it."

"I know."

"There's no real harm in what I do. Not like murder and war, which is one state murdering the men of another state."

"How's your brother at war?"

"Still alive the last time he wrote to Cristina. Donato thought I should get my portrait painted. What do you think?"

"You're of patrician birth, so you should have a portrait."

"I will."

The bell chimed five.

"Vespers," Filipa said. "Now I have to pray."

"Do you?" Clara asked.

"I think there's no harm in making love, but I pray anyway."

Clara laughed.

"Do you pray?" Filipa asked.

"Always," Clara said.

"Confess your sins?"

"Absolutely."

"We must go to Vespers so we both can pray."

"Now!" Clara ordered, and they both ran along the corridor to join the other nuns.

* * *

The settlement of Torcello straddled the main canal which bisected the island. There was a fish market, palàsi, shops with living quarters above and also apartment buildings, although many of the buildings were faded and some had paint peeling away. Next to an inn was a modest building of three storeys, and that was Filipa's destination. She climbed the narrow, creaking staircase to the attic level high up in the roof. She knocked on the brown door and got the greatest surprise. The man in front of her didn't match the picture in her mind at all. She imagined an artist to be old, grey and wrinkled, but Pietro Vercius was young and extraordinarily handsome. Young like many of the men she knew, tall and darkly handsome: long, dark hair, dark eyes and a stubble of dark beard.

"Bongiorno siórina," he said in a deep, sonorous, masculine voice. "I'm Pietro Vercius."

Filipa took a breath to get her thoughts into order. "Bongiorno signor," she said almost breathlessly. "I'm Filipa Barbarigo."

"Come in, per piasser."

Filipa entered the large room which felt cramped, given the ceiling wasn't much more than head height except for the centre. In pride of place was an easel with a blank wood panel, while to the right was a paint-spattered bench with many paint-spattered bowls of various sizes, as well as grinding implements. Furniture consisted of an old, partly threadbare couch, a couple of chairs, and a simple, double bed to the far side.

"What can I do for you, siórina Barbarigo?"

"I would like my portrait painted, and I hope we can come to an arrangement for that."

"Of course. What sort of arrangement did you have in mind?"

Filipa hesitated and felt she shouldn't. Up until that moment she picked men for her pleasure, but to trade sex for a painting seemed wrong. Even if it wasn't wrong, Filipa wasn't sure how to ask. "I'm a nun here on Torcello," Filipa

199

said to set the background. "My family had enough dowry to get me into an abasia, but not enough dowry to find me a husband. Because of my heritage I can come and go as I like and even have men in my life." She looked at Pietro Vercius. "I can give you my time in exchange for my painting."

"As a model for other paintings?"

"If you want me to, or as a lover if you want that."

"I can't take advantage of you as a lover."

"On the contrary, being your lover will give me great pleasure."

"That's not something I can do. Let's go to the inn and talk about this over dinner."

They went downstairs and to the inn next door, where Pietro recommended sardines. Filipa ordered sardines and a cup of wine, and Pietro ordered the same.

"You said you're in an abasia," Pietro said.

"Like many women of my station," Filipa said. "Either marriage or an abasia."

"We don't treat women well," Pietro said. "And yet I know that women can do as much as men, except for very physical labours. But most other things, even painting, women can do. Some women have painted, some women have written poems and stories, and some women have written songs. If some women can do those things then I'm sure that many women can, if they were allowed to."

"I agree; but this isn't something we can change."

"When I marry, my wife will help me in my business, as many wives do. She will mix paint to the right shades, she may assemble wood panels, and most likely she will do our taxes and accounts. If women can easily do these things, then it follows that women can do more complex business tasks."

"It wouldn't be in men's interests for women to do more than simple tasks," Filipa said.

"Men would lose their power if that happened. This is why men consign women to being wives and mothers, or they consign women to abasie."

Filipa was quite surprised by that and didn't quite know what to say.

"Women are the opposite of men in many ways," Pietro said. "Men are physically strong where women are soft and beautiful. Men seek power and control where women seek close, personal relationships and friendships."

Their meals arrived from the kitchen and Filipa sipped some of the coarse wine before using her fork on the sardines. They were juicy and tender.

"I have a proposition for you," Pietro said. "Although I understand if you are uncomfortable with it. An opportunity has come my way and I'm looking for a model who will pose nude for me."

"And you will paint a picture of this model?"

"That's right."

"I will model nude for you," Filipa said.

"Are you sure?"

Filipa had no hesitation to model for this fascinating man, if only to spend more time with him. "I'm sure," she said.

He tilted his head. "Greeks and Romans sculptured and painted their Gods and Goddesses nude. I want to paint the Goddess Venus like that; chaste and erotic at the same time."

"I don't really understand, but I'm happy to model for your painting."

"When you see my idea take shape you will understand it better."

"I'm sure I will. Filipa took his left hand. "You have such big hands; big and strong and powerful. I want to feel your hands on my body."

Pietro took Filipa's slim hand with long, slim fingers. "Men are the opposite of women in this way."

"I really want to make love with you, Pietro."

Pietro touched Filipa's golden hair. "You're very beautiful Filipa, and if you want to make love with me then we can. After, we can start on my painting."

"Of me nude?"

"Most men are scared of the beauty of women, and that's why they keep women locked away. When I paint you nude I'm painting the most beautiful of God's creations, as He made her."

Filipa squeezed his big, strong hand and looked into his eyes. She felt strange, not sexually aroused but something deeper, more connected, more together. "I think I could love you," she said quietly.

He smiled brightly and he was so handsome! "See how much you love me after I get you to lie just so for hours at a time!"

* * *

Filipa walked Nicolò to the door and kissed him gently on his cheek.

"Can I come next week like the others?" he asked.

Filipa didn't feel anything much, but Nicolò wasn't any different to the others. Perhaps next time would be better. "You can come next week Nicolò."

"Adio Filipa."

"Adio Nicolò."

Filipa returned along the corridor.

"He makes seven," Clara said.

"Nicolò makes eight. I met a painter in the town and I'm modelling for him."

"And you make love with your painter?'

"Sé I do. I like him a lot."

"And Nicolò?"

"Nicolò Grioni," Filipa said while she thought about him. She undressed for him while he hungrily feasted with his eyes, and then she helped him undress. She took him to bed and got him to lick and suck her till she came, and then she rode him until he was close, and then she stroked his penis until he came. But with Pietro it was different. Somehow they both were naked on the bed, and somehow he licked her and then she came, and then she found his penis in her mouth. Then he was making love with her and kissing her, and he kissed her and kissed her even after she felt him on her stomach. "I told Nicolò to come back, but I like Pietro the painter more."

"I found the same thing," Clara said. "I like Luca and Carlo more than the patricians."

"I wonder what it is."

"They're real men."

Filipa thought that was it. She had seen Pietro three times that week and they made love each time. If she didn't see Andrea or Marco or any of the patricians again she wouldn't miss them; yet she had to see Pietro. She would see Pietro on Monday where he would paint his sketch of her. Filipa felt close to Pietro in her heart. When she was away from him, it was her heart that ached for him. Her heart ached to see him soon.

* * *

Filipa winced with the pain and wished she could move. Her bottom tingled and her legs ached. She looked at Pietro with hope in her eyes, but he was busy at his work. Then he looked up and their eyes met. She saw he understood.

"You can take a break Filipa," he said. "Come here and see how you look."

Filipa slid off the couch and that hurt even more, but just for a moment. She walked behind his easel and was stunned. For their past times he used a pencil and that looked like nothing, but with paint it came alive. Too alive. "That's not me," Filipa said.

"This is you," Pietro said. "Have you ever seen yourself in a big mirror?"

Filipa shook her head. "Surely I don't look like that?"

"You do."

"Tell me about Venus," Filipa asked.

"Venus was the mother of Rome, and in a way she's the mother of all Italians. Venus is the goddess of love, sex, desire, beauty, seduction, and persuasive feminine charm. Women operate differently to men; men take what they want with force, while women get what they want through...."

"Charm," Filipa said.

"The counterpoints to Venus are the Roman gods Vulcan and Mars, who represent fire and war."

Filipa thought that was very appropriate: a woman representing love, seduction and charm, while men represented war and destruction. She looked at the painting again. "The way you posed me hides my sex," she said.

"Not quite. Look closely."

Filipa looked, and she saw a little of her sex showing above her legs.

"The pudenda is the most aesthetically pleasing part of the female form, and if I could show all of your pudenda, I would. Instead I have shown just a glimpse, to remind men that no matter how powerful they are, they first came to the world from there, and then they spend most of their adult lives returning to where they came from."

Filipa again looked at the picture and contemplated that. Pietro was right on both counts. "How is it that you came up with such a painting?"

"All paintings are done by commission, and usually they're portraits or religious scenes. But this time my patron wanted a painting of love and lust, and I suggested Venus. I told him that Roman paintings and sculptures showed Venus nude."

Filipa nodded. "Your patron must love his wife or some other woman."

"You must first know love to ask for a painting of love."

Filipa took Pietro's hand and felt calm and peaceful. She felt love for him, which was different to lust but also the same. Whenever she saw Pietro she wanted him to make love with her, and after they made love she felt she was a part of him and sensed he was a part of her. Whenever she was in his presence she felt she was a part of him and sensed he was a part of her. She always had to leave, but as soon as she did she wanted to return. He meant so much to her and her other men meant so little. She wanted to say 'I know love' but those were the hardest words to say. "I like your painting of love and lust," Filipa said.

"The day after I was commissioned for this painting, the most beautiful woman in Venèsia came to my room. You have posed for a few hours and I think that's enough. Can you come back?"

Filipa wanted to come back straight away. "I can come back tomorrow. We can make love, and then I can pose."

He held her chin and looked deep into her eyes, and Filipa really sensed his love for her. "We will do that," he said.

Chapter Fifteen

Marin tried to remain relaxed and calm at the campo but he was only half-there; his other half was in their room with Blanca. He knew she was being looked after by the midwife as well as her mother and his mother, but terrible things could happen in childbirth with the best of care. And then their baby.... So many babies were born dead or died hours after birth. Vicenzo sat with Marin for support, but he was young and didn't know what a husband, and a father to be, had to endure.

"It's a nice day and we should go somewhere," Vicenzo said.

It was a hot, June day and very pleasant, but Marin didn't want to leave the Campo.

"Come on Marin," Vicenzo said. "We can go to Piasà San Marco for a while."

Marin agreed and that turned out to be a good idea. Listening to the singers, and then buying a pie from a vendor for dinner took his mind from things. He went into the baxélega and lit a candle to pray for a good birth and a healthy baby, before they returned to Campo Santa Maria del Giglio. Shortly after the bell chimed for two in the afternoon. Sióra Agoli appeared and she didn't look downcast. She came to Marin who turned to face her.

"Congratulations Marin," she said. "You have a son."

"Is Blanca alright?" Marin asked.

"Blanca's fine."

Marin was so pleased. He followed Sióra Agoli to the chaos of their room, and in time he would rent a bigger home with two rooms. Blanca sat in bed feeding her child and that reminded Marin about how astounding women were. They brought life to the world and nurtured it, and anything that men did paled into insignificance compared to that. Marin stood close and their baby was very small. Soon their baby would have to be baptised and being a boy Marin needed two godfathers and a godmother; previously agreed with his father, his mother and Vicenzo. They also had names: Lion Marin Daniele.

Marin kissed Blanca on her cheek. "I'll arrange the baptism," he said, and left to see pàre Doro at Cièsa di Santa Maria del Giglio. On the way back Marin gathered his father and Vicenzo. They left Blanca in the care of her mother while they took the baby, wrapped in a blanket, to the church. There they met pàre Doro at the church door who inquired about the sex of their child, and then the priest blessed the child and put salt in his mouth. Pàre Doro asked the godparents to recite the Pater Noster, and satisfied with their spiritual knowledge they were allowed inside to the font. Pàre Doro asked Marin the child's names and Marin told him. The priest immersed the child who cried terribly, he was anointed and named, and then Marin's mother as godparent wrapped

Lion in the christening robe supplied by the church. At the alter Lion still cried, and above that commotion he was asked to profess his faith, with godparents answering on his behalf. With that done the christening robe was exchanged for the blanket, and they could return to Blanca where they put their still-crying baby in his cradle.

The party broke up to leave the family of three in their small but cosy room. Sadly that wasn't the end of it, because the child cried terribly but wouldn't feed. Indeed Lion was hot and feverish, which was tragic. Marin raced to the church and returned with père Doro who made an incantation as a cure. Marin waited in the background while the priest said his prayers, and he thanked père Doro with great sincerity.

Sadly that didn't work and little Lion got hotter and hotter while he cried and cried, and Marin felt so helpless. Strangely, Blanca was quite calm while she nursed him. Evening dragged into night with no improvement, and Lion cried until it seemed he couldn't cry anymore. Very, very hot he stopped breathing, just like that. Marin didn't know how he felt: stunned, helpless, confused. He should have been tired, but wasn't, and he hadn't ate but wasn't hungry. Blanca, still surprisingly, was not so upset, and Marin couldn't work out why.

Marin sat on the bed and held her hand. "He wasn't meant to be with us," she said.

"I don't understand," Marin said.

"The Lord had other plans, and we just have to accept His ways."

"I suppose so," Marin said, although he still didn't understand.

"We're young and we can try again, when I'm able. Next time will be better I'm sure."

Marin looked at Blanca with amazement. "Are you sure?"

She squeezed his hand. "I'm terribly sad our son was taken from us, but he wasn't meant to be with us. But that's not the end for you and me, and in time we'll have a family."

Deep down Marin knew Blanca was right, and in time, perhaps in just a year, they would have a family. They would never forget her first pregnancy, her first birth and their first son, but Lion Marin Daniele Curri wasn't meant to be with them for more than a few hours.

* * *

Dardi and Clario climbed the stairs to the room in silence. Dardi opened the door and led Clario inside. Clario went to the far wall and turned to face Dardi.

"Tell me about what you're doing for that man," Clario asked.

"Every Monday he gives me a sealed letter to place into the war correspondence," Dardi said.

"That's bad."

"It is, but what can I do?"

"Should we continue to meet?"

"What's done is done, and he will report our pasts if I don't cooperate." Dardi knew what the problem was. "The true villain's the Church who hates people like us, and who pressured law-makers to make sodomy a crime."

"We can't change that."

"They don't understand," Dardi said.

"They don't understand many things. If they had their way married couples wouldn't be allowed to make love, and we would die out in a generation!"

Dardi thought that was true enough, and most married couples committed mortal sins because there was no other way. "We accepted our place a long time ago, and all we can do is survive. I had to marry just to survive."

"I know."

"I like Caterina and she's a good woman, but every time we attempt to make love it reminds me who I really am. You and I are who I really am."

"I like women in a way, but that's not who I am."

Dardi pressed Clario against the wall and kissed him hard, and felt his desire stirring. That was who he was, and who he always would be.

* * *

Dardi paced the room while moans and even screams came down the stairs. His heart raced and he felt sweaty, especially being a warm, August day.

"All husbands pace during these times," Papa said.

Dardi looked at Papa relaxed on an armchair. "Did you?"

"Every time."

"Women go through so much just to bring the next generation into this world. Women are stronger than men, and men drag them down to make ourselves important. But the reality is that we can never be as strong as women."

"You always had a soft spot for women, and yet your marriage...."

"Our marriage started harder than most, but it's better now."

"I suppose those rumours will stick for a while."

Dardi heard another scream. "Caterina's wonderful and I couldn't ask for a better wife. You made a good choice."

"I know we did."

Dardi sensed someone and turned around to see the midwife looking dishevelled. He panicked. "What is it?" he blurted out.

"You're a father, siór Zorzi. A beautiful girl."

Dardi was so pleased.

"For a man who loves the strength of women so much," Papa said. "A daughter's appropriate."

Dardi ran up the stairs two at a time and into the bedroom. "Here you go Papa; here's your daughter," the woman said, and Dardi was handed his daughter wrapped in blankets. She was so tiny: little eyes, little fingers, little hands. She was tiny and perfect. Dardi sat on the rumpled bed beside Caterina who looked good. No, she looked great. "She's as beautiful as you, mia amór."

"Lucia Maria Zorzi," Caterina said.

Dardi kissed Caterina's sweaty cheek. "What you have done leaves me in awe."

"All women give birth."

"That's what I mean."

She smiled at that. "Te vògio ben Dardi."

"Te vògio ben Caterina." He looked at his daughter, so tiny and so healthy. "Lucia Maria Zorzi," he said. "I'm you're Papa."

Chapter Sixteen

Marin was pleased that Mama arranged for the family to visit for the 25th anniversary of their wedding, and when Mama asked him not only was he happy to visit; he hoped that one day he would celebrate his 25th anniversary with Blanca. Marin and Blanca walked to his parent's rooms with Blanca carrying a pot of meat stew as their contribution. Blanca kissed Mama and congratulated her. Mama beamed brightly and Marin could tell there was genuine affection between mother-in-law and daughter-in-law.

Marin went into the other room and greeted Vicenzo; now with the room and a bed to himself. It seemed strange to return home where nothing had changed on the surface, but in reality much had changed.

Shortly after, Alberto and Laura arrived and Marin got the greatest shock; Laura looked terrible! Bruises on her face, a cut above her left eye and limping slightly. She wore a forced smile which pricked Marin's interest. Laura was a good daughter, a good sister and almost undoubtedly a good wife; but she had a serious nature and smiled only when overjoyed. That evening joy was unlikely, given her injuries.

Once the commotion of visitors arriving had died down, Papa gave Mama a silver brooch to symbolise their anniversary. The brooch was particularly nicely engraved. Marin wanted to speak with Laura to find out what happened, but she had brought a pot and helped Mama prepare the family feast. There were jugs of wine on the table for the guests, where the three women laid plates of the three, different stews, although the table was rather crowded for seven. Talk flowed freely and everyone seemed to pretend that nothing had happened to Laura, while Marin wondered what could have caused her injuries. Given it was mostly her face she seemed to have been struck repeatedly and viciously, which was most unfair. Women were the property of their fathers until they married, and then they became the property of their husbands who had the right to discipline their wives. But Marin couldn't imagine Laura ever needing to be disciplined. Laura had always been helpful around the home before she married, and undoubtedly she would perform her wifely duties in her own home, and quiet, patient and intelligent Laura would never provoke her husband. Marin glanced at Alberto and had to keep his thoughts to himself. It was the celebration day of his parents.

Later the women went to the campo to wash up leaving the men to play cards at the table.

"What happened to Laura?" Papa asked while he dealt the cards for a game of taròchi.

"She fell down the stairs," Alberto replied flatly.

"Her injuries don't look like falling down stairs."

"That's what happened. Besides, she's my property now."

"She's my daughter Alberto, and always will be."

"Ask her what happened."

Papa grimaced, and Marin knew that Laura would lie to protect herself from another beating. The game continued in a strained silence, even after the women returned. Time passed and they had to head home. Marin and Blanca bid their parents farewell, and went downstairs to a fine, still, autumn evening. September was a particularly nice time of year.

"Did Laura mention what happened?" Marin asked.

"She said she fell down some stairs," Blanca replied.

"Do you believe that?"

"No I don't. But you can't interfere in their marriage, Marin."

Marin wondered about that. "If the same thing happened to you...?"

"I'm sure my brothers would talk with you." Blanca stopped walking. "Whatever you do Marin, be careful. You could make things worse for Laura. If you must; take Vicenzo to make a stronger point."

That was an excellent idea. "I'll try, and I hope I don't make things worse for her."

"I do understand. Laura has been like my sister from the time we met, and she's a good person who doesn't deserve to be treated like that."

Marin thought that no woman, no matter how she behaved, deserved to be treated like that.

The next afternoon Marin asked Vicenzo to come with him, but only when outside did he say they were going to speak with Alberto. The closer Marin got to their room, the angrier he felt at the terrible way Laura had been treated. They went up the narrow, dark staircase to the second floor where Marin hammered loudly on their door. Laura opened that door and she looked shocked.

"We know what happened to you," Marin said as he strode inside, and straight to Alberto. "You will not treat Laura in such a disrespectful way ever again."

Alberto stood. "She's my wife and I will do with her as I see fit."

"She's my sister, and there will be consequences if you harm her again."

Vicenzo came beside Marin and stood with his arms crossed. Young Vicenzo was bigger than Marin and bigger even than Alberto. "This message comes from both of us," he said. "You leave Laura be."

Alberto sat down and glowered at them both.

"Laura," Marin said. "Anytime you feel threatened, anytime at all, you must speak with me or with Blanca. Alberto; you'll show more tolerance and patience towards Laura and never strike her again. If you strike her there will be consequences. Do you understand?"

Alberto didn't say a word; just glared at Marin, and Marin didn't like that. Marin's anger was gone and he'd done what he set out to do, but he knew that wouldn't be the end of the matter. He needed to know more. "Laura, can I speak with you outside?" Marin asked.

She went to the stairwell where Marin joined her and closed the door. "Can you tell me what happened?" Marin asked.

Laura looked down. "I don't really want to," she said quietly.

"I understand. Obviously Alberto hit you and pushed you, and that's why you're limping."

Laura nodded silently and then looked up at Marin. "He's not the man I thought he was. He was charming and said all the right things until we were married, and then he changed. I think not falling pregnant is making him angry."

"That's in the hands of God."

"He thinks it's my fault."

Marin thought that could be the fault of Alberto. Women had to orgasm in order to conceive, but he couldn't ask Laura such a personal question. "This is down to Alberto, both with him and with you," Marin said quietly.

"I know and that's not the problem."

"Then it's in the hands of God."

"I hope God has us in His plans because I don't ever want that to happen again."

"If it does, tell me straight away."

"I will."

Marin led Laura inside. "We'll leave you be," he said more to Alberto, and left with Vicenzo.

"You showed them," Vicenzo said while they went down the stairs, but Marin worried about Alberto taking his anger out on Laura. Alberto may even go too far with Laura and that would be tragic.

* * *

Marin was startled to have Vicenzo at his door, and he invited his brother inside.

"There's bad news," Vicenzo said. "Laura left Alberto and has come home to live."

Marin didn't think that was bad at all, although that made Laura neither one thing nor the other. A wife couldn't become a daughter again, nor could she marry someone else. Laura must have been fearful to leave her husband like that. At least she was safe physically, but the issue between her and Alberto had to be resolved. "Has she been hurt any further?" Marin asked.

"No," Vicenzo said. "Just frightened."

"I knew this would happen," Blanca said, and Marin spun around and glared at her. "You had no choice, and you did the right thing by putting her in a situation where she's safe."

Marin's anger faded. "I don't know the answer," he said.

"I don't either," Blanca said.

The answer came from a denunciation made by Alberto to get Laura back, and I Sbirri paid a visit on Marin to get his story about the situation. Marin told the sbirro that Alberto punished Laura excessively harshly and he acted to protect her. The sbirro told Marin that Él Consìlio dei Cuarànta would speak with them both, and most likely order Laura Tanto to return home. The two sbirri left and Marin knew a wife belonged to her husband. Adam was made in God's image, and Eve was made from Adam to be his companion and helper. Not only that but wives must submit to their husbands. Él Consìlio dei Cuarànta, whoever they were, would enforce the principle that wives were subservient to husbands. After a couple of weeks, Laura was ordered to attend Palàso Ducale. Later that day she was home once more.

Chapter Seventeen

Marin knew he had to do something, and perhaps that something was to bring mortal fear to his brother-in-law. Alberto Tanto may control himself if he knew whatever he did to Laura would be returned many times over.

"You're thinking about Laura," Blanca said.

"I am," Marin agreed.

"They're married."

"She was so frightened that she left him."

"I like Laura; she's a good person. What will you do?"

"Visit with Vicenzo and my friends Carlo and Piero."

"That may work."

Marin gazed at beautiful Blanca. "It's not a happy and loving marriage."

Blanca gazed into his eyes. "Laura deserves better."

Marin went out and rounded up Vicenzo before visiting Carlo and then Piero. Either of his friends should have made an attempt with Laura. The fear of rejection when you ask that question weighs more heavily on some men than on others. They climbed the stairs, and once more Marin hammered on their door. Laura opened it and showed great shock.

"We've come to talk with Angelo," Marin said firmly, before barging his way inside. The little room was crowded with six and Angelo backed away, looking fearful about what may happen.

"Angelo Tanto," Marin said firmly. "If anything happens, you will have to deal with the four of us. Do you understand?"

He nodded silently.

"I could give you a taste of what would happen, but I won't. I know my sister and I know you couldn't have asked for a better wife, and when God wills it she will make a good mother for your children. From now on you will treat her with dignity and respect in all ways." Marin turned and faced Laura. "Can we speak outside?"

They went into the corridor and Marin shut the door for privacy.

"I didn't want to come back to misery and fear," Laura said.

Marin felt terribly, terribly sad. He took Laura's small hands, and women had small, delicate hands. "I hope I can take away your fear, but I can't take away the misery."

"I know; perhaps when I fall pregnant...."

"That will make a difference for sure," Marin said, even though he didn't believe it. "We should go back."

They went inside and Marin bid Laura and Angelo farewell. In the calle they dispersed, and Marin hoped he wouldn't have to call on his brother and his friends to help.

Laura was owned by Angelo, and her future was to forever regret the day they met.

* * *

The gondoliere berthed his craft at the small jetty just below the gardens. The island of Murano, about a mile north of Venèsia and like Venèsia itself, was a series of small islands separated by naturally formed channels, with those islands connected by bridges to allow foot traffic. The main channel of Murano was Canale di San Donato, and off that canal was Palàso Donato; the grand home of the Donato family. Alongside the palàso were large gardens, their destination on a fine, mild, mid-October day.

Dardi climbed out and offered Caterina his hand, where she joined him on the dock. She looked around. "This is quite lovely," she said.

There were a few gardens in Venèsia proper, and none of those gardens were as magnificent as the gardens of Palàso Donato. Hand-in-hand they followed a gravel path bordered by a lush, manicured lawn, with more paths branching off. One of those paths climbed a hill, and crossed over on a wooden bridge imitating a bridge over a canal. That wooden bridge was draped with green shrubs, and all around were rows and rows of neatly trimmed shrubs. The gardens at Palàso Donato would look even more magnificent when in flower in spring. A simple, stone fountain gurgled happily, while further at the perimeter were boxwood and oak trees, all immaculately pruned.

"Look," Caterina said. "There's a maze."

Indeed there was. "Later, we must get lost in there," Dardi said.

"You can go in there, and when I find you my reward will be a kiss!"

Caterina looked as magnificent as the gardens, dressed in gold silk with a black and yellow capèlo, and that pendant at her neck. There were many beautiful women: wives and mistresses, but none were as beautiful as his wife. He was proud of her. Further along tables were set for dinner later, and after dinner would come dancing. A servant passed and Dardi took two cups of wine, and gave Caterina one. She sipped her drink. "The Donato family must be very wealthy," she said.

"They're one of the wealthiest families in Venèsia."

Ahead was the heir to that wealth; arm in arm with a woman also dressed in gold silk. Her back was to them, but her long, gold-coloured hair was unmistakable. Filipa Barbarigo. Dardi strolled onto another path while hearing Donato calling for him.

"That man wants you," Caterina said.

"Sé he does," Dardi said.

They returned to the path and went to Donato.

"Donato Donato; this is my wife Caterina," Dardi said.

"Bongiorno sióra Zorzi," Donato said.

"You can call me Caterina," she said. "You have the most magnificent home and gardens siór Donato. We have few gardens in Venèsia, and none as lovely as this."

"You can call me Donato," he said. "Autumn's a pleasant time of the year, and a lovely time to have an outdoor function. I would like to introduce you to...."

"We know siórina Barbarigo," Caterina said. "Bondi Filipa."

"Bondi Caterina e Dardi," Filipa said. "You're both looking well and happy. Parenthood must agree with you."

"Lucia has made our lives complete," Caterina said.

"I can see that. Do you want me to show you around?"

"Sé."

"I won't be long, mio amór."

Filipa slid her arm into Caterina's arm and led them both along another path. "For today I'm the mistress of Donato," she said quietly.

"I understand," Dardi said.

"I don't understand," Caterina said.

"I can't be a nun," Filipa said.

"She's right," Dardi told Caterina. "Who else do you know, apart from Fantino da Pesaro and Donato Donato?"

226

"Andrea Barbo, Marco Barbo, Albano Capello, Marino Contarini and Nicolò Grioni."

Dardi stopped dead with shock. "My God Filipa!" he exclaimed. "Some of those are the most noble of patrician families. Barbo, Capello, Grioni.... Marino Contarini could buy and sell my family twice over."

Filipa looked at the ground. "They like me," she said quietly.

"Why?" Caterina asked.

"Filipa looked deep into Caterina's eyes. "Because I take my pleasure with them, and no other woman does that. But I'm a nun and that's serious, so today I'm the mistress of Donato. Caterina per piasser."

"Today you're the mistress of Donato," Caterina said.

Filipa smiled. "You're wearing your lucky pendant."

"It gave me an easy birth, and we have a healthy daughter."

Filipa smiled brighter. "I'm jealous of you! Now, I must return to Donato."

Filipa left them, and slipped her arm into Donato's arm.

"What is it with her?" Caterina asked while frowning deeply.

"She told you," Dardi said. "This is a lovely garden and we can share this space with Filipa Barbarigo. She's a pretend mistress, but there are real mistresses here too. We

227

will have a lovely dinner and later we will dance, and we will enjoy this day and remember it always."

"Sé we will." Caterina kissed his cheek. "It's time for you to get lost in that maze, and it's time for me to find you for my kiss!"

Dardi jogged into the shrubbery barely able to believe what he'd just heard. Fornication was a serious crime, and fornication with a nun was one of the most serious crimes of all. Dardi remembered the precocious girl who pestered him to play hide and seek whenever her family came to visit. Filipa was grown up now and playing a different game; a game of power and control. A game probably addictive to her, where the stakes were high and the result could be disastrous. He hoped she knew what she was doing. He really hoped that things wouldn't turn tragic for her.

* * *

Saturday was a half-day, with Marin closing his shop at twelve and heading home for dinner. Blanca looked particularly happy and he wondered what it was.

"You're looking good," Marin said.

"I'm pregnant," she said.

Marin barely believed . "That's wonderful. We must go the church and say a special prayer."

"What happened last time is what happens, and we have to hope and to pray that this time will be better."

"I know."

"Are you happy?"

"I'm very happy."

"I cooked a fish stew for dinner."

"That will be nice, but tomorrow we will eat at an inn for dinner, as a special treat."

"I would like that."

"You deserve it."

"We both deserve it."

"I didn't do anything."

"Well, you must have."

Blanca dished up, and while Marin ate his dinner he imagined a more special treat than the inn. He would buy Blanca a pendant for childbirth. He decided to do that on Monday.

The Jewish quarter of Venèsia, Él Geto, had affordable jewellers shops. After he finished dinner on Monday, Marin found a shop on Fondamenta Cannaregio. He asked the jeweller for a simple pendant and was shown a gold cross on a chain, which was ideal. He bought that for 30 lire and couldn't wait to get home that evening.

On Monday Marin came home with the pendant in his tacolinn. He was greeted with a smile, a hug and a kiss as always and then he opened his tacolinn. He took it out.

"I have a special present for the most special woman in the world," he said, and gave the cross to Blanca.

"Oh that's wonderful!" she exclaimed, and kissed him again. "This will be my good luck charm."

"I know."

"I can't give you anything in return."

"You give me enough already, and you will give me a son or a daughter in time."

"Now we can have supper, and later I wish we could but you know we can't."

Marin knew what she meant and he wished too, but that was a sin and sadly they couldn't. He wanted nothing more than to make love with his wife, particularly to hold her soft body in his arms, but that wasn't allowed. It would be many long months, perhaps even a year, before they could love each other like that.

"Now mio amór," Blanca said. "Sit at the table and I will serve you a meat stew."

Marin sat while appreciating that and everything they did together, from simple meals to starting a family, happened with genuine affection. There was no question that night in his shop was the best thing he ever did. He couldn't imagine his life being happier than it was.

Chapter Eighteen

Palàso Ducale was a massive, 'U' shaped building around a central courtyard, with the north side of the courtyard closed off by Baxélega San Marco. Entry was by a simple staircase surrounded by building works, into the reception area on the Loggia Floor. The Loggia floor was where most administrative tasks were carried out. Upstairs, the first floor had grand chambers for Él Maggior Consiglio, Él Consìlio dèi Cuarànta and the apartments of Él Doxe, including his working space. The second floor had chambers for Él Consìlio dèi Diéxe, Él Colèjo and Él Consìlio dèi Pregadi. Palàso Ducale was the most lavish building in Venèsia by a long way, and an architectural masterpiece in that its massive size seemed less imposing, given the almost delicate columns facing the public area of Piaséta San Marco.

Dardi's work area was on the Loggia floor, and he was responsible for receiving and distributing correspondence throughout Palàso Ducale. He had his own room which overlooked the central courtyard, and it was modest but still quite beautiful. Finished in brown and gold with a panelled ceiling, his furniture consisted of a lovely oak desk in contrasting light and dark timbers, a blue velvet-covered chair, and an oak bookcase which matched his desk. Él Consìlio dèi Pregadi was responsible for managing the war against Lombardy, a conflict ongoing for the past four years, and the conflict Dardi was supplying correspondence for. Dardi personally distributed key war correspondence, including forged letters, to Doxe Francesco Foscari who was taking an interest in the war. Dardi went to the Equerrie who allowed him access to the study of Doxe Foscari.

"Ah Dardi," Doxe Foscari said. "Good to see you."

Dardi handed the letter across and was about to leave when Doxe Foscari asked him to stay a moment. Doxe Foscari opened the letter and frowned while he read it, and it seemed, read it a second time.

"I can't make sense of what's happening there," Doxe Foscari said. "Filipo Visconti was going to marry the daughter of Amadeus of Savoy to form an alliance, which was of serious concern to us. An alliance like that would give them superiority on the battlefield and we would have to ready more troops. But now that marriage isn't happening."

Dardi was concerned about that. "So that's good then?" he asked, stating the obvious.

"It is, but we had ongoing intelligence that the marriage was certain, and then for an implausible reason the marriage has been cancelled."

"What reason?" Dardi asked.

"It says that Visconti finds his future wife unattractive, which is contrary to my understanding of her. She's apparently quite beautiful, and is reportedly well-educated and quite personable. It seems odd that Visconti would jeopardise his success in the war against us, especially when his wife should be a suitable match."

Dardi couldn't say anything because that would give him away. He stood before his doxe and didn't know what to say.

"Well, at least you don't need to worry about such things," Doxe Foscari said.

Dardi nodded.

"Adio Dardi," Doxe Foscari said.

"Adio Doxe Foscari," Dardi said, and he left his Doxe to ponder that contradictory letter. Dardi undertook the rest of his deliveries with his mind far away, and when he returned to his room he realised that he may cause Venèsia to lose the war. Obviously the marriage of Visconti and the daughter of Amadeus of Savoy was going ahead, and the forces of Venèsia will find themselves outnumbered and probably be defeated. They wouldn't stand a chance. Dardi knew that was wrong, even tragic, and something he had to resolve. Never again would he distribute forged letters from Roberto Geni. But that couldn't be the end of it because that was near enough to a death sentence. Dardi felt he had two choices: deal with Geni or leave Venèsia. He didn't want to leave, and that would be hard on Caterina. She was close to her sister and mother, and indeed close to her whole family, and it wasn't fair to separate that from her. No, Dardi had to deal with Geni if he could, and his next opportunity would be on Monday at Él Geto.

* * *

As usual for a Monday afternoon Dardi was in the room at Él Geto; sitting on the bed while waiting for Roberto Geni. Geni was in his forties and spoke good Venèsian, but was dour and taciturn. Dardi didn't know if Geni was married but at his age he would have been. The door opened and Geni entered the room while Dardi stood. Without saying a word Geni handed the sealed letter across, turned and left the room. Dardi had to do something, so he put the letter down and went down the stairs where he saw Geni heading away from Él Geto. Daylight was fading while Dardi followed Roberto Geni across Ponte delle Guglie at a distance, and towards Santa Lucia. Dardi knew he had to do something, but he didn't have a clue what that would be. He should have been better prepared with a knife or even his sword, because he was big enough and strong enough. Geni reached a somewhat decrepit building, opened a door and disappeared inside. Dardi hesitated for a moment and followed Geni inside, to hear footsteps on the stone staircase. Stepping carefully to make as little noise as possible; Dardi followed Geni up.

"Who's that?" Geni called with his voice echoing in the stairwell.

Dardi paused while feeling slightly dizzy, and then continued to climb. Up and around and up to the first floor to be face to face with Geni.

"What is it Zorzi?" Geni asked flatly.

"I'm not doing this anymore," Dardi said.

"That will be the death of you."

"No it won't!" and Dardi instinctively grabbed for Geni's throat. Geni tried to force Dardi's hands apart but Dardi gripped that throat as hard as he could. Geni tried to shout but couldn't, and then he made the greatest of effort to break free from Dardi's grasp. Geni stood with head down and breathing hard in the cold, silent staircase and Dardi shoved him. He fell backwards down the steep flight of stairs, tumbling and falling to hit the landing hard. Dardi braced himself with the banister and raced down to Geni who seemed dead, but maybe not. Dardi struggled to pick the dead weight of Geni up. The flight of stairs to the front door was steeper and Dardi pushed hard. Geni fell head first and Dardi went after him. Geni didn't move, no sign of life; with his head twisted strangely to one side. He had to be dead with his head like that. Dardi looked up the stairwell but nobody was around. All was eerily silent that evening when Dardi opened the door and left that decrepit building. He retraced the route to Él Geto and then took his usual walk home. He arrived home just in time for supper.

"What is it?" Caterina asked. She looked shocked.

235

Dardi momentarily panicked and then a thought came to him. "A thief tried to steal my tacolinn but I fought him off."

"That's terrible!" Caterina exclaimed. "What is this world coming to?"

"It's alright mia amór," Dardi said. "I can look after myself."

"Sé you can. Do you want to sleep early to recover?"

"No, my mind's too active. After supper do you want to play chess?'

Caterina nodded her head. "I would like that, and that will calm your mind."

"Sé it will," Dardi agreed, and he knew it would too. At least his problems were over and no more would he have to betray Venèsia.

* * *

Dardi entered the room at Él Geto where Clario sat on the bed. Clario stood and they kissed, but it wasn't Clario's usual, passionate kiss. Dardi sensed something was wrong.

"Bondi Dardi," Clario said. "How are you?"

The shock of killing a man hit Dardi that morning, and he'd just drifted through the day. "Bondi Clario," Dardi said flatly. "I'm alright."

"You don't look alright."

Dardi didn't want to talk about what happened. Strangely, he couldn't talk about what happened. "It's nothing," he said.

"There's something wrong with us, and this was going to happen sooner or later. You have your marriage, you career and I come third, and that's not where I want to be."

Dardi digested that. "I will try harder," he said flatly.

Clario moved away. "I don't think you can. You live with Caterina, and I sense she's a good woman and you're fond of her. And she's the mother of your daughter."

"But she's not who I am," Dardi said. His marriage was just something he had to do for the good of both of them.

"I know that, but she's who you are in most ways. Once we used to spend hours together, and now it's a kiss, a fuck and you're on your way back to your wife and child. "

Sadly, that was true. "I can still try harder," Dardi said, but not knowing how.

"You can't change the world Dardi, and I can't either. It's time we should part."

"But you're who I am."

"Once I was, but not anymore." Clario kissed Dardi. "Adio and I won't forget you."

"Don't go!" Dardi shouted desperately; grabbing Clario's arm to hold him. "We can make this work!"

Clario pulled free. "We can't make this work for me. I'll always come third and that's not good enough."

Clario left the room leaving Dardi standing there alone. One half of Dardi wanted to promise the impossible, and the other half knew he was being selfish. Even if he made up excuses to come home later on Tuesdays; that wasn't the solution. Dardi couldn't split himself emotionally, and his closeness to Caterina came at the expense of the closeness he once had with Clario. Clario was right and they couldn't change the world, but Dardi didn't know what he would do. He liked Caterina but she wasn't what he was, and without Clario he didn't belong anymore. Dardi left the room and closed and locked the door behind him, and for the second time in two days he walked from Él Geto to Ca' Zorzi Bon.

Chapter Nineteen

They walked home from church in silence. Carnevale was again being celebrated, but not at midday on Sunday of course. Dardi let himself into their home and Caterina followed him inside. Throughout the service his mind was far away, where Roberto Geni lay on the stairwell, dead, and Clario had left him. Dardi knew he'd done the right thing killing Geni, but he felt really bad about what he did, while Clario was right and anything else was selfish. Dardi needed something to get his mind off all of that, and sat at the sofa while wondering what to do.

"What's wrong Dardi?" Caterina asked.

"Nothing," he said.

"It seems like something to me." She sat beside him. "It has been a long time for us," she said quietly. "I miss it."

"Lucia's only five months old."

"And...?"

"Won't you fall pregnant?"

"That's why I feed her, in addition to the wet nurse."

"I understand."

"Come on mio amór," Caterina said, while heading up the stairs to their room. Dardi followed thinking that was the last thing he needed, but he didn't have the energy to argue about it. They undressed separately before Caterina lay on the bed and Dardi lay above her. He kissed her lips lightly because he knew she liked to be kissed lightly. He kissed her and kissed her before kissing her nipples, because she knew she liked to have her nipples kissed. He kissed her nipples one at a time and then moved between her legs. He licked there, smooth and hairless, licked her over and over while her breathing changed: heavy, deep and ragged. Licked her and licked her and she came with a quiet gasp.

Dardi reached down and he still had an erection. Good. He moved and she guided him into her, and he thrust into her body. He thrust and thrust, over and over, over and over and over. But nothing was happening; nothing at all. Dardi panicked; he wasn't going to come. He panicked more; when he panicked over coming he always lost his erection. Dardi closed his eyes and he was somewhere else. A body firm and muscular, a certain scent. Firm and muscular with a light coating of hair on his chest. Pressed against firm muscles Dardi continued thrusting and he felt the tingle at the base of his cock. He thrust into that body, over and over, and the tingle advanced little by little. Further and further until the length of his cock tingled. Tingled right at the tip, and he came. He thrust and thrust until it faded, and he felt good. Only when he felt smooth softness did he realise where he was.

"What's wrong mio amór?" Caterina asked.

"Nothing's wrong," Dardi said.

"Everything's good for us except for when we make love, and then you're a hundred miles away. You're inside me but not even inside the room."

"It's just me."

"I know."

Dardi felt sad at Caterina's hurt, and then it came to him. "Do you want to go to Carnevale this afternoon?" he asked.

"Of course! What's on?"

"There's always something on. Musicians, street performers; maybe we will find a ball."

"That will be great!"

"I'm sorry about us."

"Don't worry," Caterina said. "It's only making love."

They dressed in silence and went to the informal dining room. Livia the maid brought out dinner of risi i bisi; thick risotto with peas and pancetta bacon. Later, Gia the nurse brought Lucia. Caterina played with her before feeding her, and then they let Lucia sit up against the furniture. It didn't take much to entertain a baby, and then Caterina took Lucia upstairs and put her to sleep. Dardi looked at his daughter wrapped tight in swaddling and remembered another baby girl in a cot, now a beautiful woman who had five men as her lovers. It was well known that women were sexually voracious and their ravenous sexual appetites had to be controlled, which is why women were passed from father

241

to husband. But even so, for Filipa to have ongoing affairs with five men.... Dardi looked again at Lucia, and wondered if all women had the capacity to feast upon men to that extent.

"What is it mio amór?" Caterina asked.

"I first saw Filipa Barbarigo when she was about Lucia's age," Dardi said. "If you had the chance; would you do what she does?"

"I want to have just one, special man."

"I know that, but if you could have – I don't know the right word. If you could have a harem of men?"

"A woman with a harem?"

"That's what Filipa's got."

"How do you think that could happen?" Caterina asked.

"Oh that's obvious," Dardi said. "Men don't marry until they're about thirty, but they still have needs. Filipa wouldn't have to beg, and there's one of her and many of them, so she can have things how she wants them to be. But to actually do that? To actually have a harem of men?"

Caterina looked at Dardi. "To be honest if a man did that, many men would envy him, but when a woman does that there's something wrong with her." Caterina laughed lightly. "I'm happier with my husband and my beautiful daughter. Let's get ready, husband."

They went upstairs and changed; Dardi wore all black with a black cape and his black, tricorne capèﾛo, while Caterina wore a deep, dark red. She opened her jewellery box and took out the pendant and frowned. "If we find a dance I would like to wear this, but in the crowded streets at night... No, I will wear this old one," and she put on a pendant also in the shape of a cross, but smaller with few precious stones. It was still attractive though. Dardi took his Bauta mask and gave Caterina her mask, and they told the nurse they were going out for the afternoon into the evening.

Outside mid-afternoon many were dressed for Carnevale, and Piasà San Marco was busy as always. They listened to a man singing while playing a lute, a light and delicate instrument, and Dardi left a ten soldi coin in the singer's upturned baréta. They went on to a juggler and watched him dealing with five balls at once, and a small hoop on one ankle as an extra challenge. Dardi gave a donation to the juggler before they watched a puppet show, which was as much for adults as children, because the themes of the show were beyond the understanding of the young people watching and laughing. Dardi imagined in a few years' time taking Lucia to see puppets at Piasà San Marco on cold, winter's days when Venèsia was at its brightest. For sure, Carnevale was a time of contrasts.

Darkness was falling when they went to Él Lión Biànco, just around the corner from the piasà, entering the

243

inn just ahead of a man all in black, and with a volto mask covering his entire face. Dardi and Caterina both ordered chopped liver with onions, and a cup of wine each. While they were finishing their meal, the bell at Baxélega San Marco chimed five and outside was almost dark. Dardi hoped they could find a ball to make for a memorable Sunday.

"What next, mio amór?" Caterina asked.

"We should head towards Canal Grando and see if there's any dancing," Dardi said. He finished the last of his wine, stood, and took Caterina's hand. They went into the near-darkness, where the main illumination came from windows of homes all around. Behind the man in a volto mask headed in the same direction along Calle Canonica. Unfortunately the ponte ahead was under attack and Dardi paused.

"Don't you get tired of such childish behaviour?" Caterina asked.

Dardi didn't know what to say.

"Ha!" Caterina laughed. "You used to do that!"

"I may have," Dardi said. "We can go this way."

They walked alongside the canal where it was quite crowded, and much more crowded given the attack at the ponte. Dardi squeezed Caterina's hand a little tighter lest he lose her in the near darkness in the jostling crowd. It was quite busy, almost crushing, with some heading to Canal Grando and some heading to Piasà San Marco. Dardi

squeezed Caterina's hand even tighter and then someone
bumped him from behind. Dardi stumbled and Caterina
slipped from his grip. He stumbled into the low wall
separating the path from the canal, and looked for Caterina
but she wasn't there. Dardi tried to get his bearings but was
pushed and shoved from all sides. She must have gone
towards the next ponte, but she wasn't there either. He
crossed that ponte while looking all around, and then entered
a narrow laneway with little light. Dardi looked hard and
then he saw something in a doorway to the left. A dark
bundle, perhaps a person, perhaps Caterina had been
knocked off her feet and bumped her head. He went to the
bundle and it was Caterina! He knelt and saw darkness on
her dark clothing, and something bright reflecting the light.
The brass handle of a knife in her throat! Dardi pulled it out
and didn't know what to do.

   "Help me per piasser!" he cried out and someone
knelt beside.

   "What is it?" the stranger asked.

   "My wife's been stabbed!" Dardi shouted above the
noise.

   A murmur rippled through the crowd pressing ever
closer; squashing Dardi towards Caterina who was very still.
Dardi didn't know what to do.

   "Call a doctor!" the stranger shouted and the crowd
pushed even closer. A man almost fell out of the crowd and

Dardi turned to see a second stranger had fought his way out of the throng. This stranger knelt beside Dardi.

"How is she?" Dardi asked.

The stranger put his ear to Caterina's mouth while Dardi looked on with his heart racing, and feeling flushed despite the biting cold. "She's dead I'm afraid."

"No!" Dardi shouted, touching Caterina's pretty face while searching for signs of life. But she was so very still and the dark stain spread from the top of her giornea. Blood. Dardi still held the knife and someone had cut Caterina's throat. A thief perhaps, except she had nothing of value. Even the old pendant was at her throat, although hanging to the side of her neck. He wondered what had happened.

Dardi looked up and two men in hooded tabàri approached, and the crowd scattered. I Sbirri, troops for Él Consìlio dèi Diéxe, responsible for law, order and the protection of the state. Dardi knew of them and sometimes wondered if I Sbirri were any better than the criminals they arrested. He stood to face them.

"What happened?" one of the sbirri asked.

"My wife has been murdered," Dardi said.

"By that knife in your hand?"

"I took it from her throat. You can have it." Dardi handed the knife across while the other sbirro checked Caterina and spoke with the two strangers.

"Maffeo," the sbirro said. "Get help to move the body to Palàso Ducale. I'll guard the body until you return."

The other sbirro disappeared into the darkness.

"What's your name," the sbirro asked.

"Dardi Zorzi, and my wife was Caterina Zorzi, formerly Caterina Cornaro."

"I'm Almoro Canal."

Dardi nodded acknowledgement.

They stood in silence while crowds moved past, avoiding the eye of the sbirro. Eventually two sbirri emerged from the darkness and cleared a space to pick up Caterina's body and take it across the ponte. Dardi and Almoro followed up the staircase into the palàso, and down to the ground floor where they went to a small room with a small table against the wall, and two chairs.

"Sit, per piasser," Almoro asked.

Dardi sat.

"Can you tell me what you were doing this evening?" Almoro asked.

"We went to Piasà San Marco to see performers, and later had supper at an inn. Then we set off to find a dance and that's when it happened. Caterina and I were holding hands in the crowd, but someone knocked me and we were separated. I couldn't see her anywhere, so I crossed the ponte and found her in that doorway."

"I'm sorry for your loss and we'll find the man who did this. This is late Sunday so a doctor will examine your wife tomorrow, and then you can arrange her funeral. You should go home and rest if you can."

"Grassie."

"You and your late wife are from great patrician families, and because of that we will give this case our full priority."

"Grassie."

Dardi followed the corridor and up the stairs to reception, and then down the staircase into the piasà, and walked home by memory. None of it registered, not even when he found himself upstairs in their bedroom. Next to the bed where he made love with Caterina, just to please her. Only he couldn't please her. She was a good woman, no a great woman, and she was a good mother too. Dardi knew he was lucky to have her, even though he hurt her. For some reason he couldn't manufacture *that* out of thin air. For some reason that wasn't him. He sat on the bed and wondered why he couldn't love Caterina that way.

* * *

The home parish of Caterina Cornero was San Luca, and she was to be interned at Cièsa di San Luca Evangelista. The pallbearers carried the coffin from the family home of Ca' Cornaro Piscopia to Campo Manin, and into the church. Extra priests were brought in for the service, while the modest church was packed with mourners. Dardi and his immediate family: his Papa and Mama, his younger brothers Zane and Antonino, were to the left. To the right were the Cornero family, headed by Giovanni Cornero. Dardi heard not a word of the service until he realised the mourners were leaving. He headed into Campo Manin on a cold, cloudy day.

Antonino took his hands. "I'm sorry for your loss, brother," he said. At least Dardi had one sibling who cared. Zane disliked Dardi for various reasons: mostly because Zane was sent to war while Dardi worked at Palàso Ducale managing correspondence, and Zane also disliked Dardi's closeness to their Mama. Zane, recently returned from Lombardia, kept his distance.

They went to grand Ca' Cornaro Piscopia where there was to be a final remembrance for Caterina. Dardi wished it was all over. The funeral and morning seemed like a never-ending regurgitation of her death. At the heart of it, Caterina was a good person, no a great person, and she left nothing but good memories for those who knew her. Dardi wandered away from the crowd and found himself looking out the window at Canal Grando below. There, life went on.

"I know about your marriage," siór Cornaro said. "I insisted that Él Consìlio dèi Diéxe conduct a thorough investigation.

Dardi knew his father-in-law knew. After several months and in frustration, Caterina confided to her older sister Elana, who then told the rest of the family. It wasn't long before all who mattered in Venèsia knew. "A thorough investigation will find whoever did this," Dardi said. "Justice can then be served."

"You had problems with Caterina."

Dardi looked at siór Cornaro. "Our early months were hard, but we were better as time went by."

"So you say. If you're innocent then you have nothing to fear."

"I have nothing to fear," Dardi said, although he did fear Él Consìlio dèi Diéxe and I Sbirri. If they thought there was any possibility they would do all in their power to assemble a case, even just a case based upon rumour and guesswork. Both parties, the secretive diéxe and the untrustworthy sbirri, were to be avoided at all costs. "I'm sorry for your loss, siór," Dardi said. "She was your daughter well before she was my wife, and I know many will miss her and her good spirit."

"Grassie Dardi Zorzi, and we will see what happens."

Dardi lost the taste for it, so he made his excuses and left. Alone in Palàso Zorzi Bon he wondered what to do, until he heard Lucia crying for a feed. Gia left to feed his daughter in privacy, but Dardi's heart felt uplifted. Caterina would forever live in her daughter.

Chapter Twenty

Saturday once more: a half-day for Marin and then a bath at the bathhouse. The same routine, come home and greet Blanca who definitely showed at six months, and smell their dinner cooking on the hearth. Take enough money but leave his tacolinn, and then head into a cool, drizzly day for the short walk to the bathhouse. Pay the attendant, undress and slip into the tub to wash. Marin soaped Blanca, Blanca soaped Marin, and then she rested her head against his shoulder. Momentarily they were alone amidst the commotion, and he loved her so much. After a time they left the water and towelled dry, and Marin admired his beautiful wife, who looked even more beautiful pregnant. They dressed and headed home, and Marin wished he could. They went upstairs with Marin pre-occupied.

"What is it?" Blanca asked.

Marin sighed. "Nothing," he said.

"It's something mio amór," Blanca said.

He took her hand and looked into her eyes. "I want to make love with you," he said.

She looked into his eyes. "I want to make love with you too," she said.

Marin kissed her and held her, and even though pregnant she was just the same, only more beautiful. They would have to make love differently and that was another sin, but that didn't matter. He thought back to her naked at the bathhouse, and soon she would be naked in his arms and together on the bed. They would be a married couple in love making love, and never could that be a sin. Blanca turned the pot away from the fire before undressing, and Marin undressed before holding her in his arms.

"Te vògio ben," he murmured.

"Te vògio ben," Blanca said sweetly before climbing onto their bed. Marin admired her for a moment before joining her there.

* * *

Filipa kept her eyes closed while he fucked her. Harder and harder, and she pretended he was Pietro. Harder and harder and harder and he gasped loudly when he came. Hard and hard and less and less, and then he pulled his cock out of her arse. Filipa liked it when they came inside her like that. He laid his head on her breasts and she stroked his soft, brown hair.

"That was nice," Albano said.

"Sé, mio amór," Filipa replied absent-mindedly. She wished she was with Pietro.

He lay calm and still but eventually he moved and knelt beside her. "Te vògio ben," he said.

"No you don't," Filipa said.

"I suppose I don't. Did you hear about Dardi Zorzi?"

Filipa sat up with a start. "No. What is it?"

"He murdered his wife Caterina."

"That can't be."

"It is. He was found with her body and holding the knife which killed her."

"Maybe someone else stabbed her, and Dardi just pulled the knife out."

"They had a very unhappy marriage."

"How many marriages are happy, Albano? If your marriage was happy, you wouldn't be here making love with me."

"But there's unhappy and unhappy."

"Did anyone see Dardi Zorzi stab his wife?"

"No, not a soul."

"So we have a body, a knife and an unhappy marriage."

Albano nodded.

"We will see what happens," Filipa said.

"If Dardi Zorzi is the only suspect, they will torture him until he confesses," Albano said.

Filipa put her hand to her mouth in shock. "That's wrong!" she exclaimed.

"That's the way justice works in Venèsia. Do you know Dardi Zorzi?"

"I know him well, but not like I know you. He lived near me when I was young."

"We will see how this scandal plays out."

It was a scandal too. Not many of patrician birth were brutally murdered.

"Did you enjoy that?" Albano asked on a totally different direction.

"Sé I did," Filipa said, even though she didn't enjoy as much as she should have. In fact she had to imagine she was with someone else.

"Can we do that next time?" Albano asked.

Filipa wondered, and after so much beautiful love-making with Pietro she had to change her life. "We should take a pause, Albano."

"What do you mean?"

"When I want to see you again I will let Marco know, and he can tell you."

"I will miss you."

"You can make love with your wife more often."

"But that's not the same," Albano whined.

"I will let Marco know," Filipa said, even though she had no intention of ever seeing him again. In fact she wouldn't see Donato and Nicolò either. That would make her life more balanced. Andrea was nice and they always had fun playing cards, Marco was gentle and he bought her gifts, she did what she liked with Fantino, while Marino had little time to see her, but when he had the time she enjoyed the power she held over him. With those four and Pietro her life was much more balanced.

Filipa noticed Albano had dressed and she got off the bed. She kissed his cheek. "Adio Albano," she said.

"Adio Filipa," he said.

He left and Filipa sat on her bed. That was terrible news about Caterina and Filipa felt knotted up inside. Caterina was lovely person and she died too young. And poor Dardi. He would be hurting over the death of Caterina, and from what Filipa saw they had a happy marriage despite rumours. They were like two young lovers at Donato's ball. And then to be accused of murdering her! Poor Dardi, and Filipa really sorry for him.

* * *

Filipa lay on Pietro and kissed him lightly on his lips, little pecks rather than the passion of moments before. He cupped her buttocks in his big, strong hands while she kissed his lips.

"I sensed something was wrong," he said.

"No mio amór," Filipa said. "We were perfect together, as we always are."

"No, not that. That was perfect because you're perfect. I mean when you first came you seemed distracted."

Filipa sat up and looked down on him. "The wife of a friend of mine was murdered," she said.

"One of your other men?"

"A former neighbour who I've known for many years. His wife was stabbed to death and he seems to be a suspect."

"I'm sorry to hear about your friend."

"He's a good man; a lot like you."

"You should see your friend and offer him your support in his time of need. That will help him."

"Sé; I will do that."

"My patron liked the painting of Venus."

"I suppose I'm hanging on his wall."

"You're immortalised."

Filipa lay on Pietro's chest and he ran his fingers lightly up her back. That sent a shiver up her spine. "Te vògio ben," she murmured.

"Te vògio ben," Pietro said quietly, and Filipa knew he did. She lay on him and he held her, until she had to leave. Pietro lay on his side in bed with his head propped by his hand, watching her dress, feasting on her body even though he'd seen her naked countless times. Filipa bent down and kissed his lips. "Adio Pietro."

"Adio Filipa. Tomorrow?"

"Sé, tomorrow."

Filipa went out into a typical cold, wintry day with a strong wind blowing a faint drizzle. She pulled her tabàro tight around her and walked briskly to the abasia. When she reached the cloister she stopped, and remembered a conversation from just after she joined. The badésa before Barbarella left to marry a man, and then it hit Filipa. She could marry Pietro! She could leave the abasia and marry

Pietro! But she wondered how. Filipa walked to Barbarella's door and knocked. Barbarella let her inside.

"How are you Filipa?" Barbarella asked. "You seem different."

"I met a man," Filipa said.

"A man?' Barbarella asked with her eyebrows raised.

Filipa understood. "A special man. How did the badésa who was once here leave?"

"Would you leave for your special man?"

"If he wants me I will leave, but first I need to know if I can."

"You write to the Holy See and ask them to release you from your vows. They will do that but it takes time. Maybe a year or maybe a year and a half, but they will do that."

Filipa thought. For a year or a year and a half she could see Pietro every day, and when she was released they could marry and have children together. "Grassie Barbarella."

"He must be a special man."

"He is."

"It's been almost two years since you came here, and you've had an adventure during that time."

"I suppose nobody has ever been like me." Filipa looked at Barbarella intently. "It's the power," she said. "They do whatever I tell them; even Marino Contarini. It's powerful, and we have fun of course. Love's different though."

"Love's dangerous."

"Sé it is," Filipa said. "You lose reason and you can lose everything, but when it comes it's something you have to do." Filipa stood. "Adio Barbarella."

"Adio Filipa and good luck."

"Grassie."

Filipa went to her cell and took out her lute. She tuned it and then sang the beautiful sonnets of Francesco Petrarca. Francesco Petrarca knew love, even if love was tragic for him. Filipa hoped her love would turn into happiness and even children in time.

* * *

Dardi was surprised to have visitors calling so early. The maid showed them into the alcove while Dardi finished dressing, and a few minutes later he came down the stairs to see two men, one older and one younger, patiently waiting.

"Bongiorno siór," Dardi said. "Can I help you?"

"Bongiorno siór Zorzi," the older man said. "I'm Cosmo Orio and I have with me Paolo Soranzo. We are investigating the murder of Caterina Cornero, and I will ask you some questions about that."

"I don't know what I can tell you beyond what I told the sbirro I spoke with."

"Tell us what happened that night."

258

"Caterina and I went to Piasà San Marco, and then went to an inn for supper. After eating we headed towards the canal where it was quite crowded, and I got bumped and Caterina disappeared. I continued onwards and found her dead in a doorway with a knife in her neck."

"You gave that knife to the sbirro?"

"I did."

"As you know it's common knowledge that your marriage was in poor shape."

"Caterina and I had more difficulties than many new couples, but over time those difficulties eased and we became genuinely close to each other."

"We have no evidence of closeness, only the testimony of siór Giovanni Cornero, and common knowledge of course."

"Even if we continued to have difficulties; that gives me no reason to kill my wife. We could share this house as husband and wife, and I could find rooms and have a second relationship."

"Such relationships are the fantasy of many married men, but there are few women who will have such relationships. The reality for many men is prostitutes, except a few hours with a whore isn't a substitute for a good marriage. No siór; if you're in a diabolically unhappy marriage, then separation, no matter how it happens, and a marriage with a more compatible wife is your best option, but I'm sure you know that."

"After a time our marriage wasn't unhappy, so that's not relevant."

"So you say. Siór Cornero has insisted we conduct this investigation with thoroughness, and we will heed his wishes. In time we may request your presence, but until then if you can't think of anything else...."

"There's one thing," Dardi said. "One old friend, sòra Filipa Barbarigo of the order of Saint Benedict, met Caterina and I a few times over the past year. She could vouch that we were happy together."

"How you behaved when in public may or may not help your cause. We do know of an incident where Caterina and you spoke with someone at a dance, and left shortly after. That doesn't seem happy to me. So if there isn't anything else we will continue our investigations, and you will probably hear from us soon."

"I can show you out," Dardi said. He got up and let the two men out the water door to their gondola, and then returned to the alcove to think. Cosmo Orio and Paolo Soranzo were undoubtedly from I Siór di Nòti, who investigated the most serious of crimes. They were not corrupt like I Sbirri but they were dangerous, and they would stop at nothing to get to the truth of a matter. Dardi was concerned about that. If he was the obvious suspect they

260

would torture him for a confession. Dardi's heart beat fast: he would do anything to avoid being tortured, except he couldn't leave Lucia. She was only six months old and too young to travel. He was stuck in Venèsia and he didn't want to be tortured.

Chapter Twenty One

Filipa picked at her fish stew while she contemplated what to do. It was Saturday and a good time to visit Dardi and offer condolences, but she could do more than that. She had a network of lovers, some of whom worked in Palàso Ducale, and they might be able to provide information. Information would be of some use. But at the least she would visit Dardi and offer support.

"You seem distracted," Barbarella said.

"The wife of a former neighbour was murdered," Filipa said. "I will visit him today."

"That's terrible for your friend," Clara said.

"It is," Filipa agreed. "I will see him after dinner."

"Offer our sympathies," Clara said.

"Grassie Clara."

Filipa finished her meal and the last of her wine, went to her cell and slipped on a tabàro, and went into the cold. Once more she was crossing the lagoon on the way to Venèsia, where the gondoliere took her to the water door of Palàso Zorzi Bon. After paying the gondoliere, Filipa knocked and the maid let her into a sitting room overlooking Canal Grando. Dardi appeared dressed in dark blue; appropriate for a man in mourning. Filipa went to him and held his hands, while realising her hands were terribly cold.

"I'm sorry for your loss," she said. "Caterina was a lovely woman, and all of us who knew her will miss her."

"Grassie Filipa," Dardi said. "Sit, per piasser."

She sat and he sat, and Filipa wondered what to say, and then she knew. "Do they know who did it?" she asked.

"I Siór di Nòti think I murdered her," Dardi said flatly.

"Because of rumours about your marriage?"

"Sé."

"I know those rumours aren't true."

"We became closer after a time, and especially after Lucia was born."

"I could see that. I prayed for Caterina's soul of course, and I prayed for you too."

"What use is praying when God lets such things happen?"

Filipa looked him in the eyes. "God gave man free will, and one man misused his freedom to murder Caterina. That man will be judged in this world and he will be judged in the next world. We have free will and we can use that to mourn Caterina, and always hold a place for her in our hearts."

Dardi sat in silence for several moments. "I never thought about it that way. You really are a nun."

"I've always had my beliefs. I can help if you want."

"How?"

"I have lovers as you know, and I can ask them what they know, very subtly. That dreadful Dardi Zorzi who murdered his wife! To think he was once my friend! By the way, do you know what's happening with his case?"

Dardi almost smiled and shook his head at the same time. "That won't get you anywhere Filipa. Grassie for the thought."

"If you change your mind...?"

He shrugged his shoulders.

"How's Lucia?" Filipa asked.

"We have a wet nurse so she's in good hands," Dardi said. "But it's a tragedy she will never know her mother."

"I don't know what to say, but now you know you're in my thoughts and I will pray for you every night. The nuns at the abasia offer their condolences."

"Grassie Filipa for coming and you're my best friend." He wiped tears from his eyes.

"I should go," Filipa said.

"You came by gondola?"

"The abasia is on Torcello."

"I will get my gondoliere to take you home."

"Grassie Dardi."

Filipa stood and Dardi stood too. She kissed his cheek before he led her to the water door. Soon she was crossing the lagoon, and in the fieze Filipa thought of a real way to help Dardi. Nobody was beyond seduction, not even

"Perhaps something strange is happening to correspondence between Lombardy and here," Dardi said.

"Strange?" Doxe Foscari asked.

"Intercepted and forged."

Doxe Foscari nodded slowly. "Perhaps."

"All it takes is a facsimile of the handwriting of Francesco da Carmagnola, and a copy of his seal which wouldn't be hard to duplicate."

"That would explain what's going on, and once the forged letter arrives here we would never know."

"I can't think of any other reason for correspondence to be contradictory like that."

"Good, sé, right. I will make the assumption that the marriage is happening and make arrangements accordingly. Grassie Dardi."

Dardi nodded, and left Doxe Foscari. Dardi was troubled; there were more Lombardians in Venèsia beyond Roberto Geni and that could be dangerous. If they wanted vengeance for what happened, that could be easily arranged. He sighed deeply. Things could be just as dangerous for him as if he hadn't killed Geni. His situation could turn very dangerous very quickly.

* * *

Filipa dealt the cards. "Do you know Paolo Soranzo?" she asked Andrea.

"Not well," Andrea said.

269

Filipa placed the deck face down on the bed and counted her hand: 22. Andrea drew a card and she drew a card. She had 24.

"Does he have dinner at Él Lión Biànco?"

"No, but I can find out where he eats if you want."

"Grassie."

"What's your interest in Paolo Soranzo?"

Filipa didn't know what to say and then she remembered Pietro Blanco. "I heard he has a big penis," she said.

"Does that matter?" Andrea asked, looking shocked.

"Sé it does."

Andrea drew another card and Filipa drew an eight! She sighed. Andrea put his cards down and he had 26.

"That makes two games out of three for me," he said.

"You win. What position do you want for next week?"

Silence and Filipa wondered why. "I want to ejaculate inside you," Andrea said quietly.

"Alright; you deserve that. Anal intercourse next week."

"Really?"

"That's a bonus for you. Get Marco or Fantino to tell me about Paolo Soranzo, per piasser."

270

Andrea climbed off the bed, picked up his clothes and sorted them into order. "I don't know how I will be able to wait until next week."

Filipa giggled. "Until then, fantasise about it whenever you masturbate."

* * *

Filipa left the abasia early and walked to Pietro's room in the town. She knocked on the door and he opened it not with a smile but with a look of surprise.

"Bondi Filipa; I must be getting forgetful," Pietro said.

"Bondi Pietro," Filipa said. "No you're not forgetful."

"Come in,"

Filipa entered his room. "I told you about a friend whose wife was murdered and he was a suspect," Filipa said. "I'm on my way to Venèsia to find out what I can."

"What do you think you can find?"

"I will tell you what this is about. He's the only suspect, and if we don't find who killed his wife they will torture him for a confession."

"That's quite serious," Pietro said slowly.

"I'm not sure what will come from my endeavours, but I must at least try."

"Of course you must. Good luck for your quest."

"Grassie Pietro," Filipa said and kissed him. "I will see you properly as soon as I can."

"I know you will. Adio Filipa."

"Adio Pietro."

Filipa then left to catch a gondola to Piasà San Marco, and decided they would be making love only, because to interrogate a first-time lover over Dardi would be suspicious. Then she would invite Paolo Soranzo for Friday, and she could talk about Dardi. After the gondoliere berthed at Piasà San Marco, Filipa went to La Croxèra, an inn just to the north, arriving well in time for dinner. She dressed for the occasion in a tight, red giornea, cut low at her bust and split in front to reveal her gold gamurra, and also split at the sleeves. Inside the inn was relatively quiet when Filipa went to the counter.

"I would like a cup of wine, per piasser," she asked the woman serving.

The woman poured a cup. "Two soldi," she said.

Filipa put two coins on the counter. "Do you know siór Paolo Soranzo?"

"What if I do?"

Filipa put a twenty lire coin on the counter. "I will be sitting over there," she said, and glanced towards an unoccupied table. "When siór Soranzo arrives, can you tell me?"

The woman took the coin and nodded, while Filipa took her drink to the table. It was terrible wine, although all wine was terrible after the lovely drinks served by Marino

272

Contarini. Several noisy young men came into the inn; well-dressed too, and they took a big table. Filipa glanced at the woman but she didn't move. Filipa bought another cup of wine and returned to her table, glancing across whenever she heard men arriving; then the woman came across.

The woman bent down. "Four men over there," she said quietly. "The man in purple is siór Soranzo."

"Grassie," Filipa said while she looked across. Late twenties, average build, long dark hair, dark eyes, quite handsome, in a patterned purple giornea with white spots, red calsa and a black baréta. Filipa took a big breath, got up, took her drink, and walked slowly across the inn, ignoring the chaos and other men gobbling their food. She stood beside Paolo Soranzo. "Bongiorno siór," she said. "Do you have room for me at your table?"

They slid along the bench and Filipa sat. "My name's Filipa Barbarigo."

"I am Carlo Civran."

"I am Piero Canal."

"I am Alvisio Emo."

"I am Paolo Soranzo."

"And you're all having a break from your labours." Filipa said. "With dinner at this charming inn."

"And you siórina Barbarigo?" Carlo asked.

"I haven't made up my mind." She sipped her wine and put the cup down. "Who shall it be?"

273

She put her hand on the Paolo's thigh. "I have a room in Torcello that's quite cosy, if a handsome man can take a few hours away from his work." Filipa squeezed Pietro's muscular thigh and turned to face him. "Would that be you, siór Soranzo?"

He swallowed.

"You can tell your friends that you took ill and won't be able to return to work, and they can relay that message," Filipa said.

"I could."

"But will you?"

"I have taken ill and I won't be able to return to work," Paolo said.

Filipa stood and Paolo stood too. They left the inn together.

Chapter Twenty Three

Paolo lay on his back on his bed in his room, while outside was noisy and bustling. His family home, Palàso Soranzo, fronted a narrow canal, and across the road from that was Campo San Polo, busy in the late afternoon. He went for dinner with his work friends as he often did, and a few moments later was on a gondola bound for Torcello. In no time the beautiful Filipa Barbarigo was disrobing for him, and knowing what affect her display would have on him, before she helped him to remove his clothes. Then he was taking her to her orgasm just as she wanted him to, before she rode him until he was close, then taking him out and stroking his penis until he came. After that she then lay on him and kissed him, and never had he experienced love as beautiful as that. As beautiful and, perhaps, as efficient as that. It was clear that patrician nun had much practice. Later she played cards of all things, and still naked! Perhaps that easy acknowledgement of nudity was the best part. Few women were comfortable in their skin, but Filipa Barbarigo was very, very comfortable in her skin.

After he beat her at cards his prize was to return on Friday afternoon! Paolo closed his eyes and looked forward to that. But before then he would discreetly check out his lover. Barbarigo was a patrician family and Paolo was interested to find out more about their achievements.

Pietro greeted Filipa with a big smile before he held her arms and kissed her. He invited her in and beckoned Filipa to sit on his old, ramshackle couch.

"How have you been this week?" Pietro asked.

Filipa looked at Pietro in his eyes. "My friend is in trouble, and I'm helping him by telling a man in authority the truth about his marriage. I see that man tomorrow, but in the meantime...."

"True friends help their friends in need."

"That's right. We grew up next door but one to each other, so we were close neighbours. He had no sisters and I became like his sister, and he was more of a brother to me than my real brother. He's a kind and patient man and I like him very much."

"We haven't done your portrait yet," Pietro said.

"That doesn't matter. After all I'm Venus now," she said, smiling brightly.

"You were very appropriate as Venus. Beautiful, charming and seductive."

"Grassie Pietro."

Pietro took Filipa's hands and looked into her eyes. "Te vògio ben," he said.

"Te vògio ben," Filipa said.

"I mean it."

"I mean it with all my heart."

"I never imagined a woman so independent, so full of life, so easy to get on with, and so beautiful."

"I never imagined a man so talented, so genuine, and who respects women the way you do, not to mention so handsome." Filipa wondered if she should offer to marry Pietro, but she had many things happening and it wasn't a good time. She decided to love him for now, and raise marriage after Dardi's problems were resolved.

"I've always wondered what women find handsome in men. I can't look at a woman without admiring her beauty, but men aren't like that."

Filipa giggled. "You're not a woman, Pietro. I like the power and strength of a man. You feel his strength when he holds you, and you feel safe and loved. When a man's naked, his muscles, especially his arms and chest, are just gorgeous." Filipa took his hands. "I love men's hands," she said softly.

"It's just as well that men and women are made different to each other."

"Men and women fit together just so." She kissed him and he held her and kissed her, and she felt his strength even thought it was controlled. Soon he would be overwhelmed with desire for her, and that made Filipa feel giddy. His tongue touched her lips and she met it, and their kiss became ever more passionate with his hands running through her long hair. Moments later they were on his bed and kissing, and clothes were discarded while kissing continued, and he kissed her all over but especially there, all the way until she came. And just as she was he entered her, and Filipa arched her back to take all of him. He kissed her and made love to her, body to body and mouth to mouth. Filipa didn't want him to stop; she didn't ever want him to stop, not even for that. She wanted, no needed him to go all the way.

"Come inside me," Filipa murmured before he kissed her once more.

He kissed her and she held his strong, manly arms while he loved her. He loved her harder, more insistent, all the way until he came, and still he kissed her. They lay together still coupled and Filipa felt loved.

Pietro moved and stretched and that was the best ever, even if she had to get those seeds from Barbarella.

Pietro ruffled her hair. "Te vògio ben," he said.

"Te vògio ben," Filipa replied.

"Do you want dinner at the inn? Do you want to hear what I'm doing?"

"I would like dinner at the inn and I would like to hear what you're doing, even if that means we have to dress."

Pietro laughed. "You would stay naked all day, if you could."

"I would but we can't, so let's dress and have dinner at the inn."

They dressed, and Pietro took Filipa's hand and led her down the stairs to the inn. Filipa looked forward to hearing more about his life.

* * *

Paolo sat at his ornate, oak desk and leafed through the dusty volumes retrieved from the library. Famégia Barbarigo originally came from Muggia in Istria. One member of the family, Marco Barbarigo, was formerly a bishop of Verona, while the family patronised and supported Cièsa di Santa Maria del Giglio. Michele Barbarigo and Brisca Diedo had a son, Polo, away fighting for La Repubblica di Venèsia, a daughter Filipa, of the Order of Saint Benedict, and a second daughter, Cristina, married to Silvestro Navagero. Cristina had a daughter Sara in addition to two step-sons. Quite modest achievements, all in all. It was odd that younger sister Cristina was married and Filipa wasn't, although Silvestro Navagero wasn't a good match.

"Interesting research I'm sure," Cosmo said flatly.

Paolo closed the books and pushed them away.

"How are you going with your investigation?" Cosmo asked.

"There's nothing except that Dardi was found with his wife's body, which is understandable given they were out together, and rumours of an unhappy marriage."

Cosmo frowned. "We can't interrogate him just on that. The Zorzi family would never allow it."

"Sióngr Cornero is pushing for a resolution on the murder of his daughter."

"We can't torture someone just on rumour."

"I know."

Cosmo sighed deeply. "Sióngr Cornero is convinced."

"We don't have anything," Paolo said. "There might be another explanation."

"Find the other explanation," Cosmo said, before stomping away.

Paolo wondered what he was supposed to find.

* * *

Filipa helped Paolo remove his calsi while thinking about what they would talk about later. Paolo put his hands on Filipa's hips and then cupped her buttocks while kissing her, and she felt his hardness probing at her. She held his shoulders during their kiss, meeting his tongue before moving away and kneeling on her bed. He went to the bed.

"Lay down, per piasser," Filipa said.

Paolo did and he was a handsome, young man with a nice body. Filipa knelt astride his shoulders and took his hard cock into her mouth, just as Paolo grabbed her buttocks and licked her. Filipa sucked at Paolo for a moment and let him go, sitting up instead while Paolo licked her just right. She felt it buzzing stronger and stronger, building to a throb deeper and deeper, before it filled her with delight. Again and again until it faded, and she bent down to suck his cock using her lips and tongue. She heard his murmur of arousal and let him go to get on her knees instead, and looked behind. He knelt behind her and Filipa gasped lightly when he entered her, and holding her buttocks he fucked her deeply and slowly. The slowness of that was delicious; she craved more but he kept it from her. Then he touched her arse and that was delightful, as it always was. Fucking her slowly while rubbing her there. And she knew she could trust him.

"Do you want to fuck me there?" Filipa asked.

"Sé," Paolo said.

"Use a little oil from the jug beside the bed."

Paolo's penis left her, he bent down and then Filipa felt him at her arse. Slowly he filled her and like always it felt like too much; like she couldn't take it, and then he was inside her and that felt good. He squeezed her buttocks while fucking her slowly, but that felt totally different to before. Full and stretched and just lovely. He fucked her and Filipa felt that lovely tingle deep in her core, slowly building and building until her body was alive with it. He squeezed her buttocks harder while fucking her harder too, and that pushed her over the edge of ecstasy. Moments later he pounded her hardest and she sensed his peak of delight. Again and again he pounded her while squeezing her buttocks so hard! And then he was done and she was empty of him. She turned around to see him smiling brightly.

"That was good," she said.

281

He nodded; unable to speak.

"Lay down," Filipa murmured and Paolo lay on his back. She moulded her body to his and he cupped her buttocks with one hand. "I like that." They lay in silence until Filipa moved from him, and she sat up to admire his soft penis. She touched it playfully.

"How has life been for you?" Filipa asked.

"Waiting for this afternoon," Paolo said.

"Do you know Dardi Zorzi?"

His eyes opened wide. "Sé I do."

"He's a friend of mine and I'm terribly sad about the death of Caterina; she was a lovely woman. We met a few times and I liked her very much."

"Tell me about her."

"What's there to say? I met them at a dance about this time last year, and I was so pleased that Dardi had married such a wonderful woman. She was sweet, kind and had a good nature. I was attracted to her; I couldn't help myself. I think that rattled her and they left the dance early."

"Attracted sexually?'

"No, not sexually." Filipa thought about it. "You admire beautiful women of course, and sometimes you must meet women you're attracted to, even though they're unavailable. It's just something that women radiate. Do you know what I mean?"

"Sé I do."

"Well, women feel the same attraction for other women, and Caterina was so nice that it wasn't possible not to be attracted to her. I could see Dardi was attracted to Caterina and I was happy about that."

"I didn't know this before."

"I think God made women beautiful and to have an inner attraction of goodness and kindness, so that men will care for us and protect us."

"You don't need men to care for you."

"No I don't. I next met Caterina with Dardi at a ball in a garden, and I spoke with them and they seemed even happier together. Of course they had their child by then. Later I watched them playing in the maze."

"Playing in the maze?" Paolo asked.

"Dardi ran into the maze and Caterina waited outside, maybe counting to fifty, and then she went to find him. That was sweet. After that we had dinner and they were really close, like nobody else was at the table. Then we danced, and they danced from the first dance to the last."

"You had a partner to dance with?"

"Sé I did, and we danced from the first dance to the last."

"Who else was at this ball?"

"Donato Donato arranged it, and Albano Capello and his wife were there."

"It must have been a good ball."

283

"It was outside in a beautiful garden on a nice, autumn day. It was the best ball I have been to."

"How a couple behave in public isn't an indication of a happy marriage."

Filipa was disappointed with that. "I saw they were happy, and I don't think they pretended to be happy."

"Maybe their affections were real or maybe not."

Filipa was disappointed but she couldn't argue the point forever. "Now Paolo, do you want to visit me again sometime?" Filipa asked to change the subject.

"Sé, per piasser."

Filipa needed time for him to speak with Donato and Albano, if that was his plan. "Wednesday?" she asked.

"So long!"

She rustled his hair. "You're not the only man who has my affections."

"Wednesday afternoon. Can we do the same again?"

Filipa giggled. "No, that would be boring. We will do the same but differently, if you understand."

"I understand. Do you want to play cards?"

"Sé, but what can you offer as a prize?"

He frowned. "What will you offer if I win?"

"Remember when I took you in my mouth? I will do much more of that, but not all the way. Now for you?"

"If you win I will bring you a present."

Filipa got the deck of cards from her shelf and sat on the bed cross-legged. She dealt the cards while feeling disappointed inside. Her plan had fallen to pieces and she didn't know what to do next.

Chapter Twenty Four

Caligo shrouded Venèsia in mist. Normally Filipa enjoyed the eerie beauty of caligo, but not that day. She stared out of the window at usually brightly coloured palàsi, now dull and muted.

"Bondi Filipa," Dardi said.

Filipa turned around. "Bondi Dardi," she said. "I seduced Paolo Soranzo and we made love on Wednesday, but I didn't say anything because that would have been suspicious. I invited him back on Friday and we made love again, and then I told him about the two times I met Caterina and you. He didn't seem convinced."

"At least you tried."

"We have to find who murdered Caterina, because I don't think they will."

"How?"

"Tell me what happened that night. Every little detail."

"Sit, per piasser."

Filipa sat and Dardi sat.

"We made love, and then I suggested we go out to carnevale that afternoon," Dardi said. "The nurse brought Lucia to us and that reminded me of when you were a baby. We talked about you and then we got dressed to go out. Caterina decided not to wear her expensive pendant...."

"Why?" Filipa asked.

"Because of the crowded streets at night, so she wore an older pendant. We went to Piasà San Marco where there were singers, a juggler and a puppet show. Then we went to Él Lión Biànco for supper, and when we'd eaten we left to find a ball. We headed along Calle Canonica until we reached a ponte under attack, so we walked beside the canal instead. Then someone bumped me and we got separated, and I went to the next ponte searching for Caterina until I found her in a doorway further on, with her throat cut and the knife still there. Her pendant was hanging to one side."

"The old pendant?'

"Sé."

Caterina's new pendant was beautiful and expensive, and Filipa wondered if the old pendant hanging to the side had anything to do with what happened. "Where's the new pendant?" she asked.

"In her jewellery box," Dardi said.

"Show me."

They climbed the stairs and went to the bedroom.

"I Sbirri gave me her rings and the old pendant, and I put them in here," Dardi said, opening the jewellery box. Filipa watched him rummage, and with a shocked expression rummage again. "The new pendant's not here," he said, turning around to face Filipa.

"Could she have kept it anywhere else?" Filipa asked.

"Not that I know of. There's no reason for her to. Maybe she sold it."

"Why?"

"Our marriage became better over time but.... She might have sold it for money to get away."

"Not from what I saw, Dardi."

"No, it wasn't that bad I suppose." And then Dardi looked even more shocked. "When we left the inn, a man in black with a volto mask left at the same time."

Filipa frowned; that was no coincidence; nor was the missing pendant. "He was a thief who killed Caterina, only she wasn't wearing the pendant. Then he came here and stole it."

"That's easy enough to do; just pretend to be a merchant delivering something while I'm at work."

"Merchants don't go upstairs."

"That's right. How?'

"I don't know," Filipa said. "I think a thief killed Caterina and later stole your pendant, and we need to find it if we can."

"Jewellery shops buy and sell," Dardi said.

"On Monday we will check every jewellery shop. I will come here, and between the two of us we should get it done."

"Grassie Filipa; I don't know what to say."

"What were you saying about me?"

"Pardon?"

"You said you were talking about me."

"We talked about your lovers."

"Oh. You know why."

"I do."

Filipa nodded. "I found someone and we love each other, and when this is over I'm giving him the opportunity to marry me."

"Can you?"

"I can, but not now. Now it's time to help my friend."

"Grassie Filipa."

Filipa went to the window and looked out. "I love caligo; it's so beautiful." The mist shrouded everything to grey and eerie, and later it would lift to reveal all. A bit like the story of Caterina's murder.

* * *

Dardi handled La Mercerie while Filipa went from shop to shop in the parallel Dei Fabri, without luck. She never realised there were so many jewellery shops in Venèsia. She found three on that street, and in each shop she described the pendant of a gold cross with gemstones, diamonds and pearls. She said she was willing to pay good money for it, so she was confident the jewellers didn't have it. As previously agreed with Dardi, she next went to La Frezzeria, noted for making arrows but also other speciality items, but neither of the two jewellery shops on that street had the pendant. While Filipa was scouring La Frezzeria, Dardi would have been checking out Calle San Moise. They agreed to meet at Él Lión Biànco, where Filipa bought a cup of wine and went to one of the small tables while she waited for Dardi. He arrived a short while later and bought wine as well, before joining Filipa.

"You don't look like you found it," Filipa said.

"You don't look like you found it either," Dardi said.

Filipa sipped her wine. "Do you have any ideas?" she asked.

"There are two shops in Él Geto, which is where I originally bought it."

"Alright."

"Do you want dinner?" Dardi asked.

"Shrimp with polenta, per piasser."

Dardi went to the woman at the counter, and every time Filipa saw that woman she was reminded that women had more value than being locked indoors or locked behind granite walls. The two plates of shrimp were delivered by the waiter, and the food was greasy but palatable enough. With food consumed and wine drunk it was time to walk to Él Geto, where they separated. Dardi went along Fondamenta Cannaregio, while Filipa followed his directions to find the shop around the corner.

"Bongiorno siór," Filipa said to the wrinkled, old man with barely a rim of grey hair around the circumference of his head.

"Bongiorno siórina," he replied.

"I'm looking for a specific pendant and I will pay good money for it. It's a gold cross about this big," Filipa said while using her hands to mark the size. "It has blue gems on each arm of the cross and a green gem in the centre, four pearls, and small diamonds on the arms of the cross and around the gem in the centre."

The jeweller nodded before bending over behind his counter, and he placed the pendant on top. Filipa picked it up. "You do know this is stolen," she said.

"I have no idea of its history."

"Who sold it to you?"

"A man aged in his thirties with dark, greasy hair, a scar on his cheek and two missing teeth."

"Such a man would own a pendant like this?"

The jeweller shrugged.

"I believe a woman was murdered for this pendant," Filipa said.

"That's unfortunate," the jeweller replied with no emotion.

"How much did you pay for this?"

"Two lire di grossi."

Filipa nearly dropped it with shock; that was 250 ducats! No wonder murder was committed! It would retail at maybe twice that price. Filipa wondered what to do, and Dardi had to handle Paolo of course. "Siór," she said. "I will tell my companion whose wife was killed, and he will tell I Siór di Notti. They will come to your shop to get the description of the man who sold it to you."

"They will seize this pendant?"

"It's stolen property, but more important is to apprehend the murderer of a patrician lady. I don't want this pendant to be misplaced, so I will be taking it with me and my friend will return it to you when he comes with I Siór di Notti."

"You just can't take it, siórina."

"I have it and you don't, and if I were you I would be more worried about I Siór di Notti. Bongiorno siór," Filipa said, and she left the shop and went to Fondamenta Cannaregio where Dardi waited. She placed it on the palm of her hand and Dardi picked it up.

"The other shop?" Dardi asked.

Filipa nodded. "Sé," she said. "I told the jeweller you would bring Paolo to his shop to get the description of the thief. In the meantime I don't want anything to do with this, because my relationship with Paolo may still prove to be of some use."

292

"When I'm cleared; you have no need of a relationship with him."

Filipa thought about that and he was right, but there were was another issue. "I don't want him to know that I offered my companionship to clear your name."

"I understand."

Filipa looked at that the cross and felt really awful. "I know we cleared you of this crime, but I feel terrible."

"Killed for this?"

"Sé." Filipa drew a deep breath. "Adio Dardi," she said. "I must go home."

"Adio Filipa e grassie tuti."

* * *

Paolo got the greatest surprise when Dardi Zorzi was led into the chamber of I Siór di Nòti. He stood and they greeted each other formally, and then Paulo waited. Dardi reached into his tacolinn and pulled out a large, gold pendant and placed it on Paulo's desk.

"Caterina was murdered for this," Dardi said. "Only she wasn't wearing it at the time."

Paulo picked it up and it was magnificent. "How do you know?"

"My maid found it at a jewellery shop in Él Geto."

Paulo thought about where Dardi was heading. "Someone killed Caterina for this pendant but she wore a different one, so they stole this from your home?"

293

"Sé."

The jeweller would prove that or not. "Take me to the shop."

Dardi led Paolo outside and to the jeweller at Él Geto. Paolo placed the pendant on the counter and the old man looked at it.

"Have you seen this before?" Paolo asked.

"I bought it," the jeweller said. "Today a woman recognised it and took it away."

"My name's Paolo Soranzo and I'm from I Siór di Notti. You must give me a description of the man who sold this to you."

"Aged in his thirties with dark, greasy hair, a scar on his cheek, and two missing teeth."

"Clothes?"

"Neither grand nor shabby."

"Anything else?"

"No."

"Grassie." Paolo thought about what next. Verify the pendant, and he picked it up and put it in his tacolinn. "Dardi; did Caterina wear this to the ball at Palàso Donato?"

"Sé she did."

"I will ask Donato if he recognises it, and if he does we have a more substantial story about the death of your wife. I'm sorry she was killed for this."

"I wish I never bought it."

"It would have made her happy at the time," Paolo said.

"It did, but then it turned tragic."

"I'm sorry. As soon as I hear something I will let you know. Adio Dardi."

"Adio Paolo."

It was getting late so Paolo headed home. Tomorrow he would track down Donato Donato, and if necessary Albano Capello.

Chapter Twenty Five

Almoro Canal and Maffeo Basadona entered the chamber of I Siór di Nòti, closely escorting a man who Paolo recognised from the jeweller's description. Aged in his thirties with black, greasy hair, a scar on his cheek, and a couple of missing teeth. That man struggled against Almoro and Maffeo holding his arms.

"Bondi Almoro," Paolo said. "Who do you have here?"

"Bondi Paolo," Almoro said. "Mario Bondesan fitted the description you gave us."

Paulo reached into the drawer of his desk and pulled out the pendant. He stood in front of Bondesan. "Do you recognise this?" he asked. Bondesan shook his head and Paulo sighed. "I know you stole this pendant and you know it too. If you admit to the theft of this pendant and to the murder of Caterina Zorzi, you will save yourself from much pain."

"I aint seen it before," Bondesan snarled.

Paolo would give him one last chance. "Almoro, follow me to the chamber," Paolo said, and left his room to go downstairs where prison cells were located in various places, and where the torture chamber was used to extract the truth. Paulo swung the big, heavy, timber door open and entered a semi-darkened room with not enough lamps burning. He walked to one of the racks and leaned against it.

"Bondesan," Paolo said. "This is our favourite; it's simple and effective. If you hold out for long enough you may end up about two inches taller than now, but you will confess to your crimes. These spikes add extra when you get stretched, and eventually you will lose the ability to walk or do anything. You won't even be able to shit properly. The weeks between confession and execution will seem like months for a useless heap of muscle and bone tossed into the corner of a cell. Now tell me how you stole this from Palàso Zorzi Bon."

"One night when they were asleep," Bondesan said.

"How did you get in?"

"Picked the lock."

"If you could pick the lock and steal the pendant, why did you murder Caterina Zorzi?"

"I didn't murder no-one."

Paolo grimaced. "Did you use a lock-picker to steal this pendant?"

Bondesan shook his head. "No."

Not being able to pick a lock would help prove that Bondesan killed Caterina. "Almoro," Paolo said. "Take Bondesan to reception and get him to pick the lock. Give him whatever tools he needs to do this."

Almoro and Maffeo turned to leave the chamber when Bondesan shouted "I can't pick locks!"

"Who did you use?" Paolo asked.

"Don't know his name."

"Did you kill Caterina Zorzi only to find she wasn't wearing the expensive pendant you were after?"

"Don't know what yer talkin' 'bout."

"Almoro; you probably know what we need to know. He knew about the pendant and followed Dardi and Caterina Zorzi. He bumped Dardi Zorzi out of the way and dragged Caterina into a doorway where he cut her throat before realising she wasn't wearing the expensive pendant. After that he had a second attempt at stealing the pendant with a professional lock-picker."

"I'm sure we'll get that story out of him," Almoro said.

"I'm sure you will."

Paolo left the chamber and climbed from the fetid ground floor to his room where the air was cleaner and sweeter. Cosmo was there with a parchment in his hand.

"Where have you been?" Cosmo asked.

"Talking with the murderer of Caterina Zorzi," Paolo said.

"Has he confessed?"

"He will."

"You verified it was Caterina Zorzi's pendant?"

"Donato Donato remembered it."

"Unfortunately that's not the end of Dardi Zorzi's troubles," Cosmo said, handing the parchment across. Paolo read the denunciation, and surprised, read it again. He put it down.

"For the past four years Dardi Zorzi has been committing sodomy with a painter, Clario Duodo, at a room in Él Geto," Paolo said. "The room they use is on the third floor of a building on the corner of Fondamenta Cannaregio and Calle del Forno." Paolo thought about the denunciation and something made sense. "This would account for his marital difficulties."

"If his wife knew it would, and even if she didn't know she would sense that something was wrong."

"We will have to be discreet about this." Paolo thought about siór Cornero, and a scandal about his late daughter married to a sodomite. "We have to be very discreet about this," Paolo said.

"Can you be discreet when you ask your informants?"

Paolo frowned. "I will only ask those who I trust. Given the discretion involved, it may take some time to gather the necessary witnesses. If there are any witnesses to this relationship with Clario Duodo I will find them, and I will get I Sbirri to bring in Duodo if they can find him. And then we will see what happens."

"If there's truth in this denunciation, this is going to shake the Zorzi family, while the Cornero family will be devastated that their daughter was murdered by a jewel thief, while she was married to a sodomite fucking another man behind her back."

* * *

Filipa lay on her stomach, legs spread, while Paolo fucked her harder and harder and harder. She sensed his building pleasure; felt it to her soul. Harder and harder and then he gasped. Filipa shivered with delight. He lay on he and she turned her head so he could kiss her. They kissed for a moment and then Paolo lay still. She liked that; he felt good on her body. He moved and Filipa lay on her side to look at him.

"After you, no woman will ever be the same," he said.

Filipa had concerns about that. "We just share sex," she said. "What really matters is here," and she touched his head, "and here," and she touched his heart. "When you find a woman who touches your head and your heart, what we do will seem superficial."

"Do you think so?"

"I know so. Soon, your family will arrange a match for you. When that happens, take your time to get to know this girl, for she will be a girl. Find out if you have things in common. If you like dancing maybe she does too, if you like music maybe she does too. More importantly think about

300

how she touches your heart. You can refuse a match and so can the girl, although most girls will go with whoever their family chooses. So it will be up to you to find out if this girl touches you in all ways. If she does, the sex you share you move your soul."

"That sounds too good to be true," Paolo said.

"It's up to you to accept the right match."

"I will. You said you were friends with Caterina Zorzi."

"I liked Caterina a lot."

"She was murdered for a pendant, but she wasn't wearing it at the time. The thief then stole it from their house."

"Oh that's terrible!" Filipa exclaimed; pretending surprise. "I know the pendant you mean and it was beautiful. To think she was killed for that!"

"There are other things about Dardi, but at least he didn't kill his wife."

Filipa was startled by that comment. "I'm so relieved," she said, while wondering what he was talking about.

"What is it?" he asked.

"Nothing," Filipa said. "Now Paolo, do you have your present for me?"

He reached over the side of the bed and grabbed his séngia. He opened his tacolinn and extracted a shining, gold ring. He gave it to Filipa.

"Oh that is so gorgeous!" Filipa exclaimed, and she kissed his lips. "I only have four rings." She put it on the third finger of her left hand and it fitted well. "Grassie sweet man."

"Do you want to play cards again?"

"Ha! I will beat you again!"

"If you win, I will buy a matching ring for your right hand."

Filipa nodded. That was fair. "What would you want from me?"

He looked away. "To suck me until I come."

Filipa drew a deep breath. "I make love with you for my pleasure, and I would get no pleasure from that." She didn't want to be hard on Paolo and he gave her a lovely present. "What we can do is make love as we normally do, and then I will suck you to finish. Is that alright?'

"Oh sé, that would be great."

"Friday?"

Paolo shook his head. "Friday is Mama's name day and we're having a party."

Filipa had to maintain her relationship with Paolo, given what he said about Dardi. "Saturday?" she asked.

"Sé, Saturday."

Filipa climbed out of bed, took her cards, and sat cross-legged. While she dealt she thought about what she should do. She had to see Dardi to find if he knew what Paulo might be investigating.

Chapter Twenty Six

Dardi entered the room and Filipa turned away from the window. He looked surprised, given it was five on Wednesday evening.

"Bondi Dardi," Filipa said. "Have you heard from Paolo Soranzo?" she asked.

"Bondi Filipa," Dardi said. "I haven't heard anything."

"They found the thief, and either they know or suspect he killed Caterina for the pendant."

"That's good; you were right to keep your relationship with Paolo Soranzo."

"The news about the thief isn't why I came here. Paolo said that at least you didn't kill Caterina, but there are other things about you. I Siór di Notti only investigate serious crimes, so I came here as soon as you would be home from work."

"Sit, per piasser," Dardi said, and Filipa sat but he didn't.

"There's one thing it could be," Dardi said. "I was in love for many years. Clario Duodo; a young painter I met when he did the frescoes at Palàso Minotto."

Filipa put her hand over her mouth. "Another man!" she gasped.

Dardi nodded.

"Did you make love together?" Filipa asked.

"Many times," Dardi said.

"Anal intercourse?"

"Sometimes."

"You committed sodomy together!" Filipa exclaimed. "You could be executed for that! You must leave Venèsia."

"Not without Lucia."

Filipa tried to think what she could do to help him.

"A Lombardian spy blackmailed me to substitute false correspondence about the war," Dardi said. "Eventually I decided not to do that anymore. I followed the spy home and we had a fight. I pushed him down the stairs and killed him."

"What!" Filipa exclaimed.

"I thought that might be the end of it, but there must be other Lombardians."

"Those Lombardians might have made a denunciation against you. I Siór di Notti needs two witnesses, and we know they will find them. Getting yourself arrested, tortured and executed won't help Lucia."

Dardi sat and put his heads in his hands. Filipa waited with the sounds from outside clear and distinct. "You're right," he eventually said. "I must leave."

Filipa wondered how and that was easy. "My father has ships coming and going all the time, and I will ask him to smuggle you away on one."

"Do you think he will do that for me?"

"Of course he will! In the meantime it might be dangerous for you here. I would prefer you to be on Torcello."

"Where?"

"There's an unused storeroom at the abasia, and maybe you can hide there. Papa works from home mostly, and I will see him tomorrow. Then we will go to the abasia until it's time for you to leave."

"I would like Clario to come with me, if he wants to. We had an argument and I haven't seen him for a while."

Filipa sighed; that was making things hard. "I will ask Papa to arrange a passage for you, and maybe a passage for Clario Duodo." Filipa sighed again. "Can I stay here tonight?"

"Of course. I will tell the maid."

Dardi left the room and Filipa felt like someone had hit her in the stomach. Her stomach churned and ached; her heart beat fast and she felt out of breath. She'd known Dardi all her life and she never even suspected anything was wrong, although she wondered if love was wrong even if it was another man. She was a nun in love and whenever she saw or even thought about Pietro, she felt calm and peaceful. But not calm and peaceful that afternoon at Palàso Zorzi Bon! With Dardi in love with a man behind Caterina's back, there must have been tension between the couple, accounting for those rumours. But over time it seemed they reached a compromise from what Filipa saw. It was sad that Dardi couldn't be with the man he loved, but instead had to pretend to be someone that he wasn't, and even more sad that he had to abandon his daughter to save his life. He had no choice other than to leave, but that was terribly sad.

* * *

Filipa unlocked the door off the lane and let herself into her old home. She went to the alcove and asked Maria the maid if her Papa was home. If not she would have to find him at the docks. She heard creaking on the staircase and Papa came into the room.

"Bondi Filipa," Papa said while trying to smile.

"Bondi Papa," Filipa said.

"You're looking good."

"You chose a good home for me. I would like to talk with you about something."

He nodded and Filipa sat on a timber chair, and Papa sat by her. She turned to face him. "You've heard about Dardi Zorzi?" Filipa asked.

"I have and that was tragic," Papa said. "To think he could be accused of murder...."

"He didn't murder Caterina, but he's a sodomite."

"Pardon?"

"Dardi's a sodomite, and always has been."

"How do you know this?" Papa asked, looking stunned.

"He told me."

"His marriage...?"

Filipa drew a breath. "It was clear Dardi loved Caterina, or at least he liked her a lot."

Papa nodded his head slowly and Filipa knew he was digesting what he heard."

"The authorities are investigating Dardi at this moment," Filipa said. "I would like him to leave Venèsia."

"On one of my ships?" Papa asked.

"It's Dardi Zorzi, Papa."

"I know."

"We can't let him be tortured and then burned to death. I don't understand the rights and wrongs of sodomy, but it's wrong for someone we know and love to be burned to death."

"You're absolutely right Filipa." Her father rubbed his chin, like he always did when he was thinking. "I have a ship loading at the moment, to leave on Monday bound for Marseilles, and I will write a letter for the captain. We should give him a new identity. Let's call him Marco because everyone's called Marco, and Canal because that's a common surname. Marco Canal."

"There's one other thing, Papa. He wants to leave with his lover."

308

"Oh Filipa!" her Papa groaned.

"I don't see a choice."

"He was your best friend and more like your adopted oldest brother. He had infinite patience for you, and you became his adopted sister. Is this other man older or younger?"

"Younger."

"Marco Canal and his younger brother Antonio Canal."

Filipa got up and threw her arms around Papa. "You're brilliant!" she said. "I don't know for certain if this other man will be travelling, because they've been separated for a while and Dardi doesn't know."

"I understand. Marco Canal and maybe his younger brother Antonio Canal."

"Grassie Papa."

"I never thought I would say this but I miss you more and more," Papa said. "Sometimes you went exploring and we would always panic, and then you would come home and get into trouble! Sometimes you got Giorgio to take you out on the gondola, and we would be stranded! Sometimes other things; but you never caused anyone any harm. Dardi loved you, Cristina adores you, you brightened the house, and I realise now that you're my special daughter."

"Grassie Papa, and you're my special Papa. Especially helping Dardi with your brilliant ideas."

"I will get a letter to the captain, and you tell Dardi and his friend if he can find him, to report to Capitano Sacco of La Gagliana Grossa early on Monday. They will be Marco and Antonio Canal; both passengers for Marseilles."

"Grassie Papa. I should go now."

"Before you go; how's your life?"

"My life's still wonderful, Papa."

"I'm glad."

"Adio Papa."

"Adio Filipa."

* * *

Dardi thanked them most graciously and left Palàso Barozzi. Clario finished the frescoes a week previously, had been paid in full, and not been seen or heard from since. Dardi crossed San Marco and entered Clario's lodging, climbed the stairs and knocked on the door. No answer and he knocked again. All was quiet and Clario wasn't around. Dardi wondered, and perhaps Clario had a commission somewhere else. If so then Saturday would be the only opportunity to speak. Dardi went downstairs and walked to his home, and every stranger seemed menacing. Every individual was a threat and Filipa was right. On Torcello he would be safe. He arrived home, let himself in, and went upstairs to find Gia.

"Bondi Gia," Dardi said. "I'm going away for a few days. I will be back on Saturday and I will speak with you then."

"Sé siór," she said.

Livia came to the door and told Dardi that siórina Barbarigo wished to speak with him, and Dardi went downstairs.

"Papa will arrange passage for Marco Canal and maybe his younger brother Antonio Canal," Filipa said. "They must go to Capitano Sacco of the Gagliana Grossa early on Monday to sail for Marseilles."

"Grassie tuti Filipa," Dardi said.

"I know this is the only choice for you, but I wish I didn't have to arrange this."

"You're right that I'm no good to anyone if I'm dead."

"I know. Did you find Clario?"

"He must be working somewhere. I will return on Saturday for one last chance to find him."

Filipa frowned the way she did. "That's dangerous," she said. "But I won't stand in the way of love."

"You said you love someone so you know how it is."

"I know love," Filipa said flatly.

"I should pack a bag," Dardi said.

"Do that, and then we will walk to Piasà San Marco. I don't want your gondoliere to know."

Dardi was shocked. "You think of everything."

"Maybe I have a devious mind."

To juggle so many lovers, Filipa Barbarigo had to be devious. Dardi packed a canvas bag and soon they were on

311

their way to Torcello, and the further they crossed the lagoon
the safer Dardi felt. They berthed at the abasia where Filipa
led the way across a promenade to a grey door. Dardi walked
with Filipa along a corridor to her room where she invited
Dardi inside. It was a compact room: with a one and a half-
sized bed which had a soft mattress, and a blue, silk canopy
above. There were blue velvet curtains tied back from the
window overlooking the lagoon; a shelf held volumes of
books, and a trunk at the end of the bed had a lute on top.
There was one chair, while a tapestry of Campo Santa Maria
del Giglio made the little room seem more like home.

"Sit, per piasser," Filipa invited.

Dardi sat on the chair and Filipa sat on the bed.

"I like your room," Dardi said.

"It's a cell and it's cosy. I know what you're thinking."
"What?"

"Many men have shared my room and my bed."

Dardi looked around and she was right, of course.
That room had seen much activity.

The bell struck twelve and Filipa got off her bed.
"Sext None," she said.

Dardi was taken aback. "You really do go!" he said.

"Don't sound surprised, but unfortunately you're
going to miss dinner today. The last service of the day's
Compline at seven. After Compline we sleep, but you and I
will check out the storeroom.

"You think of everything," Dardi said.

"I know."

The rest of the day passed uneventfully, and after Compline the abasia was quiet and peaceful. Dardi followed Filipa around the chapel to the kitchen where there was leftover from supper. She placed some of the fish with rice on a plate and filled a jug of water, and gave them to him. She then lit a candle in the hearth and placed it in a lantern, and led the way through a tree garden to a small building about twelve feet square, and there she put down the lantern and wrestled with an old, wooden door. Inside were four old rice sacks which made for a seat or even a lumpy bed, and on the one side was a ladder. Dardi sat on one rice sack and Filipa sat on another, and there he ate his cold meal and drank some water while illuminated by a flickering candle in a lantern. While he ate, Dardi suspected the ladder went down to the lagoon. If so he may be able to enter without going through the abasia grounds, although he could never catch a gondola from there.

"I will explore," Dardi said when he finished eating. He climbed down the ladder shrouded in cobwebs. So many cobwebs; it was awful! As he suspected there was a loading platform at the bottom.

"I hoped I could come in this way," Dardi said from the bottom.

"You can," Filipa said from above. "The loading platform down there will double as a latrine for you. When you want to leave you will have to go through the abasia and catch a gondola from our jetty," Filipa said. "Some nuns rise at five to bake bread. Before they wake, come to my cell. From there you can leave for Venèsia."

Dardi climbed the ladder.

"Is this storeroom alright for you?" Filipa asked.

"It's good," Dardi said.

Filipa yawned, and they both had a busy few days.

"You should sleep," Dardi said.

Filipa bid him farewell, took the plate and lantern away, and closed the door behind her. Dardi lay on the rice sacks and hoped he would sleep, because he had many thoughts which might keep him awake.

Chapter Twenty Seven

Filipa couldn't keep her mind away from Dardi Zorzi and Clario Duodo together, and especially that their punishment was to be burned to death. She wondered why that was so. She wondered why sodomy was such a heinous sin, when other sins she thought were bad were not treated as severely. Pàre Antonio was due to hear the nun's confessions for the past year, and for sure there were a few sins to be confessed by some nuns. While the priest was at the abasia, Filipa wanted to understand more about sodomy.

After Tierce, the nuns lined up by the chapter house. The filed in one after the other, and then came Filipa's turn. Pàre Anthony was on the bench, and Filipa knelt before him with her head bowed and her eyes closed.

"My Lord God; I'm sorry for my sins with all my heart. It has been a year since my last confession, and since then I committed the following mortal sins. I committed adultery with ten different men, many times. I fornicated with a woman."

She heard his gasp. "Do you feel contrition for your sins?" pàre Anthony asked.

"I feel contrition for my sins," Filipa said.

"Your penance will be to repeat psalm fifty-one every night for the next ten years."

"My Lord God; I'm sorry for my sins with all my heart."

"I absolve you from your sins in the name of the Father, and of the Son, and of the Holy Spirit. Give thanks to the Lord, for He is good."

"I thank the Lord for He is good."

"You may go sòra."

Filipa left the chapter house but waited outside. The nuns were heard quickly with Isabella last. When Isabella left the chapter house, Filipa went inside once more.

"Sòra Filipa," pàre Anthony said. "I heard your confession."

"That's true pàre," Filipa said. "But I wish to discuss a matter with you, if you will allow me."

"Of course."

"A friend of mine has been accused of sodomy, and I was upset to hear about that of course. I hope you can tell me more about his sin."

"I can sòra Filipa. God created the heavens and the earth, and within His realm His laws are Eternal Laws. Here on earth man is capable of reasoning and has free will, and we must exercise our natural reason to discover what is best for us in order to achieve the end to which our nature inclines us. Also, we must choose what is best for our nature. The natural inclination of humans to achieve our proper end through our reason and free will is Natural Law. Natural Law is human participation in Eternal Law, using reason and free will."

Filipa had heard the terms Eternal Law and Natural Law before, but until then had never grasped what they represented. "I understand pàre," she said.

"Good. Now the key Natural Law is the fulfilment of the human activity of living. Therefore, the most basic Natural Laws are not to commit suicide, and not to kill. Natural Law commands that we take care of our life, and transmit that life to the next generation. The natural order of things is the union of the sexes in marriage in order to transmit life to the next generation of man. Further, the next generation of man would be useless unless appropriate nurturing in marriage follows, without which offspring cannot survive. The emission of semen must be directed so that both the next generation of life may result, and the correct upbringing of the offspring will follow. Every emission of semen which takes place in a way where the next generation of humanity is impossible, must be a sin."

Filipa frowned while she thought that through. "The only form of sexual relations which is not sinful is conducted in marriage with the purpose of creating life."

"That's correct sòra."

"I don't understand that perhaps a woman can have sexual relations while unmarried, taking precautions to avoid falling pregnant, and receive the penance of a prayer. But a man committing sodomy with another man is burned at the stake."

"In Genesis chapter nineteen, Lot went to the city of Sodom with two male angels in order to find ten good men. But the debauched men of Sodom wanted to have sexual relations with the male angels, even after Lot offered them his virgin daughters. In response to this, the Lord told Lot and his family to flee the city before destroying it with fire and brimstone."

"I understand pàre. The Lord destroyed an entire city because of male sexual relations. That must be a great sin."

"It's a very great sin, sòra."

"Why are sodomites burned at the stake?"

"The only appropriate punishment for such a grave sin is execution, and burning at the stake allows execution without shedding blood, which the Church cannot allow. Also, burning cleanses the soul of the sodomite, and it ensures the condemned has no body to take to the next life."

Filipa tried to remain cool and calm. "Grassie pàre for the explanation."

"De niente."

"Adio pàre Antonio."

"Adio sòra Filipa."

Filipa left pàre Antonio; went to her cell and closed the door. She sat on her bed and thought about what they discussed. Regardless of Natural Law, many did as they

318

chose. Patrician men rarely married before thirty, and in the meantime they made love with prostitutes, mistresses and perhaps nuns, none of which was intended for reproduction. Also those men masturbated, probably regularly. Married couples usually had a number of surviving children, typically three, and then they had no more. Couples took precautions to avoid pregnancy; the same precautions that a nun might take. Filipa was concerned about the fire and brimstone though, for that was a grave punishment against the inhabitants of Sodom. Although that was in the old book, the Old Testament, and much in the Old Testament was about murder and stoning. Adultery for example. In the Old Testament, both a man and a woman committing adultery had to be stoned to death, until Jesus changed that. Maybe the story of Sodom meant something or maybe it meant nothing. Filipa took a deep breath and decided to rescue Dardi from his mortal punishment if she could, and encourage him to confess his sins. If he served his penance and received absolution, he would be saved for the afterlife. If the story of Sodom meant anything, it was important for Dardi to confess his sins.

* * *

Paolo climbed the staircase amidst builders toiling away, crossed reception and headed along the corridor to Cosmo's room. He knocked and waited for Cosmo to call him, and then went inside.

"Bondi Cosmo," Paolo said. "I gave my informants time but they haven't heard anything."

Cosmo grimaced and he looked particularly ugly when he did that. "Sodomites often meet at barber shops," he said. "Starting tomorrow we check every barber shop in the city. I will do Sestiere di Castello, you will do San Marco, Lion will do Nicolotti, Priamo will do San Polo, Benetto will do Cannareggio and Donà will do Santa Croce."

Paolo was ambivalent about their investigation. Finding that jewellery thief and murderer and making him confess was worthy and would make the streets safer. But investigating the personal matters of a patrician wasn't right. And if they found something, it would serve no good purpose. All in all Paolo didn't want to be involved. His family had been part of I Siór di Noti for many generations and as eldest son that was Paulo's duty, and most of the time he was pleased to serve. But not when it involved the personal issues of Dardi Zorzi. He knew he didn't have any choice just as Cosmo had no choice; Él Consìlio dei Diéxe were gravely concerned about sodomy and they took interest in all investigations into sodomy. Cosmo and Paolo were under scrutiny to investigate thoroughly and to bring Dardi to justice if necessary. When it came to sodomy, Dardi being a patrician counted for nothing.

"I will start on this first thing tomorrow morning," Paolo said.

320

"Right," Cosmo said.

Paolo headed outside and went home, while still troubled about investigating a patrician.

* * *

All was peaceful and quiet at Abasia San Nicolai di Torcello. Filipa went to the kitchen and lit a candle in the hearth before placing it in a lantern. She served a plate of the meat stew with polenta, and with lantern in one hand and the plate in the other, she walked through the tree garden to the storeroom where Dardi had his sacks of rice for comfort. She gave him the plate and he thanked her. Filipa went to the kitchen to fill the water jug, and returned to sit on a third sack while Dardi ate his meal. She once asked him to marry her, and she now knew why he didn't do that. It was odd that for so long she thought he admired her, and that was just an illusion. He was a great actor. It was sad he had to act instead of being who he really was. Because of that story of Sodom, which might not even mean anything, he wasn't allowed to be who he really was.

"What is it?" Dardi asked.

Filipa looked at him. "I've known you for many years, but I never would have guessed you weren't attracted to me."

"No, not at all. You're a beautiful woman Filipa."

"What is it then?"

321

"I admire beautiful women like I admire a beautiful house or a beautiful bridge."

"So I'm like a house or a bridge to you?"

Dardi almost broke into a smile. Almost. "Not only are you beautiful Filipa, you're my best friend. You're a cheerful woman with a wicked sense of humour, but at the same time you're a deep thinker and a great conversationalist."

"So what is it then?"

"I'm not sexually attracted to you, and I could never fall in love with you."

"You love Clario?"

"It's like you exist for the other and he exists for you. When you've been apart, as soon as you see him you feel complete again. When you love someone it's two halves of a whole. Love's heart to heart, mind to mind and body to body."

"That's the same as when a man and a woman are in love." Filipa was intrigued by that and wondered if there were other similarities. "What do you find attractive in men?" she asked.

"What do you find attractive in men?"

Filipa frowned while she thought. "A man who stands up straight and is sure of himself; who radiates confidence and his own self-worth. Well-presented with good clothes and well-groomed too. Tall; he has to be taller than me, and handsome like you. Manly handsome especially a man's hands. I love men's hands."

"I suppose women are attracted to the opposite of themselves"

"Women find other women attractive, especially women's softness and curves."

"Feminine beauty is why men have to control you.

"Do you have the same attractions for men as me?"

"Sé I do."

"You have your daughter so you made love with Caterina."

"I did and that was hard. I really liked Caterina and she was a good woman, no, she was a great woman, but when it came to sex I had to fantasise I was with Clario or else I couldn't. Caterina sensed the distance between us and she really hated that."

"That would have been hard for you both. It's a shame we force men to pretend they're something they're not."

"That was hard for both of us, but we had Lucia which made up for that. Sadly I will lose her."

"I'm really sorry about that. Are you going to Venèsia tomorrow?"

"I am."

"Be very careful. I must go; we get up early for breakfast and then Prime, and don't say anything!"

"I wasn't going to say a word."

"Two or three times I've spent the night away from here, but otherwise I attend every service. The prayers and particularly the hymns are exhilarating."

Dardi frowned and Filipa wondered what he was thinking about. "If you couldn't go out like you do, and if you couldn't have men in your life, could you become a nun?" he asked.

That was an easy answer. "No," Filipa said firmly. "But I do understand how women can give themselves to this life. There's one other thing Dardi," and Filipa didn't want to lecture him, but it was important for him to be safe. "As you know I have relations with men and that's a sin. I confess all my sins, receive my penance and receive absolution."

"Do you want me to confess my sin of falling in love?"

"I confessed my sin of falling in love."

"Sé you must have."

"I will do what I can for you in this life, and I would like you to prepare yourself for the next life."

"I hadn't thought about that before, but perhaps you're right."

"We all have to think about what follows in the next life, and I will sleep better if you confess and receive absolution."

"I will.

Filipa was pleased with that. "Be careful tomorrow," she said.

"Sé Mama."

Filipa giggled "I'm sòra."

"Sé sòra."

"Adio Dardi," she said.

"Adio Filipa."

Filipa took the plate and lantern to the kitchen, put the candle out, and then returned to her cell. She knew she would sleep well after having that conversation.

Chapter Twenty Eight

The next morning Paolo started as he promised, and although Cosmo divided the city into the six segments, Paolo never realised there were so many barber shops in San Marco! He trudged from shop to shop to shop asking the same question over and over, and not one barber knew. Paolo reached Campo Santa Maria del Giglio by mid-morning and looked around. A dull, red building held a barber shop and Paolo went inside.

"Bongiorno siór," the barber said. "A haircut and a shave perhaps?"

"Bongiorno," Paolo said wearily. "I'm from I Siór di Nòti and I'm looking for two possible sodomites. One is named Dardi Zorzi of patrician ancestry and he's about thirty, quite tall and dark, and the other is named Claudio Duodo and he's a painter and younger. Do you know of them?"

"I do siór," the barber said, and that pricked Paolo's interest.

"What can you tell me?"

"Two men often come separately to my shop for haircuts or shaves, and always left together. They're named Dardi and Clario, with Dardi always well-dressed and about thirty, and Clario less well-dressed and in his twenties. I suspected they were sodomites but I had no proof, and they didn't do anything out of the ordinary in my shop, except arriving separately and leaving together."

"I understand. What's your name?"

"Marin Curri."

"Siór Curri; would you be prepared to testify to this in a hearing?"

"Sé I would. Sodomy's a grievous sin, and if I can bring two sodomites to justice, I will."

"Grassie siór Curri, and I commend you for this. I or one of my colleagues will return to arrange a time for you to testify once we arrest these men."

"I'm ready to do my civic duty."

"Grassie for that. Adio siór Currie."

"Adio siór."

Paolo barely believed his bad luck. Trust him to find the one barber who knew! Briefly he thought about not reporting what he heard, but he had no choice. Not only was it his duty, someone else might find out. Paolo left the shop and headed to Él Geto. There were many Jews in Él Geto who kept to themselves, but maybe there was a witness to Zorzi's and Duodo's comings and goings. Paolo reached the corner of Fondamenta Cannaregio and Calle del Forno, and found himself at a faded, grimy, yellow building with a butcher shop at the ground floor. He went into that shop which had cuts of meat and sausages hanging on hooks, and a big table splattered with blood. It smelled stale and strangely fresh at the same time.

"Bongiorno siór," Paolo said. "I'm from I Siór di Nòti and I'm looking for two possible sodomites. One is named Dardi Zorzi of patrician ancestry and he's about thirty, quite tall and dark, and the other is named Claudio Duodo and he's a painter and younger. It's been reported they rent a room on the third floor of this building."

"Bongiorno siór," the butcher said. "Sodomites you say. Men come and go, and what they do in private is private. I can tell you of two men matching that description, who came maybe once or twice a week for a few hours at a time. Otherwise their room was vacant, which I always thought odd."

"Do you know their names?"

"My brother-in-law knows the name of one of them; he bought a pendant which was subsequently stolen and then recovered by I Sbirri."

That was Dardi Zorzi alright. "Your brother-in-law's the jeweller further along?" Paolo asked.

"Sé siór."

"Would you be prepared to identify these men when we arrest them, and testify to the movements of these men in a hearing?"

"Sé siór."

"What's your name?"

"Dino Surdi."

"I or one of my colleagues will return to arrange a time for you to testify once we arrest these men."

"I don't want trouble around my shop, so as soon as your arrest them and get them off the streets, the better for me."

"Of course. Adio siór Surdi."

"Adio siór."

Paolo went outside. He had much to do: arrest warrants to prepare, get I Sbirri on the streets, and then wait for Dardi Zorzi and Claudio Duodo to be brought in for interrogation. But that could wait until later. He had more pressing matters to attend to.

* * *

Dardi got the gondoliere to take him to the water door of his home, where he paid ten soldi. Dardi went inside and upstairs to the study and sat at the desk. He took a sheet of paper and dipped the quill in ink, and wrote to his parents but particularly to his mother. It was a difficult letter to write and Dardi left out many details, but he did write that he didn't take leaving lightly, especially with his responsibility for Lucia, but he was sure they would look after their granddaughter as if she was their own. Dardi folded his letter and then took a candle in a holder and went to the kitchen where the hearth was blazing. He lit the candle and took it to the study and placed it on the desk. From the drawer he took a stick of wax and the seal, heated the wax on the candle and placed it on his letter leaving a spot of red. He stamped the seal into the soft wax before blowing out the candle and putting the wax and seal away for the last time.

Dardi took the letter to the nursery where Lucia was sleeping quietly, and Gia was embroidering. He gazed at his daughter in the cot, and with every day that passed she looked more and more like her beautiful mother. He didn't want to leave his daughter, who was young and innocent and all that was left of wonderful Caterina. Dardi wondered if there was a way to take her with him, but even if he took Gia on his journey, it was still too far to travel with a baby so young. As sad as it was to leave Lucia, it was in her best interests to be looked after by his parents. Dardi sighed deeply before turning to face Gia.

"I must go," Dardi said. "On Tuesday, take Lucia to Ca' Zorzi and give my mother this letter," and Dardi handed it across.

"As you wish," Gia said.

Dardi looked at his daughter one last time, before leaving the house. Once more he crossed San Marco and went to Clario's lodging, climbed the stairs and knocked on the door. Again no answer and he knocked again.

Another door opened and an old woman peered out. "Excuse me, siór," she said. "Siór Duodo has left."

"Do you know where he went?"

"No, siór."

"How long has he been gone?"

"About a week."

"Grassie sióra."

Dardi went down to the calle and there was one other place, although that was unlikely. In any case he needed a shave. He went to the barber at Campo Santa Maria del Giglio, but got the greatest shock when he entered the shop. Marin's mouth fell open and his eyes were big and wide.

"Can I help you siór," Marin gasped.

"A shave, per piasser," Dardi asked.

"Sit, per piasser."

The barber applied soap before clearing away three day's growth of beard. It took a while, and when Dardi rubbed his face he was most impressed. "You're the best barber in Venèsia," Dardi said.

The barber nodded.

"You may remember a friend of mine," Dardi said. "Have you seen him recently?"

"No siór, not for more than a week. That will be ten soldi."

Dardi reached into his tacolinn and gave the barber twenty soldi. "You deserve more because that was a difficult shave for you."

"Grassie siór."

"Adio siór," Dardi said, and left the shop.

Marin stood there with his heart pounding, and a twenty soldi coin in his hand. He put it in the bowl and left his shop; locking the door behind. He followed that man, Dardi, through the streets of San Marco towards the canal where three gondolieri waited for business. Dardi got into the first gondola and they set off, and Marin got into the second gondola, a light blue one.

"Where do you wish to travel?" the gondoliere asked.

"Can you follow the red gondola ahead?" Marin asked.

"If you wish."

They set off and Marin sat in the fieze with the blind open, and looked at the red gondola ahead. They left Canal Grando and entered the lagoon, heading towards Torcello. After an hour or more they reached the port where the red gondola berthed at a side door to an abasia. Marin watched as Dardi disappeared from view, and he wondered what he should do. He had to do something because sodomy was a great sin and all sodomites had to be executed. Marin remembered his former master and knew he had to report Dardi for doing the same thing. The man who came to Marin's shop was from I Siór di Nòti but didn't give his name. Even if that man gave his name, Marin didn't know how to contact him. One solution was a denunciation at Piasà San Marco. Marin decided to do that, and he asked the gondoliere to return him to Venèsia. Marin went to the rooms of Angelo the scribe, apologised profusely because it was Saturday afternoon, while assuring Angelo what he had was urgent. Marin dictated: 'Sodomite Dardi Zorzi is staying at an abasia on the lagoon at the settlement at Torcello, maybe a hundred yards from the canal'. After paying 10 soldi, Marin took the sheet of paper and slipped it into the mouth of the lion at Piasà San Marco.

* * *

Faint knocking on Filipa's door; Saturday afternoon and Paolo Soranzo. Filipa guessed Paolo was searching high and low for Dardi, who must have returned to the storeroom and was just yards away. She had to get those thoughts out of her head in case she gave herself away. She decided to give Paolo a treat and then find out what he was up to. Filipa rose from her bed and opened her door, and Paolo entered her cell. He closed the door, hugged her and kissed her in the one move. He was a nice man and Filipa was glad they'd met. He was going to make a good husband for some woman one day.

"Are you going to undress while I watch?" Paolo whispered in her ear.

"Do you want me to?" Filipa asked.

"It's like watching a present being unwrapped."

That gave Filipa an idea. "Do you want to unwrap your present?"

Paolo moved away and untied her blue giornea, and eased it from her shoulders. Then he untied her black gamurra and peeled that away as well.

"This is the best part," he said while he unlaced her camicia and lifted that off. "Sit, per piasser," and Filipa sat on the bed. He knelt to remove her garters and then her calsi, and she was naked. Still kneeling he brushed her legs apart and buried his head, and Filipa grabbed his lovely, soft hair while he kissed her gently then more than kissed her. Filipa closed her eyes and it buzzed and tingled, and grew and grew until it cascaded free. She opened her eyes and caught his eyes.

"Your turn," she said, and she stood to unlace his garments, except his hard cock made removing his mutande and calsa quite difficult. Difficult but not impossible, and she grabbed his erection and felt it warm and hard in her hand. They kissed while Filipa held him, and then she climbed onto the bed on her hands and knees, and looked over her shoulder at him. Men always gazed at her when she did that and Filipa knew why. Mesmerised by the view of her sex from behind. Paulo knelt behind her and slowly, slowly he entered her, and holding her hips he made love to her. He was a patient lover and he always started slow, and that was good. Always he teased her before picking up his pace, and Filipa put her head down and felt it coming to her again. Faint deep in her core, and then ever more insistent, until it grew and grew and came with that different type of pleasure. Fuller with him inside her.

He fucked her harder and harder and Filipa sensed his urgency. "Let me make you come," she said before moving to take his cock in her mouth. She sucked him hard while using her lips and also using her fingers. His whole body tighter and tighter and then he erupted in the most amazing gush. Filipa struggled to contain it all while she rubbed and sucked, on and on until he was done. Filipa sat on her haunches and wiped her mouth and her nose with the back of her hand.

Paolo bent down and kissed her, and their tongues briefly touched before he moved away. "Te vògio ben," he said.

"You know what this really is," Filipa said.

"It's hard not to love you."

"Grassie Paolo."

"My family's arranging a match."

"Remember what I said about touching your heart," Filipa said, while she put the palm of her hand on his heart. "If you love someone, you really feel it here."

"Really? I thought that was just made up."

"True love touches your heart."

"What about sex with my future wife?"

Filipa thought about that, and guessed that few women would do what she did. "I believe that when the door to the bedroom is closed, God turns away to give lovers privacy. He wouldn't give us these great pleasures if they weren't meant to be used, and He's not looking over our shoulders to condemn us; rather, if He does see us then He's pleased that we're using His gifts as He intended."

"If I were to talk about this with my wife...?'

"You can talk about this with your future wife, but she must be comfortable with whatever you do or else it will drive a wedge into your marriage. As long as she's comfortable then I believe God will be pleased that you're loving each other the way He made you to love. At first you don't need to worry about ejaculation inside your wife, although that will come later."

"Anal intercourse?"

"That will be the decision of your wife. With a bit of oil it's not so hard, and the more I did the easier it got, although I don't know how you can tell your future wife how you know that!"

"And what we did just now?"

"You liked that."

"That was the best ever. And you?'

"I liked the power of your manhood under my control, and I liked that you liked it. You're a decent man Paolo, and your decency shows in the way you make love. Start simple, wait for your wife to appreciate your decency, and over time you can talk about where things might go. But don't expect her to be like me first time."

"Grassie Filipa. What's a woman's first time like?"

"It hurts! You have to do it of course, and that might be difficult for you because you're so decent. For that one time just do it, and she will be grateful for that."

"Grassie tuti. Oh, I have a present for you." He reached over the edge of the bed and found his séngia and tacolinn. He took out a ring and Filipa put it on the third finger of her right hand. She held her hands up and they looked good with six rings. She kissed his lips.

"Grassie tuti Paolo," she said.

"I got my present too," he said.

"Sé you did. Are you busy at work?"

He drew his lips tight. "I am, and it's not something I want to do to be honest. But once a denunciation has been made it has to be investigated, even if I don't want to."

"That must be hard for you."

"I really needed to see you to get my mind off it."

"If you pick the right woman for your wife, you will have someone to help you with your problems at work."

"Sé, you're right."

"Do you like poetry?"

"I do."

"I will read you some poems."

Filipa got out of bed and grabbed the book Marino gave her.

"This is the best part, Paolo said.

"Being naked together after making love?"

He nodded.

"There's no shame in the most perfect of Gods creations being as He made us," Filipa said.

"I will tell that to my future wife," Paolo said.

Filipa sat crossed legged and turned the pages. "Are you sure this is the best part?" she asked mischievously.

He burst out laughing. "When you wiped your mouth like that; that was the best part!"

Filipa liked Paolo, and she was hurt that he found his investigation of Dardi's sodomy difficult. He was a decent man and his decency showed through in many different ways. She didn't love him but she liked him a lot, and she was sure his future wife, whoever she was, would be a lucky woman. Filipa read three poems before Paolo said he had business to attend to and he must leave her, although he didn't want to. He dressed, and Filipa hugged and kissed him goodbye. He left and she dressed, cosy in her small cell with heat rising through the vent in the floor. Feeling restless she went outside but nobody was around. She had to wait until after Compline, except that was so long. She hoped Dardi was alright and hadn't been spotted by any of the authorities looking for him: I Sbirri or I Siór di Nòti. The day dragged on and eventually everyone retired to bed. Filipa went to the kitchen, lit a lantern, served some food and took it to the storeroom. She opened the door and Dardi was there, and he'd shaved and Filipa thought that was a bad idea. His growing beard was a good disguise.

"Did you find Clario?" she asked.

"No I didn't," Dardi said. "I spoke with the nurse, and made arrangements for Lucia."

Filipa was upset by that. "That's sad," she said, and Dardi looked sad. He lost his wife, He lost his lover and then he lost his daughter, and he would never see them again. "With luck you will escape with your life, and while you have lost much, you could have lost much more."

"I know."

"I saw Paolo Soranzo today. He's troubled about investigating you."

"They will find something soon enough, if they haven't already. Your relationship proved useful."

"I like him; he's a good man. All of the men have been good or else I would never have invited them back, but Paolo's been the best apart from Pietro...."

"The man you love?" Dardi interrupted.

"Sé."

"You're going to marry him?"

"Sé. I must talk with him about that."

"He will be a lucky man."

"I hope I'm a good wife."

"You will be the best wife ever, and a good mother too."

"Being a mother is a great responsibility."

"You're clever and resourceful, and you will cope better than most. Cristina has a baby?"

"She does."

"Ask her for guidance. Cristina and you fit well together."

"We always have." Filipa stood. "Adio Dardi."

"Adio Filipa."

Filipa took the plate and lantern to the kitchen and put the candle out. She returned to her cell where it was cool, dark and peaceful. Eventually she would be married and actually sleeping with her husband. She rolled onto her side and imagined what married life would be like.

Chapter Twenty Nine

Filipa took a meal to the storeroom, and there Dardi waited for her as always. She took his water jug to the kitchen, and returned shortly after to close the door behind and sit on a rice sack. She thought about Dardi and his sodomy and possible burning at the stake. That was a terrible punishment for love. She didn't know if she would take such a risk, and that intrigued her. "The love you feel for Clario must be very strong," she said.

"Why do you say that?" Dardi asked.

"You would have known that if you were found you would be executed."

"That has nothing to do with love. That's just who we're attracted to, and there have always been men attracted to men."

Filipa banged her head with the palm of her hand. "Ah sé, of course. It's either men making love with men or remaining celibate, and sex is a wonderful pleasure."

"Laws about sodomy are futile. There will always be men who like men, and those men will always seek the warmth, closeness and pleasure of sex. No matter how many men they burn, they can't stop sodomy."

"Sometimes men and women have anal intercourse," Filipa said.

"That's right."

341

Filipa chuckled. "It's good birth control."

"You have...?"

"Sometimes. Do you know who they punish for sodomy?"

"Sodomy's prosecuted by Él Consìlio dèi Diéxe. They punish men who have anal intercourse with men, men who have sex between the thighs of men, and men who have sex with animals. I suppose they could punish men and women who have anal intercourse, but that hasn't happened."

"Mostly it's men who like men"

"Sé it is."

"You don't have to tell me this but I'm curious. How do men make love with men?"

"Anal intercourse is one way, and using our mouths is another."

"You take turns?"

"Most think one man is always active and the other is always passive, and me being older and a patrician would be considered the active man. The reality's different."

"I discovered using my mouth by accident, and I like doing that for the power it gives me, although we make love other ways from there. As you know, men often use their mouths on women."

"And you have anal intercourse?"

"Sometimes, and I like that too. Mostly I get men to pull out of me before they ejaculate. If they mis-time there

342

are ways to avoid pregnancy, but it's safer not to ejaculate inside."

"I understand."

She held his hand and looked into his eyes. "Sex is a great pleasure and it's something I wouldn't want to live without, but love is different. My heart aches for him when we're apart, and sometimes I ache for him even when we're together, and every time I see him I want to make love with him. I can have good sex with nothing more than mutual respect, but I can't love without making love. After we make love I feel even closer to him and I know he's closer to me. I want to see him again, and when we do we make love again."

He rustled her hair. "Love works like that Filipa."

"Love is supposed to be dangerous but it's not. It's a warm, cosy feeling that envelopes you, and you just can't let it go."

"Sé it does. Unfortunately with all that was happening with the spying and our marriage, Clario felt like he didn't belong in my life anymore. He broke up with me."

Filipa was startled; she thought they'd just had an argument. "Oh, I'm sorry to hear that," she said.

"There was too much happening at the time."

"I understand, but that must have been hard for you. And then you lost Caterina just a short time later, and now Lucia."

"I'm on my own and a fugitive."

Filipa was concerned that Dardi hadn't had the opportunity to confess. "When you get away from here, are you still going to confess?" she asked.

"You're keen on that."

"You committed sins like we all commit sins, and I will be happier when you confess."

"I will Filipa; don't worry."

"Come to my cell when you finish eating, and stay there for the night so you can leave in the morning."

"Grassie Filipa."

Filipa led him to the kitchen to leave the lantern, jug and plate, and then went to her cell. She didn't really want to wait in silence until it was time to say goodbye forever. She had no choice but she didn't want to do that.

* * *

With his bag slung over his shoulder, Dardi climbed the gangway of the La Gagliana Grossa; one of maybe 3,000 Venèsian ships in service. Él Arsenale di Venèsia built ships to the same style in hundreds and thousands, to be sailed the length and breadth of the Mediterranean and adjacent seas until their timbers were rotten, and then they were broken-up having earned their worth thousands of times over. La Gagliana Grossa was about 30 yards long and had two masts, each with a single, triangular sail. He asked for Capitano Sacco and was taken to an older man with grey hair and a weather-beaten face, although sea service probably made him look older than his years.

"Bongiorno Capitano," Dardi said. "I'm Marco Canal."

"Bongiorno siór Canal," Capitano Sacco replied.

"You can call me Marco."

Sacco crossed his arms. "Your brother...?"

"He's not coming."

"You're leaving trouble behind?"

"Possibly."

"Your clothes look lived-in but are too grand for a sailor. Come to my cabin and I will find you some discards so you can blend in. Then we will get you to work so you can blend in more."

"I have money in my bag."

"Keep that in my cabin and it will be safe there. You have a cabin next to mine."

Dardi followed Capitano Sacco to the stern and his basic cabin, with a small desk and chair, a hammock and a couple of trunks. Sacco opened one of the trunks and emptied it of clothes item by item, until he found what he wanted. He gave a blue tabàro and grey trousers to Dardi, and Dardi gave his bag which was placed in another of the trunks. Dardi changed and Capitano Sacco nodded approvingly.

"Let's get you to work, Marco Canal."

345

Chapter Thirty

The nuns were leaving the chapel after Prime when several men in dark tabàri burst through the corridor that ran through the wing of cells, and spread out around the building. One of these men came to the nuns.

"Where is Dardi Zorzi?" he shouted.

Barbarella came to the front. "Who are you and what are you doing here?" she demanded.

"We're I Sbirri and we've been sent by I Siór di Nòti to apprehend Dardi Zorzi."

"As you can see there are no men here."

"For once," sòra Augusta said.

"What do you mean, sòra?" the sbirro asked.

"These patrician nuns have men in their cells morning, noon and night."

"That's not true, Augusta," Barbarella said.

"Well, not at night, but at other times."

"Is this true?"

There was murmuring amongst the nuns in black, and clearly some wanted to add to Augusta's accusations and some didn't.

"I know Dardi Zorzi," Filipa said while she came to the side of Barbarella. "He's a friend of my family and I've known him since I was young. I also knew his late wife Caterina, and he came here to tell me about her murder and that he was a suspect. Later, he came here to tell me that her murderer had been found. A thief murdered Caterina Zorzi for a pendant, only she wasn't wearing it at the time. That thief then stole the pendant from their home."

"Did you have sexual relations with Dardi Zorzi?"

"I did not."

"He would be the first man she hasn't had sexual relations with," Augusta said.

"Quiet Augusta," Barbarella said firmly.

"Dardi Zorzi is such an old friend that sexual relations would be like incest with my brother," Filipa said. "The murder of Caterina was a tragedy for both of us, and we spent time talking about it."

"Do you know where he is?" the sbirro asked.

"I do not."

"We'll search this abasia for him."

"I don't allow that!" Barbarella shouted at them.

"You are...?"

"Badésa Barbarella della Fontana."

"I'm sorry badésa but Dardi Zorzi is a suspected sodomite, and we must search for him."

"You can let them search," Filipa said. "We've nothing to hide."

"Alright, you can search," Barbarella said.

"You nuns stay here, per piasser," the sbirro said while the other sbirri spread out. Soon doors were opened, cells peered into, a sbirro went into the chapel, and two sbirri went into the refrectory. It took them a long time to search the cloister from end to end and the storeroom as well, and all that time the nuns were held in the corridor just outside the chapel. One by one, the sbirri returned to their commander and their expressions told all.

"Are you satisfied?" Barbarella asked sarcastically.

"I'm satisfied that Dardi Zorzi isn't here," the sbirro said. "But I'm concerned about men coming and going to this abasia. If Dardi Zorzi was able to enter and leave unmolested, then I'm sure other men have come here for reasons other than to talk. For now we're concentrating on apprehending this sodomite, but we will return and pursue the matter of other men. In the meantime, I will station a man outside to ensure nobody comes or goes."

The sbirro gathered his troops and they departed.

"That was very inappropriate, Augusta," Barbarella said.

"This abasia is more like a brothel than a place of spiritual salvation!" Augusta snapped.

"That's most unfair," Diana said. "Some nuns and even the badésa are not here of their choosing. Despite that I cannot imagine a better run abasia, or a more spiritually satisfying environment. We all observe all services every day, celebrating with prayers and hymns. We have bible discussions with the badésa, and sometimes singing in the chapter house with sòra Filipa. Our meals are plain as decreed by our vow of poverty, but at the same time pleasant and filling. I'm proud to be a part of Abasia San Nicolai di Torcello."

Murmuring spread through the group of nuns, and Filipa sensed more agreed with Diana than with Augusta. Augusta and some others may have seen the lack of chastity as a sin, and some may have been jealous of not having lovers themselves.

"I thank you for what you have said, Diana," Barbarella said. "I Sbirri will return, and they will question some of us or all of us. It's important that you all tell the truth, regardless of individual loyalties. Sòri Anna, Clara and Filipa; can you come with me to my room. The rest should return to your normal duties."

Filipa followed the other nuns into Barbarella's room and closed the door. They sat on the chairs except for Filipa who stood to one side. "This matter of Dardi Zorzi is unfortunate," Barbarella said.

"That's my fault," Filipa said.

"That's not your fault Filipa. You said he's an old friend, and true friends don't turn away friends in need."

Filipa nodded.

"We must tell the truth when I Sbirri return," Barbarella said. "We're covered by ecclesiastical law and not the laws of Venèsia, so we have little to fear ourselves.

Unfortunately the men we know will be tried, convicted and sentenced, most likely to two years in prison."

Filipa was shocked.

"That's the sentence for adultery with a nun," Barbarella said.

"I feel sorry for Francesco," Anna said.

"I feel sorry for Pietro," Filipa said. "I love him and I was going to apply to leave here if he wanted me, but I haven't yet asked him. Always I was going to ask him, but I never did."

"I didn't know that!" Clara exclaimed.

"He's the most wonderful man I've ever met. He has the great views about women. To be his wife would be an honour, but that can't happen for me now."

"I'm sorry for all the men and I'm sorry for my Pietro," Barbarella said. "You can all go except for Filipa."

They left the room.

"We need to get our stories right," Barbarella said.

"We must tell the truth or else we will get caught out by the testimonies of others," Filipa said.

"I'm uncomfortable about you and I."

"I am too. What should we say?"

"You took your own virginity with a glass dildo, and tell them that I encouraged you to make love with Pietro, but don't mention I was there."

"Is that thing called a dildo?"

"It is."

"Our first time will work because only you and I know what happened, but Pietro may contradict us on the second."

"The second one is an omission rather than a lie. You're not telling them every detail."

Filipa understood. "I won't mention you were there and we will see what happens. I wish I didn't have to mention Pietro but Clara knows about him, and Donato may mention I went to see him."

"You don't have a choice, Filipa."

"I know," Filipa said. She decided not to tell them about modelling for the painting of Venus. If Pietro told them then that was an omission rather than a lie, but if he didn't tell them about the modelling then that would be better.

* * *

Paolo sat at his desk with his mind was far, far away. On Torcello, where I Sbirri were hunting for Dardi Zorzi at Abasia San Nicolai di Torcello. They may or may not find Dardi Zorzi, but they may find other things. Paolo hoped they wouldn't, but the thought of what they could find troubled him. That troubled him badly. He knew the penalty, and to be fair to Filipa Barbarigo, he knew that penalty when she took him there. He knew the penalty but that didn't stop him. Three times he enjoyed the best sex he

352

ever experienced, but that wasn't worth two years in prison. That was a steep price to pay for the brief company of the most beautiful and intriguing young woman in Venèsia.

Every time Paolo heard footsteps he expected someone to tell him the worse, or that Dardi Zori was apprehended and the raid on the abasia was over. But they just passed by, leaving Paolo to contemplate his future in prison.

* * *

The sailors tied a canvas hatch cover while Dardi stood to one side with a rope in his hand. As Capitano Sacco suggested, he tried to blend in as a sailor but knew he was getting in their way. They talked loudly, swore colourfully and shared a stivàl of wine. Once the canvas was fastened they were leaving for their long sea voyage. Dardi smirked that he was a suspected sodomite on board that ship, when on such ships sodomy was a way of life for men away from home for months at a time. Men who normally sought the company of women relied upon their own sex when nothing else was available. The authorities knew that happened but had no answer for it. Venèsia needed its ships at sea and sodomy was a part of that.

No matter how many sodomites were taken to trial and executed, it would never go away. Some men were made that way, and other men relied upon companionship of men when they had to. Trials and executions were futile.

353

Dardi sensed something and turned towards the dock to see two men in dark tabàri climbing the gangway, and he froze. They were the sbirri who attended Caterina's murder! Dardi turned away and pretended to do something useful with the rope while he knew he looked out of place. He eased away until he reached the timber rail of the ship.

"What do you want?" Capitano Sacco growled at the men delaying his departure.

"We're searching all ships readying to leave port," the senior sbirro, Almoro Canal, said calmly. "We're looking for a suspected sod...," and he stopped mid-sentence. "You!" he said.

Dardi turned around and looked down at the murky, green water. For a moment he considered jumping, and for a moment he wondered if death by drowning wouldn't be a bad way to go. Dardi felt a hand on his shoulder and he turned to face them.

"You're coming with us, Dardi Zorzi," Canal said.

Almoro Canal and Maffeo Basadona led Dardi from the ship, one in front and one behind, and then side by side to Piasà San Marco and Palàso Ducale. There he was taken up the stairs, through the reception area and along a corridor to a room with Cosmo Orio behind a desk. He stood and came close to Dardi.

"Dardi Zorzi," Cosmo said. "You nearly got away."

"Do you want to hear what happened?" Dardi asked.
"Who, where, when, how often and for how long?"

"That will do for a start."

"Then...?"

"Then we will see if there's more."

"I will tell you everything."

Cosmo closed on Dardi until he was standing toe to toe. "Even when everything has been told, the rack has the magical ability to loosen men's tongues."

* * *

One officer and a scribe returned to Abasia San Nicolai di Torcello early on Tuesday. The sbirro called the nuns in black into the chapter house one after the other, followed by Barbarella, Anna, Clara and then Filipa last. Filipa sat beside the sbirro and told him about each man: when and how they met, how often, and when her relationships with Albano, Donato and Nicolò finished. She also told him that she once made love with Pietro Blanco. All the time the scribe wrote furiously in a bound book. At the end she was thanked and was able to leave. Filipa went straight to her cell and took her lute. She sang sad love songs to the words of Petrarca. Like Francesco Petrarca she once knew love, but that was over leaving an empty space in her heart.

Chapter Thirty One

The justice system of La Repubblica di Venèsia moved relentlessly. April 1428 and just a few days before her second anniversary of entering the abasia, Filipa was at Palàso Ducale along with Barbarella, Anna and Clara. They were to testify before the Avogardori in the trial of 15 men accused of adultery with brides of Christ. Barbarella was called first, and she returned and said not a word. Next was Anna, followed by Clara and then Filipa.

Filipa was led into a richly decorated chamber in brown and gold, with several large paintings of avogardori in their dark red robes venerating Christ, the Virgin Mary and various saints. Three men sat behind a large counter elevated on a platform, a single chair faced those men, and a scribe was at a table to the left, and he had a book and a quill. Two of the three Avogardori were in their forties with dark hair and dark beards, and the Avogardoria in the centre was in his sixties or more, with silver hair and a silver beard. All wore dark red robes trimmed in white. Filipa was led to the chair and she stood by it.

"Your name is sòra Filipa Barbarigo of San Nicolai di Torcello?" the Avogadoria in the centre asked.

"It is," Filipa said.

"Sit, per piasser."

Filipa sat on the chair.

"When were you admitted to San Nicolai di Torcello?" the Avogadoria in the centre asked.

"I was admitted during the month of April, fourteen twenty-six."

"And what led to your adultery at the abasia?"

Filipa had rehearsed her testimony in her mind many times. "The day I was admitted, I saw that one of the nuns had a man in her cell. Over the next days I saw other men come and go with that nun, and then I saw another nun with a man in her cell."

"Which nuns were these?"

"Sòra Clara Rubeo and sòra Anna Molin."

"What happened then?"

"I spoke with badésa Barbarella della Fontana who told me how to take precautions not to fall pregnant. I then went to an inn and spoke with Andrea Barbo, and I took him to my cell where we made love."

"You're a bride of Christ so you committed adultery."

"I took Andrea to my cell where we committed adultery.

"Andrea Barbo took your virginity?"

"I previously dealt with my virginity using a glass dildo. After committing adultery together, Andrea and I agreed to meet the next week. The next day I went to the same inn where Andrea introduced me to Marco, who I later found to be his brother. I took Marco Barbo to my cell and

357

we committed adultery. We then agreed to meet the following week."

"So you had ongoing relationships with brothers?"

"They were quite different to each other."

"Then what happened?"

"Marco offered to take me to meet Albano Capello, and I took him to my cell where we committed adultery. Albano was married unlike Andrea and Marco, and I agreed to meet with Albano the next week. Albano took me to meet Fantino da Pesaro who was younger than the other men and single, and I took him to my cell where we committed adultery. I then agreed to meet with Fantino the following week."

"You took a succession of men to your cell, and then commenced ongoing relationships with them?'

"It happened that I liked all of these men. If I didn't like them when we first met, then I wouldn't have taken them to my cell. If I didn't like them after that, we wouldn't have continued together."

"And then what happened?"

"Some months later, Fantino took me to Palàso Locando in Venèsia and introduced me to Marino Contarini...," and there was a gasp from the men. "Marino and I spoke for a while, and after a time we went to a bedroom where we committed adultery. We then agreed to have an ongoing relationship."

"Was siór Contarini aware you were a nun?"

"Whenever he couldn't meet with me he sent messengers to the abasia."

"I understand. Then what happened?"

"Fantino introduced me to Donato Donato who was single, and I took him to my cell where we committed adultery. We then agreed to have an ongoing relationship. Donato introduced me to Nicolò Grioni, and I took him to my cell where we committed adultery. I agreed to meet Nicolò again. Donato also told me about a painter on Torcello, Pietro Vercius. I went to the room of Pietro Vercius and we went out for dinner together. Later we returned to his room and committed adultery, and we agreed to meet the next day. Some time after that I met Paolo Soranzo, and I invited him to my cell where we committed adultery. By then I was no longer seeing Albano Capello, Donato Donato and Nicolò Grioni. I liked Paolo and we agreed to have an ongoing relationship."

"Did Pietro Vercius know you were a nun?"

"Sé he did."

"Were there any others?"

"One other. Badésa della Fontana told me that Pietro Blanco was attracted to me, and she encouraged me to have a relationship with him."

"Did you think that was strange?"

"Not so many men are faithful forever, and maybe badésa della Fontana was more comfortable that Pietro Blanco was unfaithful with me just the once, rather than with another woman."

"What about Dardi Zorzi," the Avogadoria on the left asked.

Filipa knew what to say. "Dardi is a friend of mine, and he came to tell me about the murder of his wife Caterina, and that he was a suspect in her murder."

"According to sòra Augusta, Dardi Zorzi spent some time in your cell."

"Sé he did, but nothing happened between us. I met Caterina a few times and she was a lovely woman. I was upset about our loss and we spent time talking about it."

"Dardi Zorzi came to the abasia twice."

"Sé he did. The second time Dardi told me that the murderer had been found. A thief murdered Caterina Zorzi for a pendant, only she wasn't wearing it at the time."

"Did anything happen between you?"

"No, nothing." Filipa looked at the Avogadoria on the left. "Dardi is a friend who has known me since I was a baby, and that's all he's ever been to me."

"So in total you committed adultery with ten men," the Avogadoria on the right said.

"In total it was ten men."

"And at one stage you were seeing eight men regularly."

"That's right, although Marino was only able to see me every two or three weeks."

"Apart from Marino Contarini and Pietro Vercius, did you see men other than in your cell?"

"A few times I went to a room with Fantino da Pesaro, and once to Palàso Donato on Murano with Donato Donato."

"Is there anything else?"

"No, that's all."

"Sòra Filipa Barbarigo; if we could punish you for you heinous crimes, we would," the Avogadoria on the left said. "But you're covered by ecclesiastical law rather than the law of Venèsia. Church authorities will get a copy of our evidence, and history tells us they will punish you lightly for your crimes. Grassie sòra for your testimony and you can leave now."

Filipa left the room and the four nuns were led out of Palàso Ducale to Piasà San Marco on a mild, sunny, spring day. It was too nice a day to seal the fates of 15 men.

"The Bishop of Castello will get copies of our testimonies," Barbarella said while they crossed the piasà. "He will come to the abasia to determine our punishments. I will get Diana to find habits and sandals because that will make a better impression. You're too tall Filipa! You may end up showing more ankle than you should."

"That's always been my problem," Filipa said.

"For you to find men isn't so hard, but I'm shocked about Marino Contarini."

"He was genuinely nice," Filipa said, thinking back. "Sometimes we played cards together and he eventually talked me into playing chess with him, and we had surprisingly close games. I liked him and I know he liked me."

"You made him feel eighteen again."

"I suppose I did. It's hard to imagine someone that important in prison for two years because of me."

"I hope it was worth it for him."

"I hope it was," Filipa said, while thinking that her company would never be worth two years in prison.

* * *

Marin went to answer the door and was pleasantly surprised to greet his cousin Giacomo and his wife Ursa. Marin invited them in to sit at the table, and poured two cups of wine for their guests.

"How are you both?" Marin asked.

"We're both well," Giacomo replied. "How are you Bianca?"

Blanca put her hand on her stomach. "I'm fine and I'm praying for a healthy child."

"How long to go?'

362

"Maybe two months."

"That's good for you both."

"I feel like two people by this stage, so that's good for the three of us."

"I don't know how women do this," Marin said, while thinking that Blanca's good humour never changed.

"You live near the Barbarigo family," Giacomo said. "Have you heard the scandal?"

"No I haven't," Marin said.

"Their oldest daughter Filipa is a nun in an abasia, and she and other nuns were involved in a scandal with fifteen men."

"Really?" Marin exclaimed. "I never imagined such a thing."

"These women don't want to be nuns," Blanca said.

"But still...."

"There were three other women involved, including the badésa," Giacomo said.

"Would you want to do something like that?" Marin asked Blanca.

"Not really, but I'm lucky. I have a good marriage of respect and affection."

"A nun isn't married, except to Christ," Marin said.

"If she doesn't want to be married to Christ, if she was forced to be there because her family didn't have enough dowry, then who knows? But I'm not in her position so I can't say. But enough of that; it's a nice, spring evening and do you want to go for a walk to the campo?"

They all agreed and headed outdoors into the fading light, and the campo was always a lovely place on a pleasant evening. The campo was overlooked by Cièsa di Santa Maria del Giglio where he and Blanca were blessed after their marriage. That church was supported by the Barbarigo family. While Marin contemplated Cièsa di Santa Maria del Giglio, he thought about the strange ways of the nobility of Venèsia. And just then he spotted Laura and Angelo together, and went to them.

Against the odds, when Laura fell pregnant their marriage improved. Angelo didn't love Laura but he treated her with respect. For his part Marin wanted the past to be the past, but Angelo seemed never to forgive him or Vicenzo for interfering.

"Bondi Angelo e Laura," Marin said.

"Bondi Marin," Laura said while Angelo turned away.

"Bondi Angelo e Laura," Blanca said.

"Bondi Blanca," Laura said. "How are you?'

Blanca put her hands on her stomach. "We're good," she said, smiling. "And you?"

Laura put her hands on her stomach. "We're good too. Anytime now."

"A while for me."

"If you have a son, you have an heir," Marin said. "But if you have a daughter, a mother has her best friend and helper, and maybe that's worth more."

"You're sweet," Laura said.

Marin took Blanca's hand. "Blanca was once a daughter and now she's the reason for my existence."

Laura nodded in agreement while Marin hoped that Angelo understood.

"Son or daughter is in God's hands," Laura said. "Who are we to question His ways?"

"That's true Angelo?" Marin asked.

"Yes it is," he said unconvincingly.

Marin hoped Angelo understood, because he didn't want Laura to be punished for having a daughter, if that's what happened. He put his arm around Blanca and wished Laura knew love instead of fear.

* * *

Filipa met with Cristina in the chapter house rather than her cell. She wanted to be open in front of the other nuns, and especially in front of Augusta.

"How are you?" Cristina asked.

"I'm good," Filipa said. She wasn't good; she missed Pietro and wanted to talk about him, but she just couldn't.

"You created such a scandal and everyone's talking about it! Fifteen men imprisoned for two years!"

Filipa didn't want to go over all that, but Cristina was her sister and deserved to know. "I had them all here," she said, and put out the palm of her hand. "You can't imagine what that's like."

"I know what it's like to be dragged down to the depths of despair, so what you did to those men is no surprise to me."

"I'm sorry to hear about your problems."

"My problems aren't so bad. How bad will your punishment be?"

"Maybe a week or two to contemplate our behaviour."

"Is that all?"

Filipa nodded.

"Filipa, I have bad news for you," Cristina said. "Dardi was captured on the boat before he had a chance to get away."

Filipa felt like someone had stabbed her heart, and she felt her eyes go moist. Cristina reached out and Filipa buried her head with tears flowing. They would torture Dardi until he was nearly dead, and then they would execute what was left of him.

"We haven't heard anything," Cristina said quietly.

Filipa couldn't talk.

"As soon as we hear something," Cristina said. "We will tell you."

***

The Bishop of Castello wore the grandest clothes, topped by a magnificent, red tabàro and a pointed, red capèⓞ. He had an entourage of ten priests who assembled in the chapter house. There Barbarella, Anna, Clara and Filipa were led in, all dressed in the black habit of the Order of Saint Benedict. They knelt before the bishop.

"Badésa Barbarella," the bishop said. "You have been a bad example to the sòri in your care. That bad example doesn't excuse the behaviours of sòra Anna, sòra Clara and sòra Filipa. You are all to be taken to punishment cells for one week. You will have prayer books to help you to reflect on your sins, and to guide you towards better behaviour in the future. That's all."

They were led away and Filipa wondered where the punishment cells were. As far as she was aware the abasia didn't have any. She would find out soon enough.

Chapter Thirty Two

After a week in a punishment cell at Baxélega di Santa Maria Assunta, Filipa was pleased to breathe fresh air and to see sunlight once more. But she had unfinished business, and now that she had a habit she could do something denied to others, with the help of pàre Antonio who was responsible for all abasie on Torcello. After bathing, Filipa dressed in her habit and went to Barbarella's room where she knocked on the door.

"Bondi Filipa," Barbarella said. "You don't have to wear that now."

"Bondi Barbarella," Filipa said. "You now know about my friend Dardi Zorzi who indirectly led to this chaos," Filipa said. "He was captured around the same time, and would be imprisoned at Palàso Ducale. He will be executed for sodomy, and he hasn't yet confessed his sins."

"That's terrible for your friend. Come in, per piasser."

Filipa entered the room.

"I want to ask pàre Antonio to come with me to Venèsia to hear Dardi's confession," Filipa said.

"Of course," Barbarella said. "You have my permission to do this."

"Grassie Barbarella. I will go now."

Filipa returned to Baxélega di Santa Maria Assunta; a large church about fifteen minute's walk away. It was quite plain on the outside, but was light and spacious inside, with lovely mosaics right up to the domed ceiling. Filipa asked a young priest if she could speak with pàre Antonio. The priest went away, and shortly after the pàre strode into the cathèdral. Pàre Antonio was about the same age as Filipa's father, and a friendly, cheerful man with lovely smile lines around his eyes.

"Sòra Filipa," he said. "What can I do for you?"

"I'm here to ask you to hear the confession of a sinner," Filipa said. "I have a friend who will be convicted of sodomy, and he hasn't had a chance to confess."

"Is he one of the men from your trial?"

"No, he's a family friend. Actually he doesn't like women that way, but regardless of that he deserves to confess."

"Sòra; I find you disarmingly honest, and you're quite right. Every man deserves to confess."

"He will be held in prison at Palàso Ducale, and I would like to come with you."

"You're a nun in the Order of Saint Benedict, so that's possible. You really want to come with me to see your friend."

369

"I hope when that he sees me, his heart will feel settled and that will make his transition to the next world easier."

"That's a worthy ambition. We will go to the prison together."

"Have you been there before?"

"I have, and I warn you that it's bad in parts."

"My friend's name is Dardi Zorzi and he's a sodomite."

They walked together to the port and hired a gondola to Piaséta San Marco. From there, pàre Antonio took Filipa up a staircase to the reception area of Palàso Ducale and spoke to an officer. The officer led them down narrow stairs and along a narrow passage deep into the ground floor of the palàso, with the air becoming ever more fetid until the stench was almost overpowering. Filipa felt like throwing up with a smell like a latrine only many times worse, while it was damp and semi-dark with few lamps burning. Filipa heard a rumble of voices before they reached a cell separated from the passage by iron bars stretching from floor to ceiling, and squashed into this cell were forty or fifty men. It was cold, damp, stinking and crowded.

"He's in there," the officer said before standing aside.

Filipa kept away from men's hands reaching through the bars while searching for Dardi in the crush. "Dardi!" she shouted above the moans of the prisoners. "Dardi it's me, Filipa!"

"Dardi Zorzi!" pàre Antonio bellowed, and the mass of humanity parted like a wave. Dardi shuffled towards the bars, hunched over and dragging his left leg. He was thin and gaunt, unshaven, had scars on his face and hands, and was dressed in rags. He struggled to the bars and held them tightly. Filipa put her hand to her mouth in shock and didn't know what to say. The words formed; "I'm so sad for what happened," and Dardi shrugged. He was on the boat and close to getting away, until tragedy struck. "I brought pàre Antonio to hear your confession," but Dardi seemed unmoved. Filipa remembered a conversation they once had. "I want you to prepare yourself for the next life."

"There's no next life," Dardi croaked in a hoarse voice.

Filipa closed on the bars and put her hand on the scarred skin of his hand. "All of us who know you will remember you for the good man you are. Forever you will live in our hearts."

"I see no hearts."

"They would come if they could, but only I can come. Think of my family: Papa, Mama, Cristina and me. We all loved you. Surely you remember that?"

He nodded his head slowly.

"I don't know what the future holds, but I'm sure your goodness and kindness will win through in the end. You have been judged harshly by cruel men, but there's a fairer judgement to come, made by those who know your true heart. Let pàre Antonio hear your confession, per piasser."

Dardi nodded and pàre Antonio came to the bars. Filipa heard him ask Dardi to kneel and Dardi did so with great effort, struggling to get his legs into place. Filipa moved away to give them privacy, and then she turned her back and contemplated the officer. After a while she saw pàre Antonio was almost finished, so she waited before coming to the bars. She knelt in front of Dardi still kneeling.

"You will be in my prayers every night," Filipa said.

"You have a good heart," Dardi said.

"I will come back here."

"I would like that."

The officer came to them and Filipa stood. "Adio Dardi," she said, and followed the officer and pàre Antonio into the passageway once more. While she walked she had perhaps one chance, and it would be foolish to let that slip away.

"Excuse me siór," Filipa said to the officer. "There's another prisoner. His name is Pietro Vercius."

"Do you want to see him?" the officer asked.

"Sé, per piasser."

The officer nodded, and instead of heading to the reception area, they took a passage to the left. That passage led to five cells smaller in size to Dardi's cell, again separated from the passage by iron bars stretching from floor to ceiling. But it was totally different and Filipa was quite stunned. While Dardi was kept in the most wretched conditions, these cells overlooked Piaséta San Marco through windows guarded by more iron bars. There was fresh air, and the cells were not at all crowded with about ten men in each. In the corner of the first cell she spotted him along with Pietro Blanco, Luca, Carlo and Francesco; all the cittadini from the abasia. Filipa moved closer but kept away from prisoner's hands reaching for her.

"Pietro!" she shouted. "It's me, Filipa!"

She saw both Pietros' heads turn, but Pietro Vercius looked at her with his mouth open and his eyes wide. He came to the bars while the other prisoners moved away. Filipa felt suddenly uplifted just to be in his presence. Strange she'd never noticed that her heart felt lighter as soon as Pietro was near.

"Filipa!" Pietro exclaimed. "What are you doing here?"

"I'm so sorry about what I did, and what happened to you."

"When we first met you did the right thing by telling me you were a nun, but that didn't stop me falling in love with you."

"I love you Pietro and if you want me, I will leave the abasia. I was going to tell you that, but I got caught up with the problems of my friend who I told you about."

"You were doing the right thing for your friend, as a good person does. Can you really leave the abasia?"

"I can write to the Holy See and ask them to release me from my vows, and in time they will do that. It may take as long as your release from here, but my release will come."

"Will you do this for me?"

"I love you," Filipa said. "Nothing else matters."

"Will you marry me?"

Filipa wanted to grab him and hug him but bars were in the way, so she put her hand on his hand. "I want to marry you and have many daughters with you." Filipa smiled brightly. "Well, three daughters."

"A son will be good, if he's taught to respect women."

"We will have a son and two daughters," Filipa said, still smiling.

"When I'm released we will marry, and you can help me with my business."

"Until then I will come here as often as I can."

"Time will pass soon enough, and then we will marry."

The officer came to Filipa and it was time for her to leave. "Adio Pietro," she said. "I will be back."

"Adio Filipa," Pietro said.

They returned through a passage to the reception area. Filipa was glad to leave Palàso Ducale while they crossed Piaséta San Marco. They boarded a gondola and pàre Antonio asked the gondoliere to take them to Torcello. They sat side-by-side in the fieze.

"You don't need to tell me," pàre Antonio said.

"I love him," Filipa said. "I will leave the order and marry him when we can."

"I understand."

"You can't understand love until it happens to you."

Pàre Antonio nodded solemnly, and then stared into the distance while they crossed the lagoon.

Chapter Thirty Three

After Prime, many of the nuns went to the chapter house to sing. Filipa fetched her lute to accompany them, with Margarita singing first. Next was Diana and Filipa sensed someone enter the room. She glanced up and saw pàre Antonio. When Diana finished her song, Filipa excused herself and went to the pàre.

"Bondi pàre," Filipa said. "I suspect this is for me."

"I have bad news," pàre Antonio said. "Dardi Zorzi is to be executed tomorrow. Do you wish to accompany me?"

"I will. I will put this lute away and change my clothes." Filipa turned around. "I must go with pàre Antonio," she said. "I hope this meets with your approval, sòra Augusta."

Augusta's mouth fell open, but since the problem few wanted anything to do with her. The abasia had always been a place of love and kindness, and remained so except for one. Filipa went to her cell and changed into her habit before meeting pàre Antonio in the corridor. They walked to the jetty in silence, and reached the piaséta just before midday. Again they were escorted along the ground floor passageway of the palàso to eventually arrive at the crowded, stinking cell. Having been there before it was less of a shock, and Dardi was in better shape too. He limped to the bars and they stood close with his rough, gnarled hand on Filipa's hand.

"I will miss you for always," Filipa said.

"I will miss you for always," Dardi said.

"What was the worse I ever did?"

"Nothing really bad, but once you took Cristina in the family gondola to Lido di Venèsia to go camping for a summer's night. Your parents had to go with your gondoliere to find the two of you. They were really worried."

"I will only ever have good thoughts about you."

"Me too."

"I've prayed every night."

"I knew you would."

"Do you want to confess again?'

"Sé, per piasser."

Filipa glanced at père Antonio who came to the bars. They knelt and Filipa turned away. After a time she turned back and they were finished. Filipa knew there wasn't anything more to be said. "Adio Dardi Zorzi," she said.

"Adio Filipa Barbarigo," he said.

She turned away with tears flowing freely, and followed the officer and père Antonio through the narrow, damp passageway to that reception area. Outside the first floor of Palàso Ducale were two columns in red marble, known as the fatal pillars, where executions were carried out. Beneath the fatal pillars was a timber post surrounded by neatly stacked timber, with for a gap wide enough for one man to enter. Filipa glanced at that and shuddered, but interestingly the sea washed across the piaséta. Being Sunday afternoon Piasà San Marco and the Piaséta would normally be busy, but the crowds were gone while the water rose. Acqua alta, and Filipa wondered whether that was random chance or something more. She looked at the place of execution with water lapping, and the wetness had made the stacked timber useless for a fire. Also useless was the dock on Canal Grando well under water, and there was no way to return to Torcello.

"We must get away from this," Filipa said.

"Do you know where?" pàre Antonio asked.

"We can go to my home. We will be safe there."

Filipa led the pàre across San Marco to Palàso Barbarigo, and pulled the bell chain on the back door. They waited with their gowns rolled halfway to their knees, while water almost reached the top of the flood barrier at the doorway. Maria the maid momentarily didn't recognise Filipa, but then let them in where they discarded their wet sandals. Introductions were made while outside the water rose higher and higher, and Filipa went upstairs to better view. Everything was under water and she'd never seen an acqua alta like it. Maybe five foot deep, and much of Venèsia was inundated and brought to a standstill. Filipa went downstairs.

"Do you think this is divine retribution?" she asked.

"I don't know," pàre Antonio said. "But I do know this execution is wrong."

"The wood has been wet, but once this recedes they will put fresh wood for tomorrow."

"What wood?" Maria asked.

"The wood to burn Dardi Zorzi with," Filipa said.

"Oh."

After a few hours the water receded as it always did; acqua alta was just wind and tides in the lagoon, although the acqua alta that day was much bigger than any Filipa had ever seen. Filipa borrowed Giorgio and the gondola for the journey to Torcello, and at Baxélega di Santa Maria Assunta they bid each other farewell. Filipa walked to the abasia, and then went to her cell to wrestle with her conscience. Could she be there to offer Dardi moral support, or would it be worse being on Torcello while knowing it was happening? She imagined the hideousness of it, but also imagined being alone in her cell while knowing what was happening. No matter how much Filipa argued with herself, the answer wouldn't come.

Chapter Thirty Four

There was always a big crowd for an execution. They filled Piaséta San Marco and spilled into the piasà. Filipa kept to the rear, and in time she saw smoke very close to Palàso Ducale and even heard his screams. A nun in a black habit on her knees praying would seem unexceptional to those in the crowd.

Chapter Thirty Five

Barbarella escorted Filipa to the chapter house where her parents waited. She didn't know what to say or even how to deal with them. She went in alone and they were on a bench. She sat opposite with her head down while fiddling with the séngia around her waist.

"I'm most sorry for what happened," Filipa said while looking at the floor. "I did the wrong thing and I hurt a lot of men. Forgive me per piasser."

"You weren't the only one and you tried to do good for Dardi," Papa said.

"I know; but I still hurt those other men."

He sighed. "There's the bright, happy Filipa we all love, and there's the naughty Filipa who doesn't think before she acts. That's always been the way."

She looked at him. "I will do better in the future; I promise."

"Will you?"

"I have much to lose if I don't. I would like to marry," she said. "A good man who wants to marry me, and who doesn't want a dowry."

"Who's this man?"

"Pietro Vercius; a painter. He's in prison at the moment, and when he gets out he wants to marry me. I've asked to be released from my vows."

"Will you do the right thing by him?"

"I swear I will do the right thing. I love him and I can't throw that away."

"You have my blessing for your marriage and I hope it brings you happiness."

Filipa wished she didn't have to wait so long, but at least she could see Pietro from time to time.

"Do you love him?" Mama asked.

"With all my heart," Filipa said. "I ache for him when we're apart, and I feel complete when we're in each other's presence."

"By presence you mean the prison?" Papa asked.

"I'm a nun so I can visit him," Filipa said.

Papa chuckled. "That's the Filipa I know and love; the only woman who would do such a thing."

Filipa tried to smile but couldn't, but she understood his sentiment. "Grassie Papa," she said.

"I hope you have a good marriage and you're happy together. Your husband will be welcome in Palàso Barbarigo."

"He will be the father of your grandchildren; God willing."

"That too. He must be special to steal your heart like this."

"He reminds me of Dardi Zorzi."

"That was tragic."

Filipa nodded.

Her father rubbed his chin for a moment. "When the time comes," he said. "We will put on a wedding appropriate for a Barbarigo, and we will pay Pietro enough dowry to help him get established in his new life."

"Grassie tuti Papa," Filipa said.

"What happened here is what happens in many abasie, but it was found out. I'm glad that good came out of it for you, and I know you did everything you could to help your oldest and dearest friend. In time you will be a wife and mother, and I'm sure you will be excellent at both."

"I want to help Pietro with his business," Filipa said.

"I'm sure you will help him with your energy and abilities." Papa stood. "I'm glad you're well and you put what happened behind...."

Filipa stood and looked at him hard. "I was there and I will never forget it for as long as I live."

"That was a brave thing for you to do Filipa. I'm glad that you have plans for your future and I look forward to having Pietro as part of our family. We should go now, but we will visit you more often. I promise we will visit soon."

Mama stood and hugged Filipa. "Adio my daughter," she said quietly.

"Adio Mama," Filipa said.

"Adio Filipa," Papa said.

"Adio Papa," Filipa said.

383

Filipa watched them go and was pleased they were reconciled, and pleased about her father's generous offer. She was in love, and she would marry with her father's blessing and with his help. But she hoped that men who loved men would never, ever be treated like that again. That was cruel and inhumane and no fit way to treat anyone, and especially someone who simply fell in love.

Epilogue

Not so much is known about those involved with the 1428 scandal at Abasia San Nicolai di Torcello. Marino Contarini served his two years in prison, and retired from his business relatively young in order to devote his energies to the grand reconstruction of Palàso Zen, renamed Ca' d'Oro or House of Gold. Fantino da Pesaro didn't learn from his two years in prison; in 1436 he was sentenced to one year imprisonment in chains for touching and kissing a servant girl inside Baxélega di San Marco.

Abasia San Nicolai di Torcello was far from the first scandal to involve young patrician women sent to abbeys, and would not be the last. By the end of the Fifteenth Century, 15 abbeys had men travelling from afar to indulge in affairs with nuns from noble backgrounds.

At the time, women were thought to be unable to control their substantial sexual appetites, and it's interesting that, when abandoned by society and free to follow their own inclinations, many of these noble women chose to behave in accordance with that stereotype. Many hundreds of years later stereotypes changed, and women were considered naturally chaste and pure.

By early in the Sixteenth Century, the men in power of Venice thought the abbeys of Venice were out of control, and in 1521 a group of magistrates were appointed to clean up those abbeys. Windows were walled up or barred, doors were sealed, and gardens were put out of bounds. Despite this, the women inside and the men outside still found ways to associate with each other. Sometimes priest-confessors became involved with the nuns in their care, and in 1561 one of these, pàre Lion, was beheaded for his indulgences.

As time went by conditions inside the abbeys of Venice became ever more wretched for the women inside. They were sentenced to imprisonment for life without ever committing a crime, other than being born a woman. Frustrated and lonely young women gazed through barred windows hoping to catch glimpses of men passing by.

It wasn't until the defeat of Venice by Napoleon in 1797 that things changed. After a time Napoleon ransacked abbeys, expelled nuns, and turned abbey buildings into barracks or prisons. The era of Venetian patrician women sent to abbeys finally came to an end.

By the middle of the Fifteenth Century, convicted sodomites were no longer burned alive in Venice; instead they were beheaded and their remains were burned. Execution of men for homosexuality continued in various parts of the Western Christian world until the Nineteenth Century, and execution as a punishment remained on many statute books until relatively recent times. Since then in many Western countries, same-sex relationships have come to be accepted as normal, and in many countries, same-sex marriage is now available to officially and legally celebrate love regardless of gender.

www.ingramcontent.com/pod-product-compliance
Lightning Source LLC
Chambersburg PA
CBHW071200250626
47159CB00001B/152